D0249467

THE TOWN THAT DROWNED

THE TOWN
THAT DROWNED

Riel Nason

Copyright © 2011 by Riel Nason.

All rights reserved. No part of this work may be reproduced or used in any form or by
any means, electronic or mechanical, including photocopying, recording or any
retrieval system, without the prior written permission of the publisher or a licence
from the Canadian Copyright Licensing Agency (Access Copyright). To contact
Access Copyright, visit www.accesscopyright.ca or call 1-800-893-5777.

Edited by Bethany Gibson.
Cover image after "Submerged," 2009, by Liz Poage, flickr.com.
Cover design by Julie Scriver.
Page design by David Moratto.
Printed in Canada.
10 9 8 7 6 5 4 3 2 1

Library and Archives Canada Cataloguing in Publication

Nason, Riel, 1969-
The town that drowned / Riel Nason.

Issued also in electronic format.
ISBN 978-0-86492-640-1

I. Title.

PS8627.A7775T69 2011   C813'.6   C2011-902901-4

Goose Lane Editions acknowledges the financial support of the Canada Council
for the Arts, the Government of Canada through the Canada Book Fund (CBF), and the
New Brunswick Department of Wellness, Culture, and Sport for its publishing activities.

Goose Lane Editions
Suite 330, 500 Beaverbrook Court
Fredericton, New Brunswick CANADA E3B 5X4
www.gooselane.com

For my Eli

The Town That Drowned is a work of fiction. Although the background event discussed in the book did take place in New Brunswick in the late 1960s, the story does not attempt to factually recreate historical details and is only inspired by them. Place names are used fictitiously. Characters, timeline, and activities described are all a product of the author's imagination.

CONTENTS

Summer 1965

Chapter 1

~

The beginning I remember is this: my brother Percy on the old Hawkshaw Bridge. It is August, sunny and warm, and he's in a white T-shirt and jeans, with his glasses tied tight around his head with a shoelace. He is walking, carrying a bottle in one hand, and his lips are silently moving. It is afternoon. Percy is nine years, two months, three and a half days old. Believe me, that's what he'd say if you asked him.

I know he's almost to the middle of the bridge — the exact middle — because he is counting. He takes two hundred and seventy-three short measured paces from where the road turns into wood-plank platform and black metal spans, all blue sky above and blue water below him. The bottle is an emptied Nesbitt's Orange, and soon Percy will drop it into the river. There's a note inside it. And an envelope with a five-cent stamp and our address (to Percy, care of our father). In the bottom of the bottle are seven small rocks from our driveway for weight. All this is sealed in with a rolled-up rag, a piece of cork, and some wax my mother bought for her jars of chokecherry jelly.

I sit on the hill up from the shoreline and watch while the bottle falls down, down, plunges then bobs, and floats away. Percy will stay there and I will stay here until the bottle is only a glint in the sun in the distance. We'll wait as it starts its journey along the Saint John River past the houses and farms of everyone we know — past Doyle's apple orchard, Mr. Cole's giant pine tree, and Mr. Black's cows grazing. It will drift past three churches, the high school, the garage, the Legion, and Foster's Store. The bottle will eventually wind its way by Prince William and Fredericton, Gagetown, Westfield, then toss and turn through the Reversing Falls at Saint John before continuing into the Bay of Fundy.

If it makes it that far.

Because of course we won't know. Beyond the time Percy leans on the bridge rail watching, the bottle seems to disappear and almost ceases to exist — except as a number in a chart in his notebook.

He will turn to walk home, get me to untie the shoelace from his glasses (which is only to keep them from falling into the water), wait a week and start again. He will use the same brand of bottle, the same number of rocks, and the same blue stamp with the Queen. He will take the same two hundred and seventy-three steps to the same spot, and he'll always be wearing a white T-shirt and jeans.

It was just two years ago, and it used to seem that nothing ever changed. Everyone thought Percy was so different when he was really all about being the same.

But that's not to say my brother is like anybody else. His desire for consistency means he likes to make up and follow his own rules and regulations. Percy puts himself to bed every night at eight o'clock — even when the summer sun is high in the sky and I'm sure through his bedroom windows he can hear other children playing. He has only ever slept in his own bed in his own room in his own house. He never stayed at my grandparents' place when they were alive, or at my aunt and uncle's when they lived nearby, or in a hotel or tent. If we are out somewhere and it is getting late, Percy will look at his watch and declare (as if he is Cinderella), "Mother, I must go home immediately, it's almost my bedtime." When anyone overhears him there is a giggle or a "Now Percy dear" or that silly sly smile some ladies get when they're tucking a new piece of gossip away in their brains.

What other people see is a bossy, spoiled little boy. They don't know that sometimes the smallest of changes, like a drop of orange pop on his white T-shirt, can bother him so much he can't wear it any longer, that the stain physically pains him, like the spot becomes a wound bleeding not from the inside out but the outside in. They just see a boy who cries about everything. They see a boy who appears to be simultaneously strong-willed and weak.

So maybe it seems unlikely that Percy would get wrapped up in something as random and whimsical as messages in bottles, but he did. He has sent one a week from April to November (when the river wasn't frozen) for the past two and a half years. No letters have ever come back — which keeps it the same for him, I guess. Still, he has his notebook with a chart of each bottle's number and release date at the ready, always prepared for a response. He records the weather under the heading "Environment at Launch" and leaves a wide column for the "Details of Final Destination" — "Date Found," "Location," and "Other Notes." He has a map of New Brunswick in his room, and a globe he got for his eighth birthday. I will see him tracing over blue lines with his finger or measuring oceans with a ruler, dreaming, imagining, or since it is Percy, probably more like calculating, predicting.

Once he told me that in calm weather a bottle might only drift a few miles each day. That meant at least three weeks to Fredericton and maybe two months to the world's highest tides in the Bay of Fundy. The longer Percy waits without a reply, then the farther the bottle is travelling. To him it is a direct correlation. And the only possibility.

I'm pretty sure the contents of the note have more to do with the lack of response — assuming anyone even finds the bottles. Percy doesn't clue in that it might help to let people know he's nine years old, or that he should ask for a letter back with some sort of impassioned plea. His notes look like they were sent by a forty-seven-year-old weirdo amateur scientist or, worse, the government, with all the formal language Percy uses and the fact that he has them typed (by me). He makes it sound as if there is someone waiting for the bottle, expecting it to arrive like a package ordered from the Simpsons-Sears catalogue and paid COD. Percy isn't open to editing though, or suggestions. That I know from trying. The original wording of the note may as well have been inscribed in the back of our family Bible from the instant Percy finished double-checking the spelling of each word in his dictionary.

What it says:

> Please reply by mail using the enclosed envelope upon receipt
> of this bottle. Please state geographical location found as
> specifically as possible including any details that may have
> contributed to the conclusion of its journey such as driftwood
> in the area, or shore debris. Please state condition of bottle
> including cracks or breakage. Please state date of receipt, not
> date of mailing, and bottle code number: 1965-19.

See what I mean?

The code number is the only thing that changes. I type every word on the Remington typewriter I inherited from my grandfather, with Percy hovering like a wasp at my shoulder, watching for any reason

I might have to start over. I am not allowed any spelling mistakes, incorrect spacing, or double-punched keys. Percy knows how to type, but my mother insists I do it, making us spend time together — more for him I suspect than for me. In fact the whole bottle business has turned into a family project, so that Percy isn't always alone in his room reading. I type the notes and watch him do each launch, my mother takes him to buy stamps and seals the bottle with wax, and my father lets him put his name — Jack Carson — on the envelope, and sometimes drinks the Nesbitt's Orange to empty the bottle, and (as I've heard him tell my mother) tries his hardest not to swear if Percy cries when it takes over an hour to find seven tiny rocks in the driveway.

But for now I'm on the hill waiting. Percy is on the bridge and the bottle is in the water. For at least fifteen more minutes I'll sit, tilting my face to the sun, trying to conjure up enough freckles to blend into a tan. Once in a while I glance at Percy, then the opposite shore, up- and downriver, then at Percy again. I figure I'd hear him if he ever fell in. I concentrate on braiding little pieces of my long brown hair and counting almost like he does — except backwards and approximately. Twelve minutes, ten minutes, five minutes, until we can go home again.

That's probably why a man I've never seen before has managed to walk all the way up to Percy before I notice. Suddenly, as if he's fallen like a raindrop, there he is casting a shadow over Percy up on the bridge. The man's holding a big fancy camera with a tripod attached. Everyone around here loves to say that we have one of the most scenic views in the province, but I hope the man doesn't ask Percy anything about it. I hurry across the hill toward them.

Percy still hasn't turned away from the river. He's staring into the water, tracking the bottle even though the man is obviously talking and standing right next to him. I can tell now it isn't a camera the man has either, but that piece of equipment surveyors use, and I realize that's what this man is. Who knows what he's doing out on a Saturday, but I suppose he's just taking a break, being friendly to a local boy. I'm sure it won't take him long to find out that Percy's not exactly the president of the River Valley Welcoming Committee.

The man sees me coming, running, and with a big smile and a wink he says, "Now where's the fire, missy?"

"Late for supper." I nod at Percy. It's only about three-thirty, but it's the first thing that pops into my head.

Percy is oblivious, still silently staring at the water, leaning on the railing. I tell him it's time to go and touch him on the back. I say goodbye to the surveyor as Percy walks ahead of me. So far so good. We make it to the end of the bridge before it starts. It's like Percy's foot touching the roadway is the trigger. He cries.

And cries. And cries.

It's the most upset I've seen him in a long time. But that doesn't mean it's the worst thing that's happened lately, because with Percy there's often a mismatch between the seriousness of the problem and the extremity of his reaction. Little things may equal a big cry, and big things little or no cry. Major events that you'd logically think would cause a complete breakdown in someone so sensitive sometimes hardly affect him. When our cat Quilty was run over by a car last year Percy was dry-eyed. But the week before that when Quilty had knocked over her water bowl and soaked one of Percy's socks, he started sobbing. When Percy lost a button off his winter coat, he also lost his mind.

A few other problematic incidents:

The night my father wouldn't pick up the phone or let anyone else answer it because we were having supper and whoever was calling should know better and damn well let us eat in peace.

The time my cousin Sarah told him she still, at twelve, believed in Santa Claus. She said his magical sleigh just travelled so fast its speed couldn't be calculated.

The day this past February when the ceremony in Ottawa introducing our new Canadian flag with the maple leaf was shown on TV. As the old Red Ensign was lowered down the pole Percy started whimpering. Then for weeks there were aftershocks as he noticed the flags replaced at the high school, the Pokiok Lodge, the garage, and the Legion.

The one time my mother made tomato scallop. And the one time she made poached eggs. And chocolate cake with white instead of chocolate icing. And mincemeat pie. And when my uncle made the monumental mistake of not telling Percy his burger was venison until after he had taken a bite. And the one horrible, horrible time my father brought home a box of live lobsters.

Getting his hair cut. (When Percy was younger my mother just trimmed it while he was sleeping.)

The day his teacher made him sit in the corner because he had stopped working on his math problems. Percy had found a mistake in the textbook, and once he saw it he didn't know what else to do.

The minister telling him God could read his mind.

Really. So you get the idea.

Welcome to the Percy Carson show: free admission.

As I've said, Percy definitely liked things to stay the same. But outside of his own rituals (which caused enough drama if interfered with), there was all this who-knows-what, who-knows-where, who-knows-why, who-knows-when. It was as if the whole evolving, revolving world was by nature the problem since it would never stay still for him. Percy wasn't wired to understand that you can't control change, so he could never, ever catch up and adjust to anything. But even if you knew that, or thought you'd figured him out a little bit, Percy kept you guessing. Everything could be going along perfectly fine, then all of a sudden he'd wail like a two-year-old, or his lips would quiver, his shoulders shake, as if something had built up and he had to give in. I always seemed to be around to witness this, and although I used to be sure that his heart was at least cracking if not breaking, now I only think, Great-not-this-again. After a while you feel like you're living with the boy who cried wolf. After a while the urge to rush over and hug him fades away completely.

Once we're well up the road, I look back to see if the surveyor is still there. He's smoking a cigarette and slowly turning his head from shore to shore, taking in the whole river valley. It's as if he's memorizing the scene to paint a picture. Or like he's a tourist and it will be the only time he's here. I catch up to Percy just as he wipes his nose on his shoulder. Now he's toned it down to some whimpers and an occasional hiccup.

I'm not going to chance more upset by asking, but I do wonder what the surveyor said to him.

We live at the top of the road that leads down the valley to the bridge and continues over to Hawkshaw. This side of the river is Haventon, shortened from Haven Town years ago. The whole area is a long sprawling village. Our neighbours' houses are staggered along the hillside on smaller winding roads and at the ends of driveways. It's as if the houses rolled like rocks down the slope and got stuck on tufts of grass. This is what makes up Haventon for a few miles on each side of us — houses and barns and other buildings like the churches with big or little stretches of land in between. You can kind of imagine it like people sitting on bleachers: lots of them are clustered together and a few are alone, but they're all waiting for the main event. Except here the main event is simply a view of the water.

*

A car drives by and swings extra wide around us, so I know we've been recognized even before the little beep. It's Mr. Hogan, a teacher, and I manage to wave even though seeing him is just an unpleasant reminder that school starts in two weeks. In a way it's hard to believe that the summer zoomed along so quickly. But then again (with my permanent sidekick), some days seem to go on endlessly. Percy raises his hand in a delayed wave, and since he's finally calmer, I untie the shoelace that was knotted on his glasses.

"Ruby," he says. He always uses my name. "Were you aware of the fact that seventy per cent of the Earth's surface is covered by water?"

"That sure sounds like a lot."

"It's true. It is a well-established calculation," he says, although I don't doubt him. Percy reads all the time and has an amazing memory.

"So your bottles could have a long, long way to travel, right?" Even two and a half years into Project Bottle Launch I know talking about it makes him happy.

We're passing in front of our next-door neighbour's house and Percy's cheeks are still wet. I see my father back by our shed, sharpening the lawnmower blades. My father hates it when Percy cries for what he calls "no good reason." It bothers him more and more as Percy gets older. I can tell that my father does his best to tolerate it for days, even weeks at a time, by leaving the room for a smoke or a beer when Percy starts in. But then Percy will wail right in the middle of *Bonanza* and my father won't be able to hear Hoss talking, and he will have to yell — have to — "Jesus Christ, Percy!" because he had waited a whole week to find out what would happen.

"The bodies of water comprising that total are not all connected," Percy says, wiping his cheek with the back of his hand.

My father looks up.

"Still," I say. "That sounds like a lot more water to float away on than land to get caught up in."

Percy stops walking and looks at me. He is focusing on my mouth since he never quite meets anyone's eyes. He's perfectly quiet and doesn't move for several seconds. Then he bursts into tears and runs toward the house crying.

Have mercy, Percy.

That's what the other kids say when they tease him. They think of something, anything, trial and error, to make him cry, then once he's going they hold their hands over their ears as if it's Percy who's distressing them. "Have mercy, Percy! Mercy!" they'll scream between fits of laughter, sometimes hiding their heads behind the school bus seats. The way they act is a pretty good dramatic interpretation of the way I sometimes feel. If I'm there during the teasing I'll say to Percy the ever-sensible but useless "Ignore them." Then they'll yell louder and ask Percy if I'm his mommy. So clever and hilarious. Even though I'm sure they've never stopped to think how ultimately terrifying being Percy's mommy might be.

I wait until Percy makes it to the front door of the house and goes in. Mission accomplished. Then I find a rock and roll it around and around in my hand as I head back down to the water. Its edges are rough, but it's warm from the sun.

I'm not looking forward to school. At all. Sure there will be the "Have mercy, Percy," but that's gone on for years and isn't the reason why. Now I have my own problems. My own personalized dent in the joy of my existence. Something happened late last winter that everyone at school decided was enough of a reason to re-evaluate who I was. Really, with a brother as strange as Percy there had to be some eventual rub-off effect. This incident proved it. It was like my body betrayed me. It was as if after all the years of my mother saying I should try to put myself in Percy's shoes, my mind subliminally commanded my body to do something.

It was March, getting near the end of the month, but spring still seemed a long ways off. Snow was all around and the river was frozen. The three churches in the area decided to have a joint family fun party with a big supper at the Legion afterwards. There was sliding for the little kids, and skating on the river for the teens. The women took care of the cooking. The men complimented them on the beans.

My cousin Sarah — who's also my best friend — was skating with me. There were at least twenty other people on the cleared-off ice, but I could glide around with ease. I like skating. I'm good at it. Graceful even. Sarah and I were showing off a little. Sarah was madly in love with Colin Moore who was skating too, so we were jumping and twirling for him and everyone to see.

And then, near the shore, a crack.

Maybe my falling made the ice crack or maybe the ice cracked and made me fall. I just remember hitting my head and my legs sprawled in the frigid water. It was probably only about three feet deep. I was half in the river and half out. It should only have been temporarily excruciating (it's the coldest I've ever been) and later embarrassing (especially with our minister yelling, "Get her out of those clothes!"), but my knocked-out head started working against me. As people rushed toward me, I began babbling. That's the only word for it, because from what Sarah told me afterwards I was making no sense. I was narrating what was going on in my freshly frozen brain.

I could see into the river, and under the water was all of Haventon. There was our house at the edge, then the houses of our neighbours. I saw the high school and the churches. I saw the apple orchard and the garage and the Legion.

Then as if this wasn't bad enough (I hardly dare think how I sounded — "Coming up on your left now, folks, Foster's Store," like some Atlantis tour guide), I saw people swimming beside me. I waved to them and said hello. Hello Mrs. Abernathy. Hello Mr. Cole. Hello Mr. Crouse. Hello Percy. None of these people was anywhere near me at the time, so when I said their names, lying there collapsed crooked with my eyes rolled back, there was speculation that I was not only senseless but couldn't see.

My mother made it to my side, still smelling like the hot chocolate she'd been serving, and when she touched my face I came back to being me. My Uncle Kent rushed down to us with my father not far behind. They picked me up, took me to the car, and drove me to the house.

Percy stood on the shore as this was happening, not upset in the least.

From what Sarah said, I wrecked the skating party. After that everyone had to clear off the river. They went for supper early at the Legion and it was my fault the men got extra gassy from underdone beans. The pancakes were slow in coming too because the batter wasn't mixed. The big room was chilly with the heat yet to kick in. The ministers had to alter their practised rhyming grace to include a provision for my speedy recovery.

You'd think I might have been cut a little slack considering I could have frozen to death or drowned, but it was as if everyone had been waiting for an excuse to tease me and I had just presented them with the perfect opportunity.

Sarah said it was June Crouse who got everything stirred up against me because I was getting dangerously pretty. I don't know. It just seems like a nice thing for a friend to say. Boys haven't noticed me yet and I figure I scare them a little anyway. They don't even want to start up with me, probably thinking our kids will turn out like Percy. June claims she was one of the first to respond to my accident (although Sarah doesn't remember her being anywhere in sight) and the way I acted was ridiculously dramatic. It was only a fall. Little kids fall all the time. The crazy babbling proved I was strange as well as clumsy. Really, I mean look, it runs in the family.

Maybe June just wanted a new hobby. At least she comes by her teasing honestly. Her brother Ronnie is the one who coined the phrase "Have mercy, Percy" and is the ringleader in my brother's bullying to this day. Now June and Ronnie can have breakfast meetings devising things to do or say to me and Percy. To keep it coordinated and exchange ideas, you know, bond in that way.

Regardless of the reason, this isn't a twist I ever saw coming. If only I had had a little warning I was going to go haywire, I would have done it a bit more privately. If only I hadn't gone skating at all. If only I hadn't twirled or jumped, or landed on that exact patch of ice.

I'm certainly not going to ask Percy for tips on coping. Sure I was familiar with circling the perimeter of outcast territory, being forever linked to him, but it's completely different now that I've been catapulted over the fence. Weird is a disease and once you have it you have it. I'm fourteen years old and infected for good. There's no miracle cure. There's no special prescription. I am quarantined all alone on the Island of the Odd. It's a chronic condition. A lifelong affliction.

And Sarah was even here last year, always at my side, like my buffer. She would say "Forget it" whenever we heard someone imitating my babbling, and once she quickly erased a blackboard drawing of me with my eyes crossed, tongue wagging out, and skate blades stabbed in my rear. It'll be worse now that she's gone. Her family moved this summer. She's only up the river in Woodstock, but I miss her beyond desperately. Since she won't be at school when I go back she may as well be a million miles away.

Down at the shore I sit under a tall, skinny birch tree. There's something else I think about a lot when I'm not so stuck on imagining a way to reconfigure my past. It's that it seemed so real — what I saw when I hit my head on the ice and my body fell into the freezing river. It was so perfectly clear and oddly familiar. The watery distortion didn't matter. I was wonderfully above it all, swimming along happily, taking in the strangely soaked view.

I sit until I know if I don't hurry back, I really will be late for supper. Before I go I look around slowly, up and down the river, kind of like the surveyor did. Something catches my eye as it shines in the sun. It is Percy's bottle bobbing.

Chapter 2

❧

The countdown to detonation, also known as the start of school, is at one week, and today is Mr. Ellis Cole's seventy-ninth birthday. My summer job has been to help Mr. Cole around the house while his regular housekeeper takes a vacation. I go every other morning for a few hours. Being around Mr. Cole is very calming. My mother says it's because you can tell he doesn't have a worry left about anything anymore. She says his smile is genuine. Whatever it is, what does it say about me that sweeping his floors and doing his dishes has been the highlight of my summer? Today I baked a cake and put together a picnic lunch to celebrate with him. The cake is chocolate — with chocolate icing — because Percy's coming with me.

Mr. Cole's house is about a twenty-five-minute walk from ours, and if you ever visited here it would be the one house you'd want to see. It looks the way I think nice people who haven't been to our province might imagine New Brunswick to be. It's a big old white farmhouse with a wraparound porch. It has a giant single pointy gable and a line of six lightning rods with cobalt-blue globes on the roof. It's down near the river, protected on the windy side and back by a stand of pines. But probably the best thing is this amazingly beautiful flowering crabapple right in the middle of the front yard. Mr. Cole's father grafted it from two trees, so in the spring it has both light pink and deep maroon blossoms.

Mr. Cole was born in the house. He inherited it from his parents along with the farm and eighty-five acres. It's always been in his family, passing from generation to generation, since Frederick John Thomas Cole was given the original land grant when he came to the province. (I know because I did a school project on him when we were studying the Loyalists.)

Mr. Cole worked on his farm, keeping a big herd of dairy cows until he turned seventy. Then he sold off all the cows and equipment to retire and spend more time with his wife Rita. They were "just one of those unlucky couples" who never had any children. Mr. Cole had lots of hired men over the years, and a nephew, Tommy, who looked promising until he turned eighteen and became the river valley's resident hooligan, but no one to continue the family tradition. Mr. Cole and Rita had a few years together to sit on the porch and reminisce. Then Rita died. That's why Mr. Cole's alone now in his big old house. That's why the weird kids from up the road are throwing him a birthday party.

Percy is carrying the picnic basket and I've got the cake. In the basket there are three roast beef sandwiches, three hard-boiled eggs, a big bag of Humpty Dumpty chips, two bottles of Nesbitt's Orange, and a Schooner beer my mother took from my father's case. She said to give her love to dear old Ellis, who she's known her whole life. I made him a card and brought a pack of Sportsman cigarettes as a gift. I'm wearing a dress, and even though it's sweltering hot, you-know-who has on his white T-shirt — with jeans. My mother tried cutting and hemming a pair once to turn them into shorts, but Percy absolutely refused to wear them and my father got agitated about the wasted money.

About halfway down Mr. Cole's long driveway I hear, "Ruby, please stop walking now. I am tiring." So I trade with Percy — his basket for the cake. It's the first thing Mr. Cole notices as we round the corner of the house. He's waiting on the porch.

"Goodness," he says. "That's a fine-looking cake. Sakes alive, Percy, you must have used your secret recipe."

Percy of course has no idea this is friendly joking.

"I must clarify it was Ruby who made it," he says, "from a recipe in the desserts section of our mother's *Five Roses Cook Book*."

Mr. Cole smiles and shakes his head.

"Our mother says we should give you the message of her love," Percy says, getting this out of the way.

Right. Mr. Cole has talked to Percy lots of times before though and knows what he's like. And since Percy isn't making eye contact, he doesn't notice when Mr. Cole winks at me.

When she was growing up, my mother lived on the far side of Mr. Cole's farm. My grandparents' place was big too, but nothing close to the size of his. They farmed a little just for themselves, but my grandfather worked out in the woods cutting trees. Even when he was old and missing three fingers he still cut boughs and made Christmas wreaths to be shipped away and hung on the doors of tall buildings in New York City.

There was a cedar fence between the two properties. It kept Mr. Cole's cows from wandering and was the right height for my mother to sit on with her drawing book every summer day. She'd sketch little red squirrels and chipmunks, gulls that flew above the river, daisies and brown-eyed Susans, dragonflies, butterflies, clouds shaped like rabbits and angels, and once, Mr. Cole on his tractor rolling up hay. Mr. Cole sometimes took a break to admire her work. My mother says she never forgot all his kind words, and she even gave Mr. Cole that drawing of him. He still has it. It's in an old Canadian Club cigar box along with his family photos, a pressed four-leaf clover, and the good gold cufflinks he wears to church. He showed me when I came to work the first day.

I think it's partly because of Mr. Cole that my mother became a painter. Mostly she takes care of Percy and me, but sometimes when we come home from school her art supplies are out and her easel is standing by the window in the kitchen. She paints everything in happy colours. The night sky in her paintings isn't black, but purple or turquoise — and the stars are pink or orange. She doesn't paint anything the colour that other people think it should be. She turns grassy hills into yellow squiggles and the river, which she always paints lilac, is a long line of zigzags.

I love her paintings, and you know how people will ask if your house caught fire what would you take? I'd take the painting that hangs above my bed. It's of me, just a tiny doll with long blue hair sitting on the roof of our pink-and-red house. The house is high on a crooked yellow hill sitting like an island in the lilac water. I'm sure I can see the whole river valley from where I sit. My mother painted it for my fifth birthday, right before she had Percy. I think it's the best gift I've ever been given and probably the best painting she's ever done. She's never painted a picture for Percy. Her paintings bother him. Percy lives in a world where grass can only be green and the river can only be blue.

Other people like them though, and the ten or twelve she paints every year always sell right away (from a gallery in Fredericton). She was even asked to paint a picture for the visit of Queen Elizabeth and Prince Philip in 1959 so it could be given as one of the gifts from the province. She painted the river with Mr. Cole's house sitting on the shore in the distance. It's something Mr. Cole and I talk about a lot when we sip tea on his porch. My big joke is that I can sometimes feel the Queen staring at us, in our miniature paint-dot forms, when she's standing in front of the frame, way across the ocean — in her curlers and underpants. When I was younger I liked to think the painting was hanging in the royal bedroom just like my painting hangs in mine, so it's the first thing she sees when she gets up in the morning. I know it's not and realistically probably the best we can hope for is some hallway. Mr. Cole and I never talk about the fact that it may instead be in the royal attic, or basement, or castle garage. But even if the painting is in one of those places, that doesn't change how proud Mr. Cole looks when he mentions it, simply knowing it exists.

We walk from the house past the flowering crabapple tree to the water. Mr. Cole is carrying an old red-and-white star-pattern quilt for us to sit on, Percy has the picnic basket, and I've taken back the cake. For the first twenty-five feet in front of the house Mr. Cole has the grass cut short and neat, but farther out it's as tall as the hay in his old fields. It's skimming the bottom of my dress as we go. Percy's in the lead, then Mr. Cole, then me.

I'm holding the cake nice and flat and careful when I bang into something. I don't fall and the cake doesn't go flying, but it squishes a round brown splotch onto my chest. My dress is a yellow gingham now decorated with what looks like a giant cow patty.

Percy is far enough ahead that he doesn't notice. Mr. Cole does though, and I feel such a wave of heat rush to the entire surface of my skin, it's a wonder it doesn't toast what's left of the cake.

"Are you all right, Ruby?"

I nod. "But look, I can't believe it. I'm so sorry." What's left of the icing is all muddy valleys and peaks.

"It's all right," he says. "Goodness, a little less frosting is probably best anyway for an old fella like me."

Percy stops, turns and comes back.

"Ruby, it appears you have ruined Mr. Cole's seventy-ninth birthday cake. Is it still edible in its present condition?"

"Oh yes, yes," Mr. Cole says. "Don't worry, you can even have two pieces."

"Thank you for the offer," Percy says. "But I believe one will be plenty."

I hand the mangled cake to Mr. Cole and hurry back to the house to clean my dress. I try not to take long at the kitchen sink, scraping off frosting, blotting and rubbing, then I head out again to retrace my steps. Maybe I'm extra sensitive since my skating disaster, but I need to know what made me trip. As long as there's a giant hidden tree root, big rock, fallen branch, dead squirrel — anything — then it doesn't mean I'm exceptionally clumsy.

Percy and Mr. Cole are down at the shore. They haven't set anything up yet, but Mr. Cole is keeping Percy occupied. I can tell he's showing Percy the spot on the lowest flat branch of his giant pine tree where he keeps his socks and shoes, cool and out of the way, whenever he goes in wading.

I'm relieved to see something sticking up a little above the grass that I never could have noticed with the cake in my hands. It's a wooden stake. The top is painted orange and the cut wood still looks fresh, as if it hasn't been here long. Mr. Cole must have just forgotten to tell us to watch our step.

I run down and join Percy and Mr. Cole, and we sit on the quilt for our picnic. It's a little cooler by the water, but the sun is still strong. We stay for an hour and eat our lunch. Percy and I drink our Nesbitt's Orange and Mr. Cole drinks his beer. When it's time for the cake, I take a candle from the picnic basket, light it, and sing. Mr. Cole smiles and blows it out, and I wonder if he has wished for anything.

~

I completely forget about the stake — until the phone calls start. All of a sudden it's like a Haventon-wide news flash that Mrs. Donna Doyle found a survey marker at the cemetery, and at least three other people saw a man with survey equipment eating his lunch across the river by the Pokiok Falls. The cemetery stake was stabbed right above the bony toe of Mrs. Doyle's dead great-grandfather, so it didn't take her long to pull it out and pitch it into the river. She had gone to lay a wreath at the foot of his grave and couldn't have it looking like a ridiculous game of ring toss with the post sticking up in the middle. "Can you imagine? Imagine!" she had said when she saw my mother and me at Foster's Store and it was our turn to hear the story.

The real question though, was what the stake was doing there. The minister knew nothing about it. The two men who took turns mowing the cemetery lawn knew nothing about it. The old couple who lived across the road was clueless too. There were lots of jokes about ghostly mischief and otherworldly creatures. Some people loved to dwell on what could happen in a graveyard at night. I wouldn't be surprised if in a few days it turns out that Mrs. Doyle ripped up that stake and stabbed it in the evil heart of a vampire. That's what I'd say if I was the type to repeat gossip. Believe me, the more foolish or fantastic the story, the better.

Considering the disrespectfulness of the placement of the stick and the lack of communication about the whole thing, soon enough it becomes the local consensus that it could only have been done by the government. That also takes care of explaining the surveyor — the one that other people saw near the Pokiok Falls and Percy and I saw on the Hawkshaw Bridge.

People are calling my father, thinking he might have some information. It's because he works for the government in Fredericton. He works for the Department of Labour, but people either don't remember or just ignore that. They always seem to assume he might have a clue about almost anything the politicians decide or do. It probably doesn't help that he once told the minister's wife that the premier's office was in his building. Now everyone figures he has access to secret information — like he spends all his time trying to overhear plans, attempting to look casual, just hanging out smoking in the halls. Maybe occasionally he does know something. But when people call I hear an awful lot of "Well, your guess is as good as mine. I'm afraid I can't help you there. I just don't know."

He always sounds friendly enough, but then after he hangs up he'll say to my mother, "Christ, why can't they just leave me?" She'll sometimes say "It's because they respect you Jack, you know that." Then, "There are worse positions to be in. You shouldn't complain." I don't know if that's exactly the case, respecting him, or if it's more that people are nosy. But I think my mother tells my father that people respect him because it makes him swear less and feel good. It may be true or it may not be. Or it may be true for an entirely different reason.

Mr. Cole said once that there were a lot of men around who would like to be my father. And not because he works for the government, but because he's married to my mother.

Regardless, it's just the way things are around here. Everybody knows everybody and since nothing wildly exciting seems to happen, no one's head gets so filled with new information that they forget all the questionably significant events of the past. Like Mrs. Cummings swallowed a pin once when she was hemming her daughter's wedding dress. It's still in her, poking around, and if she ever drops dead then a prick to the heart will be the cause. Mason Higgs has webbed fingers and once shot a three-legged moose. Mrs. Robbins is considered lucky because she won the door prize at the St. Patrick's Day tea two years in a row. It's why I don't hold out hope of anyone forgetting about my head-bonking any time soon. But adults don't tease each other. No one goes around saying to Mrs. Cummings "Hey, I think I just heard something pop. Are you feeling okay?" then laughing maniacally. That's the difference.

On the topic of the enthralling stake, everyone eventually agrees the best guess about its purpose is that the old Hawkshaw Bridge is being replaced. It was built in the early 1900s, and in the winter the steep road that leads down to it is always a slippery mess.

That keeps everyone happy for maybe a day, but as soon as that mystery is solved, new questions start. Where will the bridge be? Do you think it'll be called the Haventon Bridge this time? What will happen to the old one? How long will it take to build? Who will lose part of their land for a new road? What will happen at the end of our road with no bridge there anymore? It's all I hear when I go anywhere with my parents — the only people besides Percy that I spend time with these days. Bridge. Oh goodness, the new bridge. Did I mention the bridge? The Hawkshaw Bridge is falling down, my dear ladies.

You'd think they were talking about some magical bridge connecting New Brunswick to PEI the way it's always the centre of conversation.

It's the night before school starts and I have better things to think about than the bridge. For the past few days I've had an increasingly strong feeling like I'm living in that second before the teacher calls on me when I have no idea of the answer. Tomorrow is going to be enough of a problem without worrying about some transportation upgrade that may or may not happen years in the future. But I overhear my parents talking about the bridge as I lie in bed and as usual my mother's concern is Percy. She's saying his bottles, his charts, the river — these are all the things that make him happy. There's no way he won't find out about the bridge at school tomorrow, even though we've done our best up to now to keep it from him.

"It's just a rumour," my father says. "And it's no different than any other damn thing the kids make up to get him going."

"But it is different, Jack, you know that. The new bridge could be miles from here. What would he do then?"

"Maybe he'll grow out of it," my father says. This is something I've been hearing since Percy was three. "And besides, it might not even be true."

"You really haven't heard anything at work?"

"No."

"Nothing at all?"

"Christ, Lily."

It's quiet and I'd bet my father's taking a long drink of his beer.

"Jack, you'd tell me, right?" The tone of her voice is slightly different. "I'd just like to know so I have a chance to explain it to him."

I hear someone get up, I'll guess my father, and go to the kitchen. I listen for a few more minutes, but no one is saying anything else. I try to clear my head, but it's not easy. Attempting not to think about June Crouse lying in wait for me in the morning means wondering instead about the survey stake in Mr. Cole's yard (which I haven't mentioned to anyone) and the other one at the cemetery. I'm no engineer, but they're so far from each other I really don't know what either could have to do with a new bridge. I understand why anything to do with the river gets people around here excited, as it is the one thing we have in common. From all of our yards, or driveways, or upstairs windows, it's a blue line in the background. Maybe I'm sick of hearing about the new bridge, but I do wonder if everyone could be wrong.

Chapter 3

June Crouse and her brother Ronnie might not be able to see the river from where they live. Their little house is way down the Four Maple Road, back in the woods, and even if there was a spot in the house with a view of it, chances are someone would always be standing in the way. They have four brothers and two older sisters — April and May. If Ronnie and June ever get tired of picking on Percy and me, there are certainly other Crouses to take their places.

They're always the first ones on the school bus and the last ones off. They spread themselves out over the back four rows, both sides. They all have brown hair, oblong faces, and grey-blue eyes. I suspect most of them could use glasses because they have this creepy, unfocused way of staring at you from a distance, like when we get on the bus. They have thin noses and small, dark, almost purplish lips. It works on the girls, who most people around here agree are pretty. But the boys look strangely dainty, almost like old-fashioned dolls. None of them ever looks happy. Imagine that first thing in the morning — times eight.

I try to ignore them the way I always told Percy to by sitting in the very front seat. Percy's beside me, in near the window with his new *Bonanza* lunchbox on his lap. I know he's about to ask what I'm doing here (since last year I never sat with him) when June Crouse yells. The front door of the bus is barely closed and the driver is only starting to pull away.

"Hey Ruby, weren't you supposed to drown this summer? Isn't that what you promised?" Then her voice changes. It gets higher-pitched and closer-sounding. I'm certainly not turning around, but I figure she's standing. "I'm so crazy I'm going to live in the river with all the fish. I'm going to move there and swim all day long. I think I'll meet a nice perch for a boyfriend."

The Crouses laugh, as do, by the sounds of it, quite a few other kids between her and me. The bus driver hollers at her to sit down. Wonderful. I can already feel my fingernails digging deep half-moons into the palms of my hands. We aren't even thirty seconds into the school year. Percy is staring out the window. There's a view of the water behind houses, meadows, roads, and trees.

"It's not nice to break promises, Ruby," June calls. "Didn't your mother ever tell you that? Besides, everyone heard you say it, right?" Her brothers and sisters are probably nodding. Then she starts singing "Beyond the Sea" really loud. Soon it sounds like most of the bus has joined in.

I take a very quiet, deep breath to see if it helps. Nope. Again. Not really. Only a little bit of me manages to think, So you had all summer and that was the best you could come up with? And the rest of me feels different and small, and though I would never do anything as truly crazy as drown myself, I do wish I could squeeze into one of Percy's bottles, drop into the river, and float far, far away.

I guess this is the problem with visions: they are open to interpretation. You can make them seem better or worse, harmful or harmless, meaningful or meaningless. As more time passes, anything can be distorted, changed, remembered or forgotten, emphasized or dismissed. I didn't say much from what Sarah told me, but that just means that June has more leeway to fill things in.

All I did was hit my head and act disoriented and delusional for a few minutes. It's not like I haven't heard of other people around here doing it before for any number of reasons. How many people had gone delirious with fever? What about our minister — confused and seeing the devil after inhaling smoke when his shed caught fire? Mr. Young who lost his finger during the tug-of-war at Woodstock Old Home Week? Matilda Brewer sleepwalking? Mr. Lowe as he was having a stroke? Mr. Moore from painting the whole downstairs of his house without opening any windows?

I'm sure it didn't help that I mentioned June's father, Alton Crouse. He's one of the four people I saw swimming beside me and said hello to. Hello Mrs. Abernathy. Hello Mr. Cole. Hello Mr. Crouse. Hello Percy. Maybe June thought I chose those names to say and that they meant something. Maybe she thought my mere mention of him tainted his reputation in some way.

Except there wasn't a lot left to taint. Everyone knew Alton Crouse drank and did outrageous things. I think people stopped being shocked a long time ago — now it's just more of the same. But Alton still goes on in detail about every new exploit to anyone who'll listen. I've overheard him more than once down at the garage where he sometimes works. There's a lot of, "And Jesus H. Christ, didn't I —" this or that. I've always wondered what the H stood for. Herman? Hugo? Hallelujah? As far as Alton goes, my father says that stupid and poor are a bad combination. My mother just says, well, as long as his children are out of the way and safe.

One roasting-hot night a few summers ago, Alton Crouse used his chainsaw to cut a hole in the side of his house. When he woke up the next morning there was a little red squirrel sitting by his foot on the end of the couch, and he swore at his wife for not sewing up the rip in the screen door. Another time he took every label off every can of food in his cupboard, figuring he'd use them for cigarette rolling papers. For a month every supper was some surprise combination.

And he mistook his own dog Shadow for a bear once when it was out by his garbage box. He got his gun and shot it while the rest of the family was at church. He took the body and dragged it out to the road, figuring it would look like the dog was hit by a car. Except that the bullet hole was in the side of the dog facing up, clear as day.

Alton Crouse and Mr. Cole's nephew Tommy often got things going too. They'd drink and play cards until they got bored or wanted to go outside. Then they'd dare each other to do things like they were ten years old — something tame like knock on a neighbour's door in the middle of the night and ask to borrow a cup of sugar, or something worse like slash the tires of a tourist's car parked across the river at the Pokiok Lodge. One morning Alton Crouse was passed out on the steps of Foster's Store and later claimed he was just hungry and had wanted a bag of chips. Once he was found passed out behind the wheel of his old Ford Fairlane. Everyone said thank goodness he was in his own driveway and hadn't gone somewhere and crashed the car.

I survive the rest of the day and the bus ride home again. When Percy and I arrive at the house, my mother is in the kitchen having tea with Miss Stairs, our neighbour and my mother's old friend. My mother's easel is set up near the window and I can see faint pencil lines on the canvas, the very beginning of a painting.

"Mother," Percy says, "did anything arrive in the mail for me today?" He has stopped in the doorway, wary while Miss Stairs is here. I know this because one time she made the wrong move and said he was handsome while ruffling his hair. Percy needs to find out if he's had any bottle replies though, the same question he's asked every school day for the past two and a half years.

"Not today, Percy," my mother says.

He turns and runs past me to go upstairs.

"How was school?" my mother asks. "Was it okay without Sarah there?"

"It was fine," I say and then head to my room to change from my school clothes.

When I come back down to the kitchen Miss Stairs is gone. She visits my mother pretty much every day while we're at school, but when we come home she often doesn't stay long. Percy must have heard her leave, because he's at the table drinking a glass of milk.

"So was it really all right today, Ruby?" my mother asks again.

I nod convincingly.

"Percy," she says then. "What about your day? Did you learn anything interesting?"

"Yes."

"Did you learn things from your teacher?"

"Yes."

I walk over and look at my mother's canvas. The lines she's drawn might be a building, a church maybe, with a tall pointy steeple.

"Did you learn anything from your new textbooks?"

"Yes."

Percy can be quite the conversationalist. My mother is curious if anyone told him about the all-important bridge, but is being careful so she doesn't let the news slip herself.

"Did you learn anything from the other students?"

Percy looks up, confused. "No," he says. "Mother, I do not understand."

"I was just wondering if you overheard anything," she says.

Vagueness doesn't work well with Percy. He seems to think for a few seconds, then drinks his milk. My mother must figure so far so good when he sets down his glass.

"June Crouse told Ruby that she was supposed to drown herself," he says matter-of-factly.

Perfect. I think I just felt all my blood do a giant U-turn so it could head for my face. I shoot Percy the evil eye, but it means nothing to him. He probably doesn't even register or comprehend it. I swear if you told Percy you were dying, he'd only respond by quoting how many years you were falling short of the average life expectancy.

My mother looks startled, but I shake my head. It gives me a few seconds to think. "She was just talking about last winter," I say. "I was lucky I didn't drown." Ah, nothing like reminiscing about good times with friends. I can tell my mother doesn't buy it though, because one thing you can count on Percy for is truth and accuracy.

"Change is hard sometimes, Ruby," she says. She comes over and smoothes some of my hair from the side of my face and tucks it behind my ear. "But you're a beautiful, smart girl with a good head on your shoulders. I'm sure you'll figure it out."

I force a smile. I wonder if my mother really believes that Sarah leaving is the root of the problem. But I'm sure that's easier than thinking you've raised another outcast. It certainly would be nice to figure it out. Between my parents and Sarah I'm always hearing how I'm the one who never misses a thing. It's like they're positive that I got a double dose of social comprehension since obviously none was given to Percy. I think I'm this way because compared to the effort involved in trying to decipher the complex puzzle that is my brother, figuring out everyone else seems easy. Except not this time. Not even close. It's one thing for me to quietly gather how things work around here, watch and listen, and quite another to find a way to change anything, reposition myself, cancel out the past and attempt to fit back in.

My mother smiles at me, then turns to Percy. I go up to my room.

I'm going to work on my woodcarving for a while. Yes, woodcarving. And I am supposed to be the normal one.

One summer day when I was ten I found a wooden owl floating near the shore of the river. I was walking along the water's edge looking for rocks to put around the Johnny-jump-ups in our flower garden, when I noticed a strangely shaped driftwood log with two perfectly round eyes staring at me. The eyes were really two knots, and the beak was a small stub where a larger branch must have broken off. The roundness of its head and bit of curve to its wings was just wear from all the time floating in the water.

I almost threw it back. But I held it, and closed my eyes, and when I opened them, once again I saw the owl first, and a piece of driftwood second. I hadn't lost the idea of it, like how a shape in a cloud can change in the time it takes you to point it out to someone else. I took my owl home.

I went to the kitchen and got a pencil and our sharpest paring knife. I drew a faint line down one side of the owl to help define the shape of a wing. I took the knife and without any idea of technique, sawed away as if I was slicing a burnt loaf of bread. I sawed and sawed until I heard my father say my name.

He'd been watching from the doorway. He picked up my work-in-progress. "Hmm," he said, looking it all over. "So whoo, whoo do we have here?" But before I could respond he said he thought he had something that would help. He went to our shed and came back with a long, thick brown piece of felt, which he unrolled on the table in front of me. Tucked inside were little chisels and knives and files and gouges. They'd belonged to my grandfather. My father showed me how to use each tool, and then I practised on sticks of kindling for two weeks straight, every spare second I had, before touching the owl again.

The final result was even better than I could have hoped. I knew I'd done a good job when I saw a chickadee startle and veer away from our front step where I'd left the carving. My father said I had a natural talent. He finished the owl with three coats of Varathane and mounted it on the wall near our front door, perched above a hook. It's still there today.

I know girls typically don't carve wood, but back before I bonked my head, I didn't worry quite so much about doing things that were different. Sarah likes to crochet and I didn't see how woodcarving was any worse than making granny square after granny square, pot holder after doily after afghan. Besides, it wasn't anything I did or even acknowledged in public. I worked alone in my room and I didn't wander around with incriminating sawdust on my dress. Plus, when Sarah lived here, I would sometimes go months between woodcarving sessions.

Lately I've been unrolling the brown felt more and more. And when I'm not carving, I spend a lot of time searching for another piece of driftwood that looks like an owl. I pick up what I can, and then practise gouging out scrolls and flowers, and fancy letters and numbers. I feel better, calmer, with something sharp in one hand and a powerless piece of wood in the other. Random happy memories often pop into my head when I'm not doing anything but focusing on my carving. Today I think about when I went to New River Beach and looked for sand dollars. I remember making a special gingerbread Christmas lighthouse with my Grandmother Carson. And once I wore a white dress to the church's Easter Sunday service and an old lady asked if I was the bride.

I work for about an hour before throwing the finished product in our kindling bin like I always do. We must have the fanciest woodpile in the area. I should probably think of a real project to work on, something worth keeping. If my social status doesn't change, maybe I will.

*

It still seems odd that Sarah is gone because virtually no one around here ever leaves. I walk by her old house sometimes, and the new owners, the Johnsons, will be in the yard with their baby crawling in the grass. The Johnsons changed the colour of the shutters already—from green to black. Every time I go by the house now those shutters are a reminder. You're all alone. Sarah's not coming back.

Uncle Kent, my father's brother, got tired of driving the half-hour to Woodstock for work, and according to my mother, Aunt Patty reluctantly agreed to a change of scenery. There was the required gossip at first, and whispers of financial problems, sickness, or divorce, because no one could figure out why Uncle Kent would leave his beautiful house, friends, and extended family. But my father said once Kent had made up his mind, it was to be.

Uncle Kent responded to every argument by saying that sometimes it was just nice to control your own life, rather than sitting around waiting for something to happen. Eventually people accepted that and the rumours died down, even though my father told him it was a bit philosophical and not exactly something you'd say without a beer in your hand. Uncle Kent put their house up for sale and it sold in three days. Sarah cried for a week.

It's been more than two months since I've seen her. Sixty-eight days apart after our whole life of being together almost every day. She spent the summer at her mother's sister's in St. Stephen while Uncle Kent fixed up and painted their new house. She's back now in time to start her new school. It's an understatement to say that I can hardly wait for her visit on Saturday.

~

Tuesday morning is a repeat of Monday, and Wednesday is a repeat of that. June Crouse demands that I drown. Her singing is getting better though, more in tune. I even found myself humming "Beyond the Sea" as I got dressed for school. Today's bus ride will be no different I'm sure. June with the Crouse family back-up band. Drown. All together now! Drown. You promised, drown. Go live with the fish. Please. At least with all the attention on me, Percy's getting a reprieve. Maybe this will make up for all the times I ridiculously sputtered, "Ignore them." If someone said that to me now, I'd scream.

Percy looks out the window, maybe counting trees. He seems as if he doesn't have a care in the world, and for as much as I can figure him out, this might be true. He doesn't seem to know about the new bridge — or if he does, he hasn't bothered to let my mother or me in on it. My mother is relieved and has given up her questioning, but him not hearing about it really doesn't surprise me. Not too many of the under-ten crowd, or even the under-eighteen crowd for that matter, sit around talking about transportation infrastructure issues. Even though Percy isn't normal and might care about the bridge, it's going to take one of the so-called normal kids to tell him. I'll say now that this is highly unlikely. They generally think on a smaller scale. Personal stuff. Friends. Family. Things like, "Wow, you must be really hard to live with, Percy. I hear that just to get away from you, your sister is going to drown herself."

At lunchtime in the classroom, I say hi to Adele Stanley on the way to my desk. Adele always wears her hair in two perky pigtails, only dresses in pink and purple, uses "Oh jelly jam!" as an exclamation of both excitement and frustration, and walks by sliding her feet along, never lifting them even an inch. As far as I know she has no excuse for how she looks or talks, but the shuffling she blames on her parents for always putting her in heavy shoes when she was a baby. She's not in Percy's category of strange, but I think if you asked someone from away to observe Adele and me each for ten minutes, then bestow an award for "Most likely to be the outcast," nine times out of ten I wouldn't win.

Adele looks up, but doesn't stop chewing her tuna fish sandwich. She doesn't nod or blink or attempt to swallow her food to speak. She licks a glob of mustard (yes, tuna fish and mustard) off her lips. She takes another bite and turns away from me so precisely her pigtails don't even swing.

Oh jelly jam indeed. Even Adele Stanley can't chance talking to me.

Current attempt: failed. Current status: unchanged.

I head for the washroom. It's not even the middle of September and I've already spent enough time there to realize that once every few minutes, all three sinks drip in perfect unison. Help me. Help me. Help me now.

Miss Stairs is visiting when I get home from school. Percy sees her, asks about the mail from the doorway and goes to his room. My mother has her easel out near the window again but the canvas still only has pencil lines. There's a new circle in the sky that looks like she traced around the base of her teacup. The way my mother's paintings go it could end up being the face of God peeking above the church steeple, but for now I'll assume it's the sun.

Miss Stairs brought some lemon squares and I try one. We have a steady supply of sweets because she brings them every time she comes. Miss Stairs doesn't have any children of her own. She's not married. When my mother says this she always adds "yet" (especially when Miss Stairs is nearby) because she's a good friend. I guess it could happen, although Miss Stairs is already thirty-three and I've heard her joke to my mother that there's not exactly a fresh supply of men around here. Her parents died in a car accident ten years ago, and she lives in the house she inherited from them. I vaguely remember being in it a long time ago. I remember playing on an angled staircase with a great big landing. I think it was before Percy was born. But now Miss Stairs never invites us down. She says she doesn't like to interfere with my mother's family commitments, keeping her away from home.

Miss Stairs fills us in on all the latest Haventon news like she always does. The minister's wife started taking singing lessons in Fredericton (I hope it helps) and Mr. Foster bought a new blue Ford Mustang. Just before Miss Stairs leaves, my mother calls for Percy. Miss Stairs brought him seven empty Nesbitt's Orange bottles and my mother wants him to thank her. Miss Stairs saves all her bottles for Percy. He puts them (and all the ones our family keeps) along the window ledges in his room. When the sun passes through them late in the day, the light they throw ripples and sparkles like water on his wall. It might be why he keeps them there. There are always eight on each window, the number never changes. The extras he keeps in the closet.

I know Percy will be reluctant to come, but in a few minutes he'll take the bait. My mother passes Miss Stairs the lemon squares. She doesn't take one, but I eat my third while we wait.

"Oh," Miss Stairs says all of a sudden. "Now oh my soul, I can't believe I forgot to tell you this. Isn't that funny now." She shakes her head and smiles. "I guess it's because it happened to me and we've been going on about everyone else."

My mother looks up attentively and I put the last bite of square on my plate.

"I found something," she says. She looks like she's just called "Bingo." I wonder if she's found Captain Kidd's treasure, which has long been rumoured to be deep beneath the water at the bottom of Pokiok Falls. Well, really not something that good. It's probably going to be a new way to get stains out of your laundry, but she looks pretty thrilled.

"I found a stake," she says. "I went for a walk along the shore not far from Ellis Cole's place and wouldn't you know, I tripped on it in the tall grass."

Great. Back to the wondrous stakes again. But at least it's nice to know that I'm not the only one who trips on the things.

"A survey marker?" my mother asks.

"Yes," she says. Miss Stairs is beaming.

My mother doesn't look even a fraction as enthusiastic as Miss Stairs does.

"For the new bridge," Miss Stairs goes on, nodding vigorously at my mother, then me, perhaps trying to encourage the reaction she wants. "It has to be. Maybe we'll be getting it sooner than we think."

My mother smiles a little in acknowledgment but turns to look at the door. I turn too. Then Miss Stairs.

Percy is standing there.

"Percy," my mother says. Then before she can think of whatever else she might have planned to say if this happened, Percy starts to speak, looking over at Miss Stairs.

"That the surveying being done is for the purpose of a new bridge is only speculation at this point," he says. "It is not inevitable, nor a known fact."

Percy is standing in the doorway as if he's a teacher delivering a boring math lesson. "And besides," he says, "if such construction were to take place, a project of that magnitude may take years."

Yes. Well, that solves that. I almost want to laugh. This is usually about the time that my mother would get a judgmental glare if anyone but Miss Stairs was here. Miss Stairs has known Percy since he was four days old though, and held him as a baby, even if now he doesn't like her to come too near.

"Well, I suppose that's right, Percy," Miss Stairs says. "I shouldn't be so quick to jump to conclusions." She smiles at my mother, who looks incredibly relieved.

"But if it's true, do you think a new bridge would be okay?" my mother asks.

"Yes, Mother," he says, although there is a questioning tone in his voice as if he wonders why she's asking. Percy does much better with facts than opinion.

"Good," she says. "Good, good." She looks at me and smiles. So often with Percy she's happy when she's wrong about things. I know he isn't an easy little guy to understand, but I do sometimes wonder how she must feel being his mother when the only choices are potential disaster, disaster, or disaster averted. I'd like to know how Percy found out, but I'm sure it's best now to keep the subject closed.

"Miss Stairs brought you seven more bottles," I say and point to the end of the table.

"Thank you," he says.

I stand up to help him, but Percy tries to scoop them all at once using both arms. Two fall off the table, smash against each other on the floor, and one breaks.

Percy starts to cry.

On Friday at school, June Crouse is wearing an old blouse of my mother's. It's pale pink with yellow and white flowers, and I know there's a little blotch of purple paint on the right wrist. The church gives clothes to the Crouses (and a few other families) that the rest of Haventon donates. No one ever mentions it to them though or makes fun. I don't understand why not, except that maybe with the church's involvement any meanness about it is perceived as a sin. It just seems like a missed opportunity. My descent into delirium happened at a church function, but there's certainly been no divine intervention for me. My mother looked way better in the blouse than June does. But my father never liked it, and the ruffles on the cuffs were always getting in the way when she painted, or dangling in the water at the kitchen sink.

It's because of the blouse that I know June is outside the stall when I use the washroom at the end of the day. I can see the flowers through the little hole by the lock. June and someone else came in after me and are standing, probably fixing their hair in the mirror. June's best friend Linda Small, who I bet it is with her, is always telling June she's the prettiest girl in our grade. June sometimes sneaks some of her mother's lipstick to enhance her looks, but the rusty tin-can shimmer doesn't do much in my opinion. I've heard her offer it to Linda other times in the washroom, although Linda isn't as brave.

I wish they'd leave. They're making me feel like I have to pee again, but I know there's not a drip left in there. I'm sure they're waiting for me. June likely wants to get in a little warm-up with the badmouthing before the main show on the bus. I may as well get this over with. I push open the door.

I see a blur of pink, hear laughing, and suddenly water gushes down over my nose, rolls off my chin, soaks into my blouse and skirt. June and Linda dumped it from four large coffee mugs that they must have taken from the staff room for just this occasion. The water is ice cold and hurts when it hits. I suck in a loud breath at the shock of it, and instinctively bring my hands up to cover my face. The water that missed me splashes on the floor. June and Linda laugh even more.

"Bring back any memories?" June asks.

Out in the hall the principal is announcing, "Last call, two minutes for the buses." He gets closer, passes by, then walks away. Linda looks nervous, but June doesn't even blink. June grabs Linda's hand and they are gone in a split second.

Now I will have to walk home. I look in the mirror and see a sort of sad, angry scowl on my face. I rip off a piece of paper towel and try to rub my hair dry. I sit on the floor until my heart rate goes back to normal. I tilt my head back against the wall and close my eyes.

*

Once there was a six-year-old girl who fell down an old well. It was out along the Allandale Road. It was on a deserted property that used to be owned by the girl's great-grandparents. The girl and her father were there looking for rosebushes to transplant. The thing with old wells is that even though they're almost always boarded over when a family is done with them, after a while the boards get wet and rot. And moss grows. And weeds cover them up. And those softened boards become a trap.

The girl was running along, and I can imagine her golden hair flowing out behind her, her blue skirt rippling. She is laughing, smelling the flowers she's picked as she goes. She is happy, even joyous, carefree. Then whoosh, straight down the well. I can think of it so vividly I can feel it. The drop. The lung-emptying scream. The smell of must and mud. The terrible scrape of the boards against her arms.

When I was younger I used the story to scare myself — which was probably why Aunt Patty told Sarah and me about it in the first place. It was a warning. But the horror of it isn't what I'm thinking of now. It's the happy ending. You see, that girl's skirt caught on some of the old nails and she didn't fall to a disastrous death. Sure there was the shock and lots of crying and screaming, but then, using all her strength, that girl was able to pull herself back up again.

The sun is warm enough that my hair and clothes should be dry by the time I get home and I won't have to make up a story. I pass by Mrs. Brewer's flower garden, which is planted beside her house in a huge square. She has every colour of flower and little clumps of cedar hedge that her husband trimmed to look like an arch, and two pyramids and, a bit ambitiously, a three-legged, lopsided elephant. She has a fancy white trellis and a dark-green metal birdbath in the shape of a shell. Lots of people go to her garden to get their graduation or wedding pictures taken — using it as a backdrop for the happy times they want to remember.

Looking at it now is making me feel worse. I turn away from the flowers and instead start to look for dead butterflies that have hit car windshields and blown onto the roadside. It happens a lot. After only about fifteen or twenty paces I see a swallowtail with a tattered wing. Then several little viceroys. It doesn't seem to take long to get to our house, so I keep going. I walk and walk. And walk. I wonder how far I would have to go before I came to a place where no one knew me.

~

When Sarah and I were little we used to pretend that a big pointy rock at the very back of her yard, where the grass sloped down to meet the river, was the peak of a buried mountain hidden years ago by Mother Nature. I think we got the idea from our vacation Bible school teacher who was always saying that what we couldn't see for ourselves, God would reveal. But God is a boy and Mother Nature is a girl. (Sarah had to sit in the corner of the church basement for fifteen minutes once just for asking if Mother Nature was God's wife.) Plus the rock was pink granite, which made it seem feminine. Or as near as I can remember that's what I figured when I was seven years old.

It stuck out four feet above the few other flatter rocks around it, and Sarah and I took turns balancing on its top. We pretended we were Mother Nature's daughters. Sarah was called Summer and I was Winter. We'd braid our hair with twigs and stems of flowers. Sarah pretended to have one brown eye and one green to represent her season of earth, growing and grass. I didn't have to pretend as my eyes are ice blue.

We would spend hours near that rock playing, then go off searching for daisies, brown-eyed Susans, purple vetch, or devil's paintbrushes. We were both expert wildflower arrangers, and each Sunday night

when our families got together for supper, Sarah and I would make a
bouquet. As we got older and sometimes had to watch Percy, we'd tell
him to sit by the rock. When we went fishing in Uncle Kent's rowboat,
the rock was how we kept track of our location from the water.

Two weeks before Sarah left we walked down to the shore and
laughed about all our memories. We hadn't been near the rock in a
long time, and we could see a lot of dirt had been washed away from
its base. It was obvious that only enough of the rock was buried to
keep it secure and standing. This was suddenly hilarious. We had
thought it was the peak of a whole mountain.

"Still, you never know what was under there a hundred or thousand
years ago," I said, seeing if Sarah would go along with it.

She smiled. "That's right, my dear Winter, I guess you never know."
She touched the top of the rock but looked sad for a second and I
remembered she was leaving.

Now she's here again, finally, sitting across from me on the bed. She
took my old knit rabbit called Rabbit, and because she always does,
she put him in her lap. Sarah got her hair cut. It's trimmed all the way
up to her shoulders. She has a wide headband in it, which is another
new thing. But other than that, I can look over to our reflections in
my dresser mirror and pretend it's all back to the way it used to be.

Until she starts talking.

Sarah's already made three new girlfriends and spotted the boy she
might want to marry. He has white-blond hair like little kids do, and
he's tall and has green eyes and his father owns the Main Street Grocery
and three other office buildings. Sarah's new room is big and pink and
it faces the street, so she can watch car headlights as she lies in bed at
night. She can walk to school and to stores and a movie theatre. She
and her new friends went to a restaurant after school yesterday and
apparently I would die for one of their chocolate milkshakes.

"Aaand," she says. And I swear her eyes get bigger and her whole body tenses like she's going to levitate off the bed. "My friend Anna has a big colour TV!"

I don't know what to say. Oh, really? Lovely. And meanwhile, June Crouse dumped ice-cold water on me. I should smile. But I feel the urge to pull the quilt out from under us, put it over my head, and go to sleep — instead of feeling even a twinge of happiness for my best friend.

Of course though, Sarah says "Your turn, Ruby, what about down here? Tell me everything."

So I talk about the shutters on her old house, Mr. Cole's birthday, Mr. Foster's new car, and as a grand finale, all the rumours and speculation about the survey stakes and the new bridge.

"I miss you, you know," she says when I'm finished. "But really, nothing else around here, you're about it."

"I miss you too." I reach over for Rabbit and twist his long floppy ears around my fingers.

How can a cold metal bridge compete with three new girlfriends, a future fiancé, a movie theatre you can walk to, and lethal chocolate milkshakes?

The fact that Sarah, Aunt Patty, and Uncle Kent are visiting has no impact on Percy's weekly bottle launch, other than it means that both Sarah and I go with him. I typed his usual bossy note this morning; he's already found his rocks and had my mother seal the bottle with wax. Percy comes to my bedroom door. Knock, knock. Count to three. Knock, knock. Same as always. I tie his glasses tight around his head. When he leaves, Sarah and I follow about twenty paces behind him.

It is overcast with a squiggly line of dark rain clouds in the distance. The breeze is picking up and I tuck my hair behind my ears. Sarah and I talk as we walk, but otherwise the road is quiet. Not a single car passes us. Sarah insists we go onto the bridge rather than wait on the hill. It's like she's a tourist already and needs to see the view. Percy counts his two hundred and seventy-three paces to the middle. We go probably a hundred. Sarah leans forward on the railing so I do too.

The river is navy, darker than usual with no sun on it, dark and calm and deep. Percy drops his bottle and it plunges, then bobs, sending out circles of little ripples. Sarah and I watch it for a while, then she crosses the bridge to look upriver, leaving me. There are three crows chasing an eagle off in the distance. They seem to swoop and almost peck at its feet. To get away, the eagle lands on top of an old pine tree. It's a long way down the shore, but I'm sure it's the one that marks the edge of Mr. Cole's property.

That's why I figure the person standing just beyond it is Mr. Cole. He is distant and small, small enough that I could block all of him with my thumb from up here, but I'm almost positive it's him. He's staring at the water. I wonder how long he was there before I noticed him.

Sarah crosses back to my side and starts dropping a few pebbles that she picked up. They make such quiet little splashes that Percy either doesn't notice or doesn't care. Since we'll still have to wait for him, I drop some too. Percy's leaning on the railing, tracking his bottle, but I wonder how well he can see it. It seems to be getting darker and I'd love to get back to the house before it rains.

Finally I hear, "Ruby, I am ready to return to our home." Sarah turns to go, but I look once more downriver. Mr. Cole's still standing in the same place. Then, a few seconds before I do, he leaves.

It starts to rain before we're even off the bridge platform. It pours. We run, but soon we are as wet as the river.

*

For supper we're having chicken and potatoes, broccoli casserole, corn, and peas. Aunt Patty brought some rolls, Lady Ashburnham pickles, and pickled beets. Each time there's a break in the conversation, Aunt Patty goes back to telling my mother about their new house — curtain by curtain, towel bar by mantel moulding, room by room. Uncle Kent sometimes joins in to verify something, like the width of the baseboard in the living room. (Sarah and I did a perfectly synchronized eye roll when he said that.) My parents are laughing and joking with Aunt Patty and Uncle Kent. My father has been nodding a lot if he's chewing, or saying, "Good, good" if he's not. Everyone, including me, and I'll even throw in Percy since it's hard to tell, seems happy to be warm, dry, eating, and all together.

When the phone rings, my father says to ignore it. My mother starts to smooth Percy's hair, and although he cringes at the noise, Aunt Patty asks how his bottle launch went today, which is enough to distract him. The phone stops after seven rings. Percy continues on with the weather conditions present at the time of the drop (a slight breeze and imminent precipitation) when the phone starts again.

This time my mother pushes back her chair. "It must be important," she says.

"Just leave it," my father says.

"But what if something's happened?"

"To who? What?" my father asks, sounding slightly annoyed. "Anyone that matters is here. And the house certainly isn't burning down, so whoever isn't considerate enough to let a man eat in peace with his family can wait."

Percy's covering his ears, squeezing them tight like he's trying to flatten his head. The phone is still ringing. It's very close behind me on a little round table in the hall.

"I don't mind getting it," I say.

"No. They can call back," my father says.

It rings. And rings.

Now tears are starting down Percy's cheeks. My mother's still smoothing his hair and Aunt Patty's rubbing his back.

Ring. I haven't been counting, but it's probably going on ten or twelve times. Sarah looks at me.

"Leave it," my father says again to no one in particular.

Ring.

Percy lowers his head, brings up his knees.

"Jack, please," my mother says.

My father looks at Uncle Kent.

"Christ," my father says and gets up. I pull my chair in close to the table so he can get past me. The ringing stops.

My father sits back down and other than Percy's little sobs everything is quiet for several seconds.

"There you go, Percy," my mother says, and he stops crying except for a hiccup. He rubs his face with his napkin.

My father continues eating. So does Uncle Kent. Aunt Patty refills Percy's glass with water from the pitcher and offers him a drink.

"Something must be happening, Jack," my mother says.

"Well, if so, we can find out after our dinner and dessert are finished," he says. "You've made a wonderful meal and we're all here together and I won't have anyone spoiling it."

My mother looks at Percy. His face is still red.

"Who would like dessert then?" she asks.

Even though it's blueberry cobbler, one of my favourites, I don't think I'll be able to eat. My mother's right. Maybe I'm more attuned lately to always expecting the worst, but it does seem like something is shifting out there somewhere. I look past my mother through the window to the beating rain.

My mother has time to go to the kitchen, dish out everyone's cobbler, carry it all to the table, sit down, and start to eat. The rain is getting louder and Uncle Kent is talking about how his trip home will be a slow one.

I hear a sound, like a bump, and I can tell Percy hears it too because his fork stops midway to his mouth. Then I hear another bump, like someone stomping their foot on the step.

More stomping.

A knock.

"Unbelievable," my father says.

But my mother goes straight to the door.

"Vergie," I hear her say. "Goodness, you're soaked, come in."

Miss Stairs steps in and in the light I can tell she's not only wet from the rain but that she's been crying.

"Oh, Lily!" she says. "Why are they doing this? How can this happen?"

My father stands up quickly. Everyone can hear her. Sarah looks around at me, Uncle Kent, Aunt Patty.

Percy says "Ruby, is that Miss Stairs at the door? Why has she come at suppertime?"

"Yes, Percy," I say. "I'm not sure why she's here."

I'm drawn out toward my mother and Miss Stairs.

I hear my father say "Patty, will you take him out to the kitchen and turn on the radio?" He means Percy. Sarah and Uncle Kent go to the kitchen too.

"I'm so sorry, Lily," Miss Stairs is saying. "Bothering you with your family, but I never —"

"It's all right," my mother says. "We should have answered the phone."

My father brushes past me.

"What is it, Vergie?" he asks. "Are you hurt?" I can tell he's trying to sound concerned, but there's something about his questions that makes him seem annoyed.

Miss Stairs takes a shaky breath.

"You don't know?" she asks. There's not one twinge of the excitement that I'm used to hearing when she's the first one to tell us gossip.

"Know what?" my father asks.

The phone starts to ring again.

Chapter 4

~

It isn't Miss Stairs who finally tells us, but my father. When he gets off the phone he comes to the living room. He brings everyone with him, even Percy. My father doesn't look sad, or scared, but there's something different about his expression that I try to memorize to figure out later if I need to. Is it confusion or concern? I think his eyebrows are twitching. It's not a look I've seen on his face before.

The facts are these: there isn't going to be a new bridge. The surveyors and the stakes they left behind are for a project much larger. A dam is being put across the river at Mactaquac, about fifteen miles from here. It's going to be of a size and a cost that's hardly imaginable. The dam will be a hydroelectric plant constructed to produce energy for the province. The water on our side of the dam will be backed up, causing flooding. It won't be like a spring flood; it will be permanent. The river is predicted to almost double in width. Land we can now walk on will go underwater.

As far as what will happen to people's houses, my father tells us they will be expropriated — which means taken away without a choice, he says — by the government. People will be forced to sell their homes, barns, farmland. Houses will be moved or destroyed, dismantled or burned. It's already been decided. The dam and the flooding cannot be changed. Everything we see when we look around now will be drowned.

My mother cries quietly. Tears start down her face at the word *flooding*. Uncle Kent puts his arms around Aunt Patty and Sarah. My father goes to my mother. I go to Percy. He seems very uncomfortable, glancing back and forth at everyone. I squeeze beside him in the chair.

"Ruby," he says. "Do you think my bottles would become permanently damaged passing through a hydroelectric dam?"

"I don't know, Percy," I say.

And I also don't know if it's okay that I only feel relief. This perma-flood isn't anything I could have guessed, but considering the dramatic lead-up, I thought it would be something a lot worse. No one's dead. No one's even hurt. A government-funded chance to move? Yes, please. Sign us up. I try to block out the sound of my mother's crying as I imagine packing my bags for Woodstock.

~

But keeping with the usual trend lately, soon enough I realize that I'm the odd one out. I seem to be the only person in the whole area who thinks any good could come of this. All the excitability that the survey stakes and the bridge caused now seem like calm, rational, nice-sunny-day-isn't-it type conversations compared to this. A foolproof way to tell that an event is truly awful is when you lose count of how many long-dead people you've heard are probably rolling in their graves. There's a lot of "Thank goodness" or "Thank God" so-and-so isn't alive to see this. It seems to be where every conversation goes. Over the next few days I hear it again and again at the store, the gas station, church, and in our own house.

And you can only hear so many times about people rolling in their graves, in the cemetery right down by the water, before someone — in this case I think it's Mr. Foster — wonders, Wait a minute, what about those graves? What will happen to them? Will they be moved? What about the churches? What about the school? What about the roads? How far will the water reach? Will it reach this house? That house? How will the prices for the houses be decided? What about the new roof on this house? The new kitchen in that one? What about the animals? What about the trees? What about Pokiok Falls? Then, When will it happen? Where will we go? And most of all, I hear, Why? How? Why are they doing it? My father asks, How can the politicians see our homes, this space we live and breathe in, only as squares on a map on a table in a big fancy conference room?

My mother repeats that some people simply won't accept it, they say it's ridiculous, the magnitude of it. Our province is small, some dare say unambitious, it is too big a task. We were wrong about the bridge, we must be wrong about this too. And even I'll admit, the more I hear, the more it sounds like an insanely gigantic, nearly im-possible job. But it's true.

Miss Stairs works part-time at Foster's Store, and on Saturday after-noon, probably about the time Percy was dropping his bottle in the river, she'd been finding out. Any sort of news always passes through the store and through her, sooner if not later. It's where she hears about everything — from pregnancies to new hairstyles gone wrong — which she repeats to my mother. Miss Stairs heard from our minister's wife after the original source, Paulette Hogan, told her.

Paulette Hogan and her husband Don live in Upper Queensbury, right along the river. Their house is so close to the water that Miss Stairs said once that you could look out the window and convince yourself you were on a boat. Don Hogan is Mr. Hogan, who's my teacher at school. He doesn't have any children of his own to embarrass, so when he tries too hard to impress us, he doesn't seem to realize he's doing it. Mr. Hogan always calls everyone by their full names, which he's memorized from the school register. "Well, hello, Ruby Persimmon Carson," he'll say. "And good morning, June Joy Crouse." There are boys with middle names like Clair and Bliss and Lynn and even Cheryl who mutter things under their breath when they see him coming. Mr. Hogan also likes to say "Merry Christmas" as a greeting regardless of the season. "Merry Christmas, Linda Leah Small," he had said the first day of school, grinning like an elf.

Paulette Hogan works in Fredericton as a secretary. She makes the drive each day like my father, except she works at the university. She works in a central office for all the professors in the Department of Political Science. She answers the phone, types their letters, sorts mail, listens to students' complaints, that sort of thing. Because of her position, Miss Stairs says Mrs. Hogan sometimes has access to private and important information. She knows things like how much money the professors make. It's the same as with any secretary (I know because Aunt Patty used to work as the church secretary). It's just part of the job to keep all the important information to herself. Which Mrs. Hogan always had, for seventeen years, up until this.

A professor needed her to type some notes for a press conference, on little cards so they were easy to read, as if he was giving a speech. A government project was being announced and he was asked to comment on the "political and public impact" according to what Mrs. Hogan said. The professor also gave her a huge document with several sentences on several pages underlined. He wanted those things copied onto cards too. The document was the study, the plans, describing everything that would be happening to our river valley. Mrs. Hogan had it in her hands, saw it with her own eyes, read every word, excused herself early after the last card was typed, could hardly drive home, couldn't eat supper, couldn't sleep that night, then went to the minister's house the next morning, white and weak.

This is the story that Miss Stairs told us, and the one that is repeated over and over for the next week. As usual, some parts of it change the more it is told. Mrs. Hogan or else the minister's wife is said to have fainted. Sometimes the document becomes an overheard conversation or phone call. The professor is an alcoholic or else doesn't believe in God. Or is forty and still living with his mother. Or is the premier's first cousin.

So my father paces and my mother arranges, rearranges, and arranges the kitchen cupboards. She cooks large Sunday-sized dinners — chicken or roast, potatoes, gravy, squash, carrots, peas, corn — for four nights straight, but barely eats any of the food herself. She finishes her painting, faster than ever. The circle I had seen was the sun like I thought, but for the river instead of the usual lilac she uses a navy so dark it looks black.

Even at school, the talk of all this is unavoidable. Mr. Hogan is Mr. Popularity now with the whole staff because of Paulette. All the teachers chatter about the dam every second that they're not writing on the blackboard or explaining our lessons. As soon as we're working, they slip out into the hall. We all listen even if we pretend not to. I can tell because no one ever sharpens their pencil in math, and I never hear a page flip, or feel the floor wiggle like it does when someone nearby is erasing something really hard.

The teachers ask the same questions that I hear my parents ask each other. How can they do this to us? How can they sleep at night? How can they decide for us without asking? How could they keep it to themselves? The "they" is, I suppose, everyone who lives far away and goes to work each day in buildings where decisions are made and sleeps at home at night in beds in houses that will never be drowned. Everybody around here is angry about not just what's going to happen, but also not being told about it. Plus it's something we never ever could have guessed.

That's what it all comes back to. No one could have known. I couldn't have known.

Or could I? Did I?

I'm awake in my bed like every night since Miss Stairs came to us because this is what I think: I might be psychic. Of course I remember what I saw when I banged my head and soaked up the freezing-cold river. I can't help but think of it again and again. Wasn't it this? Wasn't it the entire place underwater? It's kind of capital-C Creepy.

How am I supposed to convince myself that everything will eventually get better, that someday I'll be declared all clear of the weird, if my own mind is embracing the idea. What if everyone is right about me? Because being psychic really is just plain strange.

If I'd known I was going to develop a special power, then invisibility would have been nice. Or if I had to limit it to powers of the mind, then I would have gone with thought control. I'd have tried it out on June first. "Hey Ruby, weren't you — wait, I mean — aren't you going to come on back and sit with me? I'm just dying to hear all about your summer!"

Anyway.

Just the idea of being psychic starts me digging my fingernails into my hands, so for now I'm trying to forget it. I should concentrate on the other problems I have rather than thinking up new ones. What I saw wasn't a message, the river didn't know either, it wasn't whispering a warning. I'm just stuck on this lately because this flood business is all I hear about. It's water, water everywhere from the time I get up until the time I go to bed.

My mother says that this is the start of the one event that people around here will forever use to mark before and after. I can certainly understand everyone feeling angry and sad — having this ultimate rude interruption come out of nowhere. I'm well aware of what it's like to realize that you're way, way off in your speculation about how your life was going to be. But at least with this, everyone is in it together.

The official announcement finally comes. The words come from the premier's mouth. It's a time of bold change, a look to the future of our province, a brave sacrifice by some for the benefit of many. I see him on TV, in our living room, with my parents and Percy sitting near me.

"Christ," my father says. "The bastard."

It will make New Brunswick strong, the premier says, harnessing this powerful water resource. It is an opportunity to move forward, this new energy. He goes on and on and I look to my mother, my father, Percy.

My father is smoking now, staring out the window. My mother is nodding slowly, listening intently as if she will be asked questions later about the speech. Percy is tapping his knee with his thumb, counting to himself quietly.

There's a meeting. It's at the Legion. My father wears the suit he wears to church and my mother puts on a burgundy dress. She pulls her hair back into a little roll at the top of her neck. She wears lipstick. I heard my parents talking and the clothes are so the government officials will realize they're mistaken if they think that it's only simple country folk they're bossing around. Miss Stairs comes to the door in a green dress and a huge dazzling amber rhinestone leaf-shaped brooch. She's driving to the school with them. I'm not allowed to go. I'm babysitting Percy. This will involve losing one game of chess to him (no matter how hard I try), then doing whatever I want while he completely ignores me and sits in a chair and reads.

My parents are gone well over three hours. As soon as my mother's in the door she asks about Percy, even though she knows that at eight o'clock he would have put himself to bed.

"There's a small chance we might be safe," my father says finally. "We might be high enough up and out of the way."

"Maybe," my mother says cautiously, looking around the kitchen, taking it in. "But it will be a while until we know for sure."

I nod slowly as if I'm also considering this information, hoping only for the best.

Then she says it will be a long, long process. The dam won't be finished until the fall of 1967 — two whole years from now.

Translation: I'll tell June to quit planning my farewell party.

So much for something good coming out of something bad. So much for a quick escape.

And it really begins. The whole place moves past the point of no return. It's like something changes in the air around here. It turns into a scary movie with spooky music playing in the background, and in floats this mysterious grey haze. People wonder, wait as if in a daze. My father says that this is what it feels like to know your whole life is someone else's calculation, your family a number in a list on a page.

Chapter 5

~

My mother's waiting on the front step when Percy and I get home
from school. She's going to visit Mr. Cole and wants us to come too.
She'd like to check on him considering everything that's happening—make sure he's doing all right. I quickly review my afternoon
plans: sit alone in the kitchen, sit by myself in the living room, sit solo
in my bedroom. It can all be squeezed in later. Percy doesn't want to
go, but he agrees when my mother says he can choose a book to take
and he sees the divinity fudge she's made.

We walk to Mr. Cole's. It's hot for late September and my mother
has on a short-sleeved pale-blue blouse and pedal pushers. Percy was
allowed to change from his school clothes into his white T-shirt and
jeans. I'm still wearing my purple top and slacks. I carry the fudge
so my mother can hold Percy's hand. Even though it looks almost
ridiculous at his age, my mother wants to be sure he doesn't run off.
Percy can surprise you sometimes when he's deep in his own world,
lost in thought.

At Mr. Cole's someone's car is in the driveway, but my mother says it must just be Miss MacFarlane, his regular housekeeper, since finishing everything often takes her late into the afternoon. Mr. Cole is sitting alone on the porch sipping tea when we go around front, and I can tell that my mother is happy he doesn't already have a visitor.

Percy immediately announces, "My mother has told me it is acceptable to read only after I acknowledge you." He nods his head as if doing just that.

Mr. Cole laughs. Percy looks confused for a second but then sits on the steps.

"Well, let me get you some tea," Mr. Cole says. "You will stay for tea, won't you?"

"I'll get it," I say. "I still remember where everything is."

Inside someone is upstairs moving around — Miss MacFarlane I guess. The teapot has cooled so I turn on the stove. While I wait for the water it seems to get quieter in the house. Then I get that feeling like someone's watching me. Miss MacFarlane probably wonders who's down here making a mess, but when I look up she isn't there. I make the tea and check out in the hall before I go back to the porch. No one's around and it's noisy again upstairs.

Percy joins us temporarily to eat a piece of fudge, but soon enough he goes back to the steps. My mother, Mr. Cole, and I talk back and forth, drinking tea, until we're interrupted by the opening of the door.

"Uncle Ellis, you should have told me we had guests." The man's voice is loud. I startle a little and jiggle my cup against my saucer.

"Tommy," Mr. Cole says. Tommy has a silly grin on his face. "Why yes, I suppose," Mr. Cole goes on. "You must forgive an old man for not thinking though. It's just I've been here by myself for so many years now."

Tommy steps ahead and puts his hand on Mr. Cole's shoulder.

"Tommy's been staying with me some just lately," Mr. Cole says to my mother. "Since the announcement."

"Yes, yes, all this horrible upset coming," Tommy says, shaking his head. Then, as if he's just remembered, or as if a switch has just been flicked, his grin is instantly gone. "Family's got to stick together," he says and nods.

I look at my mother. She doesn't roll her eyes but smiles politely and looks at Mr. Cole.

Tommy Cole is tall and thin with a scruffy beard and brown hair that looks like he cuts it himself. He's maybe twenty-five. He's really Mr. Cole's great-nephew, but everyone just says nephew, probably since there's nothing great about Tommy. When he was younger he used to help Mr. Cole with his farm, but that was a long time ago. After Tommy finished high school and his now-dead father moved out West, everyone says Tommy stayed because he didn't have enough ambition to pack his suitcase and go. Although it's a horrifying image, I know that on the night of his graduation he got drunk, jumped off the Hawkshaw Bridge naked, and nearly drowned. This, Tommy declared, was a life-changing moment. He'd spent plenty of his time already getting bossed around — by Mr. Cole, his father, his teachers — and he didn't want any time wasted against the gamble of what little he might have left. Tommy loves to repeat this story. Everyone's heard it. I found out about it in elementary school before I even knew what *drunk* meant. It's like Tommy thinks it's some important river valley fable. But most people say that stupid drunken antics shouldn't be counted as a diviner of fate. Since it was obvious Tommy had already turned bad along the way, it seemed a bit too convenient. Some people say he should have drowned.

Tommy doesn't have any sort of regular job. He works on and off at other people's farms, on construction crews, picking potatoes upriver in season, or sometimes painting a house — just long enough to make a little cash, until whatever he's doing is half done or he quits.

Mostly Tommy survives on schemes. He's a good smuggler (rumour has it he uses the one-man-one-dog Forest City crossing to Maine), so he makes a bit of money selling American liquor and cigarettes. He sometimes picks the dump for anything he can sell to the second-hand dealers in Fredericton. He picks fiddleheads and apples and raspberries and blackberries — off other people's land.

Tommy lives in a fixed-up hunting cabin down the same road as Alton Crouse. This might have been how they met, although my father says they seem like the type to have found each other anyway. (He also said once that they were in a dead heat for the position of village idiot.) Tommy got on the wrong side of my father when he was helping a man my father hired. They were renovating part of our porch so we could use it as a sunroom. Somehow our cat Quilty got sealed behind the drywall. I was nine and figuring she was gone for good, I began her memorial service preparations. It was only a poem, but still. Then a few nights later as I was drifting off to sleep, I heard meowing. I thought for sure it was the ghost of Quilty coming to say her final farewell. Except my father heard it too and followed the sound to the new sunroom. He punched his fist through the wall and out she hopped. Wow, it seemed like magic. Or a miracle. As I got older and overheard the story repeated when Uncle Kent and my father sat out in that room and smoked, I knew it was really "half-assed" Tommy who had entombed and almost killed her.

Tommy sits down and helps himself to the last four pieces of fudge. Mr. Cole offers him some tea, but Tommy refuses, which is fine by me since I don't want to get it. Mr. Cole excuses himself and goes in the house. Tommy calls after him saying since he's up, he'd take a beer.

"So, Lily," Tommy says after Mr. Cole goes in. "You're looking as lovely as ever."

People say this type of thing to my mother all the time (Mr. Cole told me once she is considered a legendary beauty), but there's something about the way Tommy says it that makes me wish he'd gag on the fudge.

"Thank you, Thomas," she says.

"And is this the new improved younger version?" He turns to me. "How old, may I ask, are you?"

"Fourteen," I manage. I try to smile politely like my mother did before. Mr. Cole could come back out any second.

Tommy shakes his head slowly. I concentrate on a housefly about to come in for a slippery landing on his hair.

"And your special boy," he says to my mother, talking as if Percy isn't here. "He's nice and quiet at least."

Percy turns around. Tommy bends a little and does a baby wave like Percy is two.

"Hel-lo," Tommy says. "Hel-lo."

I worry that Percy will cry simply from the stupidity and proximity of Tommy.

"Mother," Percy says. "You referred to him as Thomas, but is this the same Tommy Cole that my father has said is unemployable?"

I look over at my mother so I don't laugh. She nods just slightly, because it's a well-known fact that you always have to answer Percy.

Mr. Cole comes back out at the same time and Tommy doesn't get a chance to do or say anything. Mr. Cole must not have heard Tommy's request for a beer.

"Ellis," my mother says. "We'll have to be going soon, but I did want to know that you were doing all right with the news."

Mr. Cole looks out to the river. "Sakes alive, it certainly isn't anything I thought I'd see in my lifetime, I can say that much."

"Now don't you worry your pretty self about good old Uncle Ellis," Tommy says. "I'm with him here now and I've got it all under control."

My mother looks at Mr. Cole. I can tell she's concerned.

"With all due respect to you both, I'm fine," Mr. Cole says. "But it's so kind of you to come today, Lily. I am so fortunate to still have you thinking of me after all these years. To think you're that same little girl who used to sit on my fence." He shakes his head.

"Yes, thank you, Lily," Tommy says. "Now may I offer you a ride home?"

"No thank you, Thomas, I think we'd prefer to walk."

"Well at least let me walk you to the road then." He gets up and goes past Percy down the stairs. It's obvious we're not going to be able to leave without him.

My mother hugs Mr. Cole and we say goodbye. My mother takes Percy's hand.

Tommy doesn't say anything until we're around the corner of the house and starting up the long driveway.

"So how's your husband, Lily? I must say I've heard an awful lot of people say lately that he must not be the bigwig he thinks he is. Important government news like this and a little secretary finds out before him."

My mother seems to ignore this.

"Work all those years, you'd think he'd be in some kind of a position to know. Commit all that time to a job. It must really burn him up that no one bothered to tell him." Tommy shakes his head like this is perplexing. "Have you ever been to his office, Lily? How do you know he's not just the premier's janitor or something?" I feel like tripping him. "Something sure doesn't seem right there," he goes on. "You'd think a big-deal man would know big-deal news."

Again my mother says nothing as we walk the last few steps to where the driveway meets the road. Her eyes are slightly squinted like when she is thinking really hard, trying to concentrate on something.

"Thank you," she says to Tommy. "But now before we go I just —"

she pauses to take a breath. She looks down at Percy and seems to decide something. "Please take the very best care of Ellis, Thomas. He really is a dear old friend and I hate to have to worry about him." She smiles the most beautiful smile. "And I'll be sure to give your best wishes to my husband."

Tommy looks surprised as if he has just remembered his name is really Thomas. My mother doesn't wait for a response and we start off. Percy lets go of my mother's hand for a second to wipe his off on his jeans. We're well down the road before Tommy calls after us. "Don't you worry now, Lily," he hollers. "You just remember, blood is thicker than water! You hear me? Blood is thicker than water!" I imagine his face is red since he's yelling so loud I can hear an echo of it over the river. But I don't turn around to check. I wish he'd go back to his cabin in the woods. Poor Mr. Cole.

There are slices of bread along the side of the road as we walk. Every few hundred feet there will be a piece — some are whole wheat, some are white, and then once in a while there's a dinner roll. I've seen the bread here lots of times before, sometimes with chickadees pecking at it. The slices were a mystery to me for a long time, like a giant-sized re-creation of Hansel and Gretel. Then one day while I was walking, Mr. Washburn drove by with the back of his green Ford half-ton loaded with old stale and reject bread (from the Noble Bakery in Woodstock). He was taking it home to feed his pigs. The bread was piled loose and some pieces flew out along the way. It was kind of disappointing to find out that was the true source, because pig food isn't exactly interesting or romantic. Now we step over the occasional slice like it's a rock or weed without even mentioning it as we go on our way.

My mother does mention Tommy though. She tells Percy and me not to pay any attention to what he said about our father.

~

I'm starting a special woodcarving project. I've been whittling away at a frantic pace lately and the kindling bin is getting to the point of overflowing. I'm pretty sure my father has been rescuing some of my practice pieces though. I've seen him looking through them as he sits alone on the step of the shed some nights, smoking. Sometimes he wets his thumb and rubs it over the wood to bring out a design. He'll turn pieces over and over in his hands or compare two side by side. I think he kept a piece I carved with each of our family members' initials. It was a small oval stick of driftwood and I thought after that it would make a neat Christmas tree ornament. But I couldn't find it in the kindling bin, and we haven't started burning anything yet in our woodstove. I know my father likes my carving. Plenty of times before he's suggested doing a specific project again, like the owl, that I might want to save.

I'm keeping my ambitious plan to myself for now, but I'm sure my father will soon notice the lack of additions to the kindling bin. I'm already going on my first piece. I'm working away on a bit of water-greyed pine. The wood is soft and so easy to work with. There's just something about watching the little sliver of wood curl as I press and guide my chisel. I can focus my eyes so completely that it's all I see. Once a gouge is made it can't be erased like a pencil line, unravelled like yarn or painted over. Once a bit of wood is chipped off or chiselled away, the only way to fix a mistake, or straighten out or smooth what you've started, is by going deeper.

And today as I work I think about a beautiful red trillium I saw once blooming in the woods. And when I was ten I got to hold a two-day-old baby because his mother had taken him to church. His miniscule fingernails weren't any bigger than one of my freckles. He was so warm, and he looked right at me and didn't cry. Then just because I'm on the topic I figure, I remember my mother saying that when she was pregnant with me she craved chewing ice.

Percy and I go to school. (It's an inescapable obligation that must be fulfilled.) I haven't made any new friends and I know better than to even try. Our area's so small there's limited choice and everybody's already doubled or tripled up. It's not like there's a bunch of other social rejects I can band together with (Percy's already my blood relative). I suppose I could hope that someone else does something disastrous to sabotage themselves, but it hasn't happened yet.

I've always done well in my classes, but so far this year I'm wildly surpassing any previous results. It's not through any special effort on my part, it's just that doing homework, memorizing textbooks, and spending hours on projects and essays isn't a big deal anymore. I can't whittle all the time, and the evenings and weekends Sarah and I used to spend having fun must be filled somehow. I've been reading more than usual, making use of the limitless resource known as Percy's bookshelf. Plus I'm always well rested. I go to bed early, and I have no problem sleeping in or napping on the weekends. This means that at school I sit there wide awake, paying attention. If I wasn't already an outcast, I might worry what these new habits of mine could set me up for.

Although I was hoping that now with this big tsunami-type problem hanging over us, the little problems known as Percy and me would seem insignificant and be forgotten. But, please. I've come to the conclusion that instead we're the perfect stress relief. School is an escape from worried, edgy parents, and what better way to work off a little extra anxiety than to badmouth us. I swear Ronnie and June have never been so popular. It's like they're providing a public service.

It doesn't help that we're studying colonial New England in history class and spent a day discussing the Salem witch burnings. It's giving June new material. Back then I could have been burned without question. I could have been burned for my babbling — even without anyone figuring out I might be psychic.

And, speaking of that, the more I analyze it, the more I think I am definitely, absolutely, unequivocally being a bit too generous in my assessment. I didn't say the water was going to rush over us, flood out all our houses, or permanently change things. People like accuracy and need specifics in their predictions. An old lady out in Temperance Vale who reads tea leaves never says "Well, you may meet a man — someday." It's more like "You will marry a tall red-haired man within three years and have two of his children." Or that's the type of thing that Miss Stairs says she says anyway.

But, just to be on the safe side, and to try to get my mind off this once and for all, a few afternoons ago I decided to check my possible powers. I had Percy help me, since a psychic test really isn't something you can do alone. I went to his room and asked him to silently think of a number between one and a hundred.

"Ruby, I must ask why you are requesting this," he said.

I did predict that much would happen.

"It's just for fun, a guessing game."

Percy was clearly suspicious, but he set the book he'd been reading beside him on the bed.

"Although I will do as you ask, without evidence of my chosen number, I do not know how you will tell without a doubt that I am being truthful."

Percy is the most truthful person I know, but telling him that wasn't going to help.

"How about you just write some numbers down for me and we'll fold up the papers so I can't see them."

Percy agreed and soon I was back in my room with five little white squares. I sat in the middle of my bed, legs crossed, perfectly still with my eyes closed. I held the five little papers out in front of me, cupped in my hands. I didn't feel anything different churning in my brain. I thought and thought and then somehow, for no specific reason, I came up with 72, 43, 31, 19, and 22.

I took a deep breath and unfolded the papers.

Percy had chosen 1, 2, 3, 4, 5.

I should have known. Straight ahead, ordered, and really quite predictable.

Not only wasn't I psychic, but my attempt to conjure up some mind-reading ability was cancelling out my common sense.

~

June and Linda are waiting for me in the hall after math class.

"So did you ride your broom to school today?" June asks. "I don't think I saw you on the bus."

The reason she didn't notice me was because today's selection was "Have mercy, Percy," which she supported by joining in.

"Did you miss me?" There. I did it. My legs feel a little weak.

June looks surprised.

"Why, yes I did," she says, hardly missing a beat. She's obviously better at this than I am and it's got to be from all the practice. "I thought maybe you'd finally drowned yourself."

Linda laughs.

Lovely. I'm quiet because one line was all I had in me. My mouth goes dry.

I walk away down the hall. At least it was a start. That's what I'm going to try to remember. (Because it took days of planning in my head to do it.) I turn around and see June and Linda talking with two other girls. At the same time I trip over a book bag that someone's left on the floor. To catch myself, my hand makes a loud slap against a metal locker.

There's an instant quartet of laughter. My face stings as much as my hand.

Yay. Three cheers for me. Okay, so make that a false start. I wonder if you can be disqualified from your own life?

As usual, Miss Stairs is in the kitchen when we get home from school. She's been here every weekday since the announcement. I'm pretty sure she's been coming earlier in the day too. Our house has been a little messier, like my mother doesn't have the time to clean it. My father's been noticing this too, and even if Miss Stairs isn't the problem, she's who he's been blaming. I sometimes hear her name when they argue after I'm in bed. My mother will ask over and over "Well, who else does she have, Jack?"

My father doesn't like how Miss Stairs is clinging so close. I think what really annoys him isn't the mess, but the fact that without asking him, my mother agreed that Miss Stairs could meet with the government men here when it's time for her house assessment. Miss Stairs says she can't handle the idea of letting strangers in to nose around her home only so they can take it away. My father says he doesn't know how in hell they're going to do a proper evaluation without seeing it. Which sounds logical enough. I really don't mind Miss Stairs hanging around so much. She's someone to talk to besides my family.

Today Miss Stairs brought three new scarves with her to show us. They are sheer in pastel colours with faint printed flowers: one pink, one mauve, one yellow. She says she bought them this morning in Fredericton. She shops a lot. She sometimes jokes that she works at Foster's Store just to get the employee discount. She always has something new to wear and sometimes, even for no special occasion, she'll bring a teacup as a gift for my mother.

I say the scarves look pretty and watch as my mother encourages her to try one on. Miss Stairs chooses the mauve one.

"Beautiful, Vergie," my mother says.

"She's right," I say.

"Well then," Miss Stairs says, "I guess this is the one I'll wear to the big church service."

Which is on Sunday at two, after everyone has gone to their usual church in the morning and had time to go home and eat lunch. The afternoon is a special service that all three churches in the area are joining together to have because of the changes coming. The ministers thought it would be a good idea to get everyone together to pray. I'm not so sure. The last time the churches got the bright idea to do something together was the skating party. But my parents say the whole family's going.

We drive to the high school, where it's being held. The wooden chairs usually saved for assemblies are lined almost to the back of the gym and it's already quite full. There's organ music being played through the school's intercom system, probably to set the right mood. It's loud so you can hear it over everyone's chatting. I see Miss Stairs in her scarf, and the Johnsons with their baby, Mr. and Mrs. Foster from the store, Mr. Cole — and Tommy. Adele "Jelly Jam" Stanley is shuffling along to a seat. Linda Small is with her parents and twin brothers. Even the Crouses are already here, Alton included, which is in itself a small Sunday miracle. They're taking up their own row.

Some people turn when we come in and of course there's whispering. It could be about any one of us — me for my weirdness, Percy for his weirdness, my mother for her beauty or the fact/justice/irony/bad luck she's stuck with Percy (and maybe now me), my father for his lack of any significant information about the flood. We sit at the back where there are still empty seats.

There are four large bouquets of cattails decorating the stage. The principal's lectern is in the middle with three chairs to the right of it. Hanging from the front of the stage is a large banner that reads "Learning to Accept What Will Come." There's a tidal wave painted on the side in front of the "L" for "Learning." It's as high as the whole banner. I bet it was our minister's wife who painted it. It seems to project her brand of drama. There are smaller waves across the bottom of the sign, but they don't look as ominous. They make the words look like they're out in the river floating.

During the service itself there's lots of talk about persevering, being strong, and not being given more than we can handle. It's all a test of our strength, our faith, you get the idea. I'm glad there's no mention of Noah. We say a prayer together, sing a couple of hymns, then with one more reminder that we're all in this together, and we'll all get through this together, we're released to the tables filled with sweets.

Percy hates mingling because of the unpredictability of anyone being able to come up to you at any time, so I quickly take a lemon square likely made by Miss Stairs before he gets upset and we have to go. I'm not much into mingling either these days, so I just stay out of everyone's way and lean against the wall.

I can overhear two men talking — Linda Small's father and someone else. They're discussing some of the upcoming house assessments. The Smalls live quite a ways downriver, and her father says he's already received an official phone call.

"They're coming by tomorrow night," he says. "Their secretary, a Muriel Abernathy, called and said she and three more of them would be coming — get this — at our convenience." He laughs.

The other man shakes his head.

"Muriel Abernathy?" he says, making sure he's got the name right, probably so he can repeat it later.

"Yep, that'd be her."

"Nope, can't say I've ever heard of her."

"Well, you will," Linda's father says.

I wonder why her name seems so familiar.

Chapter 6

~

After my grandfather died when I was nine, my Grandmother Carson made a quilt. She'd never quilted before, but as soon as his funeral was over she started cutting up all his old shirts into miniscule hexagons about the size of a quarter and sewing them together. She sat in her kitchen rocking chair working on it for days, and then weeks, and then months. By the time she was finished the quilt had 3,122 hexagons (Percy counted), and she seemed happy again. My mother said she'd worked through her grief. She said the quilt was the perfect thing to concentrate on, rather than dwelling on feeling sad. At the time I didn't understand what my mother meant and I only wondered who would end up with the quilt. Of course I wanted it, but she kept it for herself. (And then when she died two years later it went to Uncle Kent.)

My mother was telling the story to Miss Stairs the other day and it got me thinking. I sometimes, or probably most of the time, feel like I'm in grief. I'm not going to start a quilt because I already do carvings, and I'm sure my mother would worry if I started hacking up my wardrobe into tiny bits. But I realized I kind of do have a new hobby already, which is keeping up with all the developments in the preparations for the big Haventon flood. Now that it's going along, it's getting pretty interesting. It's way better than hearing about who dyed their hair or found a family of raccoons in their attic.

Plus it's easy to do. I listen carefully when Miss Stairs is visiting, and I tag along with my parents wherever they go. All the new bits of information are spreading full speed ahead lately. Our phone seems to ring at least twice each evening. And when I sit in the kitchen doing my homework after supper, I always leave the window open, because often someone will stop in the yard and chat with my father.

The government team has a map that shows the whole area to be flooded. All the houses are on it as little squares, along with the schools and the gas station and Foster's Store and the Legion and all three churches (marked with crosses). Everything that will end up underwater is coloured blue. Anything that will be safe from the flood but will have to be moved because it's going to be too close to the new shoreline is green. Areas that the government has picked for new roads, public buildings like the new school, and "future development" are grey. What's left is yellow. But according to Linda Small's mother, who was among the first to see the map, there is very, very little yellow. She said she cried when she saw all the blue.

Everyone around here wants to see the map, and Mr. Foster has a petition addressed to the premier that people can sign demanding a copy be posted publicly. He says no one should have to wait until the government purchasing committee finally shows up at their house with their one ratty map. Mr. Foster wants a copy of the map posted in the front window of his store where anyone can look at it any time. Miss Stairs said she doesn't know of anyone who doesn't agree and didn't sign the petition, even though Mr. Foster joked to her that the map would also be pretty good for business.

Some of the other news we're always hearing is what the options are for people's houses. There's no choice about selling if you're in the flood plain or another area the government wants, but after that there are decisions to be made. Some people may be able to buy back their houses and move them elsewhere. People with farms or large pieces of land may be able to move their homes back on their own property. Some houses that are too big, or are built in some way so they can't be moved, will be torn down or burned. Some people may build again, or move somewhere else completely, like Woodstock or Fredericton, or — the biggest, biggest news flash of all — to the new town.

Which is going to be built by the government for everyone, all up and down the river, to gather together in. The town will be somewhere near here since we're in the middle of the whole disaster zone. There's also going to be a huge new pulp-and-paper mill built not too far from here, and the town will provide housing for the workers. The verdict on the town and the mill is still out because it seems everyone has enough to deal with. And did I mention the new Trans-Canada Highway being built on the other side of the river? If we are told next that our area has been chosen for a model alien colony, everyone will probably just say fine, whatever.

Miss Stairs gets her phone call from the government purchasing committee, now widely known as The Four Horsemen of the Apocalypse. They want to come to her house on Friday after supper, but somehow, at least for now, she gets them diverted to ours. She tells my mother she played the old maid card — oh yes, she's a comedian — and explained that she wanted her dear friends there to hear the news and support her. The Horsemen will still have to take photos and measurements of the house and land, but whether they know it or not, she's insistent no one's getting in. My father seems to have warmed up a little to the idea, and I figure it's because he wants to see the map like everyone else. He's agreed to sit at the table when they come. I'm not allowed, even though with only three of them and Four Horsemen, they're outnumbered.

I devise a plan to bake cookies so I'm in the kitchen when they arrive. It's the best place to listen to the conversation from the dining room, and since there's only a French door between the two rooms, even with it closed I'll be able to see them.

My mother and Miss Stairs wait at the dining-room table while my father answers the door. I hear Miss Stairs tell my mother she's very nervous and I'm glad — not that she is — but that I can clearly make out what she's saying. I get the flour and sugar out of the cupboard so I'll look busy. I see my father go by with the government workers following — three men and a woman.

For a long time one of the men goes through what must be a rehearsed spiel, reviewing everything we know already. Nothing interesting happens until my chocolate chip cookies are all made and in the oven. Then I hear another man say, "Now let me get the map." There is the sound of a large sheet of paper being unfolded. I stand perfectly still and don't make a sound. Chairs move back from the table.

At this exact time, Miss Stairs says, "Does anyone find it a bit warm in here?" And my mother opens a window. It's October, but one of our yard-obsessed neighbours is giving his lawn a final mow. The sound is distant but just loud enough to make it nearly impossible for me to hear. I feel like running down the road and telling him enough already. Once the whole place is flooded his grass is going to be on the bottom of the river, and no one is going to remember how it used to look.

I strain to hear them for the eight more minutes my cookies are baking, but no luck. I take the cookies out, eat five or six of them, then use up the rest of the dough. I have the second batch in the oven before the mower finally stops and I can make out the conversation in the next room again.

"Well, that certainly isn't the typical way to do it," a man is saying. "We must have complete information in order to do a proper assessment."

"Ma'am," another man says. "With all due respect."

"That's Miss," Miss Stairs interrupts.

"Miss, in order to evaluate properly we must measure and photograph both the inside and outside. All sorts of factors can affect the value given — number and size of bedrooms, type and quality of finishing, quality of electrical upgrades, built-ins such as cupboards and the like." I think he's trying to hide how annoyed he is by sounding official. He's deliberately pausing between each little phrase to take a breath. "Surely you must understand."

"Understand? Understand like you do, I suppose, to be told one day right out of the blue that you have to sell your dead parents' house only so it can be destroyed?" Miss Stairs's voice gets a little shaky at the end.

"Ma'am."

"Miss."

"Miss, please. We're only trying to do our jobs."

"Well then. Let me save you the time of traipsing through my house. You can go down there and do all you want outside, measure and take pictures to your heart's content, but anything about the inside that you need to know, you're going to just have to ask me now.

"Come on," she continues, sounding annoyed. "Number of bedrooms: three. Flooring: maple hardwood. Built-in pantry." A pause. "I don't see anyone writing this down."

For several seconds there's complete silence.

"Well, it's hardly conventional. And I must say it will likely result in a significantly lower assessment than you may be entitled to."

"I'd rather be entitled to my privacy."

I walk by the door. Miss Stairs is sitting up straight in her chair and my mother is beside her smiling. My father's taking this time to study the map. The Four Horsemen look agitated and confused.

The timer goes for my cookies and as if on cue, the lawnmower starts again outside. I can't believe how curious I am about what they're saying in there, but the sound of the mower is making my body feel itchy on the inside like some strange torture. I eat four more cookies in about a minute and a half. Then I put several on a plate and almost launch myself into the dining room. My father is startled and gets a scowly look when I open the door.

"May I offer anyone a chocolate chip cookie?" I ask. "They're still warm."

"Oh, lovely, thank you," my mother says. My father's face relaxes.

"This is our daughter Ruby," my mother says to the government committee. They nod. I wonder why there are four of them. I think I only ever heard two of them talking. Maybe it's for their own safety. I bet the reaction of Miss Stairs has been tame compared to some.

"Why don't you leave them on the table," my father says.

"Certainly," I say. I make my move. The map is on the table. Percy would love it. The detail. The scale. The complexity. The colours. But he's upstairs reading. I set the cookies down and using as much childlike innocence as I can conjure, I ask, "Is our house on here?" I trace my finger along the edge of a huge blue area. I look expectantly at the government man sitting beside my father.

"Your house?" he says. "Now, let me see." He scans the map with his finger as well, dragging it through all the blue, then green, and finally stopping on a square. "Here."

The green danger zone comes up to the very edge of one of the lines, maybe even finishing underneath it. But the square itself is yellow.

"Looks like it's going to be a nice piece of waterfront property by the time all this is finished," he says.

"Mr. Comeau, I am so sorry to interrupt, but we're only authorized to divulge information about the property in question here this evening, which is the home of Miss Vergina Stairs." It's the woman talking. It's Muriel Abernathy, the secretary that Linda's father mentioned. She's a big woman, maybe fifty years old, and now her face has flushed red. It's the first time I've heard her say anything.

"Sorry," I say.

"That's all right, dear," she says. "It's just we have strict orders to follow." She folds her hands tightly on top of her notebook.

I leave the cookies and go back to the kitchen. At least I saw the map — and our house on it.

And I saw with my own eyes that Muriel Abernathy is a real person.

Because I had wondered a long time. Back when I hit my head and said the names of the four people I saw swimming beside me, Muriel Abernathy was one of them. I only said, "Hello Mrs. Abernathy," but with a name like that it has to be her. For months it bothered me and I thought it surely made my mental state seem a lot worse — mixing in an imaginary person. But now that she's real? It's kind of like our house being safe. It seems wrong not to think that it's good news, but I can't say I'm feeling that glad.

Later, when I finally fall asleep, I dream I'm sitting in the sunroom and Quilty is alive again on my lap. Our house is up on stilts with the water below. Sarah comes down the river in a canoe to visit, knocks on the window, and then we're on the roof. I look around and there's water on all four sides of us. Our house is an island. It's almost like the painting my mother made me. Except there's no hill below the house, only the lilac river. The house is pink and red and my hair is blue. In the dream, Sarah says, "Hey, look," and points below us. A hand has risen out of the river and is waving. I wake up.

My mother hasn't been painting at all lately. She hasn't gone to Fredericton to buy any new canvases and her easel and supplies are put away. The last painting she did was the one of the church with the river turned navy black. But even that she rushed through, like she was just trying to get it over with, and I don't think she liked the way it turned out. It's at the bottom of our hall closet.

Instead she's been moving things in the house. She switched the dining-room curtains with some she had put away in her hope chest, so now when we eat we smell cedar. Percy and I came home from school one day and the kitchen table was turned around. Another day, our baby pictures were missing from the sideboard. The rocking chair in the sunroom has been angled to a different window. An old rug that Uncle Kent and Aunt Patty gave us when they moved went from the porch to our shed, rolled up for garbage. Percy hasn't been happy at all about any of this, so as a compromise when my mother reorganized the pantry for probably the fifth time, she let him put the soup and vegetable cans back in alphabetically.

My father hasn't said anything about the rearranging, which says a lot — especially since lately he seems so easily annoyed. Maybe he understands that with all the changes going on outside, my mother changing things inside evens it out. But that's probably thinking up something too fancy. I think she's just nervous and fidgety. I think she's not painting because it requires too much concentration.

My father tries to soothe her. Sometimes, across the supper table, as if responding to something no one else has heard he'll say, "We're safe, Lil." Then again, "We're safe." I know this means from the flood waters, but Percy always looks up from his plate confused and doesn't start eating again until my mother says, "I know." Except what I don't think he sees and I do is that there's always this look on her face (this one I think I have figured out for sure) that says although being safe may be wonderful, it's just another thing that makes our family different. It's just another mark against our family.

As for my father, lately he's been drinking more beer than usual, and sometimes he lights a second cigarette right off his first. In the past three weeks he's chopped through our entire woodpile, turning more than we can ever use into kindling. He's definitely a bit thrown off, but I think years and years of the reality of Percy have already put a serious twist in his expectations. As his son, Percy's been both visible and invisible. Everybody notices Percy when he cries publicly, but no one seems to miss or ask about him when he's not there. Percy would never go with my father to do the things the other boys do, like go hunting or fishing, learn to play baseball, or swing an axe. I don't think my father needs our home's safety from the rising river to remind him we're different. I think it's something already permanently accounted for. I don't know if the flood coming is affecting my father much more than him worrying about how it's affecting my mother.

My father met my mother the summer he was twenty-two and she was eighteen. My mother says that because my father's four years older she wasn't really aware of him before they met. My father claims he knew about my mother the day she was born.

That July my father's parents went to Maine for a few days, and my father and Uncle Kent were left in charge of the house and my grandmother's prized canary. All they had to do for the bird was feed it and change the papers in its cage. So yes, the canary, Orillia, escaped not only the cage but the house within ten minutes of my grandparents turning out of the driveway. Neither my father nor Uncle Kent can remember exactly how it happened, but putting the cage on the Hoosier cupboard next to the open kitchen window probably wasn't the best idea.

News of the escaped bird travelled fast over the next couple of days. People saw the canary perched with sparrows on a telephone wire, taking a bath in a puddle, chasing some chickadees at Doyle's apple orchard, and having the time of its life. At first my father thought Orillia's adventure was well deserved and funny, but then as he considered it, he knew my grandmother would be sad and the canary couldn't survive outdoors once the weather got colder.

Meanwhile, my mother was bringing in laundry from the clothesline when she saw a blur of yellow. Orillia and the chickadees were flying from the clothesline post to the roof of the back porch to the lowest branch of the maple tree where my other grandparents hung their bird feeder in the winter. My mother had heard about the missing canary at church. She grabbed one of my grandfather's shirts from the clothesline and flung it over her arm. She ran to the shed for a handful of sunflower seeds and then went to the base of the maple tree like she did in the winter — to see if the smart chickadees would remember her.

My mother waited, still as frozen water. She stood as the chickadees and Orillia hopped from branch to branch in the maple tree, gradually getting lower and closer. She stood there with her arm out straight, my grandfather's shirt draped over it — and the seeds flat in her hand. My mother silently watched the little streak of yellow and her black-capped friends.

Finally one of the chickadees landed for a second on my mother's hand, just long enough to peck one seed. My mother didn't move and a few minutes later another one tried. Then another. And another. Next it was Orillia's turn. My mother saw the canary flying right toward her and held her breath. As soon as Orillia landed, my mother used her other hand to flip my grandfather's shirt up over top of the bird. The canary tried to fly away, but the weight of the shirt was just enough to hold her. My mother grabbed Orillia's little feathery body through the shirt swaddling and gently wrapped the rest of the fabric around the bird to keep her from struggling. My grandmother could hardly believe it when my mother went inside. They drove straight over to my father's house.

My father answered the door and, as he tells it, he was so stunned by my mother's beauty up close that at first he didn't notice the canary chirping in her hand. After the bird was safe in the cage, my father insisted he take my mother out to eat as a reward. They went to the restaurant in the Pokiok Lodge. The rest, I guess, is history.

It's one of those stories that's told again and again in our family. Sometimes other parts are added depending on who's doing the telling. Uncle Kent will sometimes laugh and say my father was lucky he wasn't home instead to answer the door that day. He'll also claim that my father owes that bird everything because half the men around here, from Basil Brewer to Alton Crouse, had wanted to ask my mother out. My father will say he would have let the canary loose sooner if he'd known what was going to happen. Sometimes my mother will tell me I was almost named Orillia. And Percy for sure if he'd been a girl. When I was younger and my grandmother was alive, she used to say the same thing every time at the end of the story — as if it was from a book. It was a quote she'd memorized from somewhere. She'd say, "Now you see, if you keep a green bough in your heart the singing bird will come."

If there was a thermometer to measure the level of annoyance and agitation in the air, then right about now I think the area would be setting a hundred-year record. Part of it is because the evaluators have been a lot of places now and some of the assessments coming back are far from generous. Part of it is that the surveyors are everywhere and multiplying. Percy and I sometimes see them along the side of the road or in someone's yard as we ride on the school bus. One field had so many stakes in it that it looked like a giant pinball game.

The Four Horsemen of the Apocalypse are easily the most hated people around. (They make Percy and me look like prime candidates for Mr. and Miss Congeniality.) Sure most of our neighbours aren't exactly loving the premier right now, but he hasn't been sitting in people's dining rooms. Everyone thinks the Horsemen are too efficient in their jobs as bearers of bad news. They ask questions as if they're just asking for your name and number for a door-prize entry form. (Miss Stairs does a surprisingly funny imitation.) They are rude and fast and act like they have a right to be there. The men have lit cigarettes without asking if it was okay and several times while looking through different houses have stopped to use the washroom.

The four of them drive around in a shiny new black Buick Skylark — the men in suits and overfed Muriel Abernathy with three rings on her fingers. It only reminds people how much money is being spent on this. My father said they're a symbol of the fortune it's taking to ruin our lives.

Leonard Black refused to even let them in. When Mrs. Abernathy called to make an appointment, he hung up. Mr. Black has a small farm with about a dozen cows and two goats. When the Horsemen went to his place, Mr. Black stepped onto the porch with his twelve-gauge full of birdshot, told them it was private property, and threatened to call the RCMP. Mr. Comeau said fine, but that they'd be back.

And there's one assessment that everyone in Haventon knows, and keeps talking about, because it — more than anyone's — seems to prove a point. The Johnsons, who bought Uncle Kent and Aunt Patty's old house only five months ago, are losing the equivalent of their whole down payment. They're a young couple just starting out and they have a baby. Even with everyone feeling bad about their own situation, the Johnsons are generating a lot of compassion. I heard my mother tell Aunt Patty about it on the phone and she said after to my father that Aunt Patty felt sick. But my mother was saying there was no way she could have known, how could she, how on Earth could any of us — it was just one of those things!

~

It's a Friday night and I've been sleeping horribly lately, so my mother said we could stay up late and watch TV. She offered Percy the chance to stay up too, but it was like he was late for an appointment with his bed once the clock struck eight. It's about eleven-thirty now and my mother and I are sitting on the couch in the living room. My father's in the sunroom with a beer, smoking. My mother's been asking about school during the commercials, but I haven't said much of anything. She didn't sing or hum along to any of the performances on *The Tommy Hunter Show* like she usually does, so I figure she's already worrying and thinking. She keeps asking if I'm tired, and every time I say no, she says that she isn't either. It's like a competition. We'll probably be sitting here until we have to stand for "O Canada!" at sign off.

There's a knock on the front door. My mother and I both startle a little.

"Jack," my mother calls. But my father's already come in from the sunroom.

"Just stay here," he says. Before he's even out the other side of the room, the single knock has changed into insistent pounding.

I lean ahead as my father opens the door.

"Jack, Jack Carson, just the fellow we came to see," a man's voice says. I'm pretty sure I recognize it. This can't be good.

"It's all right, Lil," my father calls. "I'm just stepping out for a few minutes."

This, and likely the banging that came before it, wakes Percy. He yells for my mother.

I go to the kitchen but leave the light off. I sit at the table near the window and I can see my father and the two men outside. They've parked their old car close to the step — on the grass even — and now they're sitting on the hood. It's Tommy as I thought — and Alton Crouse. Tommy has a bottle of beer. Alton has a nearly empty bottle of what is maybe rum. This is how most of the stupid stories about them start. Once upon a quart of rum.

My father's standing with his arms folded across his chest. Even without considering that it's late at night and they showed up out of nowhere, these two have that instant effect on people.

In the dark I pull my chair right up close to the window so I can hear them.

"Christ, Tommy, it's almost midnight," my father says. "Whatever the hell you want just spit it out, then go. I don't have time for your damn games."

"My," Tommy says and turns to Alton.

Alton laughs.

"Five minutes Tommy, and only because your uncle's a good man and I'm not going to cause him grief if I don't have to."

"Grief? Goodness, Alton, we don't want any grief, now do we? No, no. We just came to talk." Tommy clinks his beer bottle against Alton's quart as if he's making a toast. "But since you mention my uncle and him being a good man, why couldn't you have tipped him off too?"

"I don't know what in hell you're talking about," my father says.

"You couldn't help an old man out? Let him have a chance to live out his last years happy? What, old Ellis isn't worth it 'cause he looks at your wife the wrong way?"

"Who doesn't?" Alton asks and they both laugh.

"I'd watch your mouth there, boys."

"Now Jack," Tommy says. He takes a long swig of his beer, empties it, and tosses the bottle into a rosebush. Probably just hoping to get this over with, my father ignores it.

"I saw the map," Tommy goes on. "I saw it down at Ellis's. And it seems while the rest of us are all gettin' pulled under, you're sittin' up here high and mighty on dry land."

"And?" my father says impatiently.

"So you're gonna play dumb, eh? Well now Alton, what d'ya think?"

"I got nothing better to do," Alton says. "Go ahead Tommy, you tell it so nice."

"So, Jack Carson, big government man. Big government man like you, it never did seem right to me that no one told you a damn thing. I couldn't imagine that somehow you didn't know 'bout this long before it was coming. But then I tell you once I saw that map, and everybody's numbers got to coming back so bad, I got to wondering. Now let me see, I said to myself. Let me see." Here Tommy furrows his brow and looks up to the stars as if for effect.

Then I get thinking about Jack's good old brother Kent. Wasn't it so strange that after all those years he just up and moves? Sells his beautiful house right down by the river. Hmm.

"Your brother's old house will be one of the first underwater," Tommy says. "And them poor Johnsons with their itty-bitty baby paid all that good money to Kent only to lose it here — what — a few months later?" He shakes his head. "So you knew and you didn't need to help yourself, but you made damn sure he made some good cash and got himself clear."

"Jesus Christ, Tommy, that is a load of bullshit! That's why you two are over here bothering me? Get the hell out of here."

"I thought it sounded pretty damn smart to me," Alton says.

"So how long have you known, Jack? Months? A year? Two?" Tommy asks. "What, you couldn't share the wealth?"

"Christ, Tommy, you have no goddamned idea what you're talking about. And both you and Alton live way the hell back in the woods nowhere near the goddamned river, so I don't know why you think this is any of your concern. Christ, even if you two did live down here, neither of you have ever worked hard enough to earn anything worth losing. Now get the hell off my property before I call the RCMP!" My father is yelling.

I'm still close to the window, but I'm sure my mother and Percy can also hear some of this upstairs.

"Once that map goes up at the store and everybody sees your house sittin' free and clear, people are gonna wonder," Tommy says.

"People don't think too much of a man only taking for himself," Alton says.

"Well you're right there about one thing, Alton," my father says. "That's exactly what we say about you around here, drinking your own children's food and clothing money away."

Alton pushes up off the hood of the car like he's going to lunge at my father, but Tommy puts his arm across Alton's chest, blocking his way.

At the same time my mother turns on the light in the kitchen and suddenly I'm on display.

"There you are, Ruby," my mother says. "They're just drunk." She walks over to me. "Don't mind —"

But from outside, Tommy's voice. "Well my my, looks like we've got ourselves a pretty little audience."

My father turns to look at my mother and me, and Alton uses this distraction as an opportunity to get up, jump the two steps, and throw a punch. Alton's awkward and slow, so as my father swivels back, Alton only catches him on the edge of the face near the eye. When my father swings he doesn't miss and punches Alton in the jaw. Alton is thrown backwards into the driveway. My mother gasps.

"Now get the hell off my property," my father says. "And Tommy, you remind your old buddy Alton here when he sobers up and sees that gravel stuck to his cheek that he was the one who started this. Him and you and your bullshit theory." My father touches his hand to the side of his face and looks at the blood on his fingers.

"We'll just see if everyone thinks it's bullshit or not!" Tommy yells.

Alton stirs and starts to pull himself up by grabbing the bumper of the car.

My father comes in.

He looks at us as he goes to the kitchen sink. He wets a dishcloth, then holds it against his cheek.

"Let me," my mother says.

"Ruby, it's long past your bedtime now," he says.

"They're not good men," my mother says to me. "Neither of them. And you know how all the flood upset has everyone out of sorts." She's blotting my father's cut.

I can hear the car backing out of the driveway.

"Come here and let me give you a kiss goodnight," my mother says.

As she kisses me on the forehead, I am close enough to my father to see the vein in his neck throbbing.

I lie in bed and although I try so hard not to, I think of what Tommy said to my father. I tilt my head way back so I can see the bottom of my painting, our house alone on an island in the water. I'm sure my father didn't know anything, but the way Tommy told the story, with our house being high enough up the hill that we're safe, and the coincidental timing of Uncle Kent leaving, he did sound almost convincing.

Percy wakes in the night. He doesn't cry or scream and it's only because I'm still awake that I hear him. I can tell that he gets out of bed and turns on his light. Then I hear the clinking of bottles. I roll out of bed and go ask what he's doing.

"I woke up and I am not tired so I have decided to reorganize my bottles," he says. The box of extra bottles from the closet is sitting beside his desk and he's taking them out one at a time. Five are already in a straight line and he's adding a sixth.

I sit on the desk chair beside him.

"You should probably try to go back to sleep," I say. It's two in the morning according to Percy's alarm clock. "You don't want to be tired when you send off your bottle tomorrow."

He stops what he's doing and looks down at his feet. He's thinking about something now. A question.

It reminds me how he's almost been forgotten in this. He hasn't been upset by what's coming, because as near as I can figure, that's just it, it's still only coming. Until the future's here, he doesn't need to deal with it. Percy's reactions are more instantaneous — one problem at a time. This is my latest guess as to the workings of his mind, because he's the only one who's behaved consistently (since it's hard to say normal for Percy). The same little things keep bothering him, and for now at least, this big looming thing isn't.

"Ruby, who was the man our father hit?" he asks.

Aha. I give it a few seconds. Percy looks up.

"It was Ronnie Crouse's father," I say.

Percy nods slowly and reaches for another bottle. By the lamplight I wonder if I can see the slightest smile.

"And June Crouse's father too," he says.

"Yes, you're right."

I'm pretty sure he's smiling. I am too. I'd love to wink at him, and then we could laugh, but I know he wouldn't understand.

My father has a black eye for a week. During this time I go to the gas station twice, church once, and the store once with him, but no one asks how it happened because they already know. Some people stop and say hello to my father, but it never comes up in their suspiciously brief conversations. Some people have only nodded and kept going. We got home from church twenty-five minutes earlier than usual last Sunday for exactly this reason. My mother says people have a lot on their minds and are keeping to themselves. But there seemed to be the usual milling and mingling after the service, just not in our direction. Percy was glad, but as for my parents, I'm not so sure. I know first-hand that once an idea's been put out there, regardless of the source, it doesn't take a genie to make it come true.

Autumn continues and leaves fall from the trees. On Halloween our house gets egged and all our car windows are soaped for the first time ever. Percy dresses up as a mummy for the fourth year in a row. My mother wraps him in the same strands of an old ripped-up bedsheet. At our school party I wear a beautiful Queen of Hearts costume that my mother sewed by hand. No one except Mr. Hogan seems to notice or care. He gets this silly look on his face and greets me with "Happy Valentine's Day." I manage a smile for his effort. June Crouse comes as a witch with a dress made from a black garbage bag. Everyone thinks it's oh-so-clever. It's because she says she's me.

Mr. Foster finally gets his map for the store. Miss Stairs says most people think it's only a crumb being thrown to us, but still it's there. Percy stood outside and stared at it one day while my mother took almost an hour to get groceries. She asked me to stay with him, but I knew as soon as I saw it that there'd be no way he'd wander off. The Four Horsemen of the Apocalypse still carry their map as they make their final rounds, but no one schemes about stealing it anymore. More assessments are coming back and now the Horsemen don't even get polite nods of acknowledgment when they're out and about. Miss Stairs isn't her usual friendly self when they stop in the store for a pop or bag of chips. They'll be around for weeks though, finishing everything. Then there's Leonard Black's place. He's refused them four times.

Fall turns to winter. Haventon turns white with snow and the river freezes. (I mostly stay inside and completely avoid skating.) There are other things going on in the world outside the river valley, but you wouldn't know it. It's only at school in social studies that we hear about the war in Vietnam. And that a woman's been elected prime minister of India. And a Soviet Luna spacecraft has landed on the moon. Miss Stairs says that at the store no one seems to care that Mr. Foster wrecked his new Mustang by hitting a deer. Anyone she mentions it to just changes the subject back to decisions to be made.

At our house there are no decisions, but I can still feel the uncertainty. There is something about the tone of my parents' whispers, which I can sometimes hear as I sit on my bed in the dark and whittle at night. Even without the suspicion surrounding my father, it's like my parents can't be thankful for the reprieve until all this is over. No one can feel happy for you when they're feeling so bad for themselves. My mother says it's like being the family of a plane crash's only survivor.

Even with this thing uniting our whole area, I feel we're on the outside looking in. I wish our house did have to be moved, not only so we could get out of here, but also to be a part of it. I think Percy and I could be excused a little if we really were all in this together. But this is making it worse. I am not like everyone else. I swear something reminds me of this at least once a day.

For example, I'm pretty sure I'm the only one who cares about the heart attack and death of Muriel Abernathy.

Spring 1966

Chapter 7

❧

Mr. Wesley Ball is the first to take the government's offer, and even though it will still be more than a year until he absolutely has to be out, he decided to get it over with now. He and his family have packed up everything they're taking with them and word has gone around that anything left that anyone might want, they're welcome to take it before the house is burned tonight. Mostly this means things like doors and light fixtures, but they also had to leave some furniture. The Balls' new place in Saint John is small, and they only had enough money for one trip with the moving truck anyway. It's what Mr. Ball tells Miss Stairs when I'm in Foster's Store getting sugar and he's buying matches. He says he'll be damned if he's going to let anyone else light up the house.

"So are you coming tonight?" he asks her.

"Oh my soul, I wouldn't miss it," Miss Stairs says.

He grins and nods. "And everyone, everyone, please, come," he announces, turning around to me and the other five or six customers in the store. "Come and bring your families."

It's a bit strange. I mean, he's acting almost as if he's throwing a big party. But then I guess who knows how you're supposed to act in a situation like this because when else does this situation ever come up?

"Ruby Carson," he says to me, "I can count on you, right?"

I was planning on it. But up until ten seconds ago I would never have said so with excitement in my voice for fear of putting another strike against myself: aspiring pyromaniac.

"Love to," I say.

No response.

Mr. Ball stares at me, expressionless. Two seconds pass. Three. I fight the urge to flee.

"Marshmallows!" he says. Now his eyes are twinkling. He isn't joking. "Let me buy you a bag so you and Rhona can roast them tonight!"

Rhona is his daughter, who hasn't talked to me since June Crouse tangled up all my lines of communication.

I politely refuse, saying it's not necessary, but he is insistent and goes down the aisles to look for a bag. Wonderful. Now I'll have to take them. I'll choose to look ridiculous rather than forget them and feel guilty. Of course I'm only included in this public event by doing something exclusionary.

I see Mr. Ball coming back with not one bag but two. I squeeze out a smile. I was standing in the wrong place at the wrong time. Mr. Ball hasn't done more than say hello after church or smile at me for years, but now I'm part of this memory he's making, his daughter's friend in good old Haven Town where everyone knew everyone and everyone helped everyone out. I thank him for the marshmallows and say I'll be there tonight.

Rhona Ball put her winter boots on once when she was nine or ten and there was a mouse in one toe. She had them almost all tied up before she felt something wiggling. She screamed and hopped and kicked and flung herself backwards and burned the whole palm of her right hand on the woodstove. She finally got the boot thrown off and when it landed the mouse ran out, unsquished and unharmed. If it had been me, I never, ever would have told the story at school, but everyone wondered how she'd hurt her hand. To this day, she won't put on shoes, boots, even sandals, without first stepping on the toes, then turning them upside down and shaking. She does it every day changing from her boots to shoes at school. Sometimes she makes other people paranoid and they look too. There hasn't been another mouse, even though once last year a piece of cheese that a boy either put in as bait or a joke shook out. I bet she will keep looking for the rest of her life. This might be the one and only thing I'll remember about Rhona Ball.

I buy the sugar and leave Foster's Store with it — and the marshmallows. I look at the map in the window for a bit, then start the walk home. I don't get too far before Miss Stairs pulls her car up beside me. She's finished her shift and offers me a ride.

"But one stop first," she says. "Wesley Ball's."

I'm already in the car so I'm not going to refuse. She's probably glad she caught up to me because she wanted to go, but not alone.

It isn't far. We drive down into the new flood plain. The Balls' house sits on an acre back at the end of a long driveway. It's a two-storey white house with a little porch on the side. There's a spray-painted chipboard sign as we turn in: "Fire 6:00 Help Yourself Til Then."

Miss Stairs parks and starts to get out, but I don't budge. I'm coming to the burning tonight, but this is different. I've never been in the Balls' house and now we're going to walk right in?

"I know it's odd," Miss Stairs says. "But it'll be fun to have a little look."

I see other people through the windows upstairs and someone walking out the door with a bathroom sink. Miss Stairs walks around to my door and opens it.

*

Inside the lights are off because the power's already been disconnected. Even though there are no curtains left on the windows, not much light seems to be coming in and it's dark. And cold. Other people are walking around quietly, sometimes whispering. It feels gloomy, without any of the thrill you'd expect when you're somewhere you probably shouldn't be. Miss Stairs and I look through the living room, the dining room, and the kitchen. Then there's the loud sound of wood being pulled with a crowbar and the eerie quiet is broken.

We go upstairs. We walk through three bedrooms and I figure the one with the purple-striped wallpaper was Rhona's. Out her window I see another car pulling up the driveway. Mr. and Mrs. Hogan are leaving. Tommy Cole is throwing a piece of moulding in the back of Mr. Cole's truck. He has a mountain of things piled up. A crowbar is hanging from his belt loop.

Miss Stairs touches me on the shoulder. She hasn't said anything since we came in. I've just been following her along. We walk downstairs and she heads for the front door, which is fine by me. Tommy's still in the back of the truck fixing the load as we walk by and thankfully doesn't see us.

We get in the car and tears start to well in Miss Stairs's eyes as she looks in her purse for her keys.

"I wouldn't be able to do that," I say, "just let anyone wander around — even in my bedroom."

Miss Stairs dabs her eyelashes with her pinky finger. "That's what Wesley wanted though, to share what little was left."

"Could you do it?"

She looks out the car window back to the house.

"Maybe," she says. "Maybe." A pause. "Once it was empty."

She starts the car.

Miss Stairs is quiet for most of the drive home, but when we pass a surveyor walking along the road she waves (I think she's one of the very few people around who bother) and she seems to perk up — as if she's just remembered something.

"You know Ruby, even though a lot of people are leaving, there will be lots of new people coming in too — men to work on the construction."

"On the new town," I say.

"Yes, and more on the dam. And the new highway. And the mill they're building." She turns to me for a second and smiles and nods.

"It should mean some new kids at school," she says. "I'm sure there will be some new families — some more chances to make friends."

Again she turns, smiles, and nods. It's a bit much how convincing she's trying to be, like she's told herself to snap out of the depressing mood of the Ball house so now she's going overboard with the optimism. But it's probably just how she's found some goodness in all the changes. New people, new possible husbands, are something for her to look forward to.

We pull into the driveway. As I get out of the car Miss Stairs says, "Be sure to tell your mother you were talking to me," even though I can see her already, waving to us out the window.

I know all about Miss Stairs's wedding fantasy. She talks about it a lot with my mother. It's a story they keep telling, editing, subtly changing, embellishing, streamlining, and perfecting. Sometimes when they're bored, or when it's dark and rainy, they get a bit adventurous and talk about exotic locations with white sand and palm trees or churches with gold-gilded angels and three-storey-high stained-glass windows. Neither of them has ever been to places with these things. The usual story they tell is better anyway.

Miss Stairs and her future husband will stand beside the Pokiok Stream, up above the Pokiok Falls. They'll stand under an archway of bent twigs; purple, pink, and white fresh lilacs and lupines (picked only a half-hour before the ceremony), since the wedding will be in June. The smell will be wonderful and the sun will be shining. My mother will be the matron of honour in a pale mauve dress. When they started telling the story when I was younger, I was the flower girl. Now I've been promoted to junior bridesmaid. Percy used to be figured in as the ring bearer, but now no one tricks themselves into believing he would enjoy that.

With the sound of the falls splashing and churning in the background, Miss Stairs and this usually tall, dark-haired future husband will repeat their vows. Her dress will be long and white with lace sleeves. She'll wear a necklace inherited from her mother, rhinestones, but good ones, clear sparkling crystal except for a centre one of pink. The necklace will be "the old." A gift from her future husband, earrings she hopes, will be "the new." A small pearl-encrusted hair comb from my mother will be "the borrowed." The water nearby will be "the blue."

The reception after will be at the Pokiok Lodge and the wedding night will be spent in one of the cabins. I've heard about it so many times I used to think it would come true. But now the dam is putting a big twist in the climax of the story. The Pokiok Falls will disappear into the rising river. The lodge and cabins must be moved or burned. It's sad that they're messing with those little forest cabins. Sarah and I used to imagine they were a village of playhouses. They're gingerbread-house cute — tiny, white, with a single gable and a little porch. But I suppose if the falls are gone, it takes away the best reason tourists had to stop here. Even if the cabins weren't in the flood plain, there'd be no need for them anymore.

I haven't heard my mother and Miss Stairs go through the wedding fantasy since all of this started. I wonder if Miss Stairs is still holding on to it in her head or if she's made adjustments. Maybe she does

dream that somehow in the next year and a half she can meet one of
these new men and get married before the flooding. It doesn't seem
likely to me, but not much that's happened around here lately ever
seemed likely. So who knows what Miss Stairs considers possible or
probable? You really don't know what other people think about. You
can't know what other people are saying to themselves when they're
sitting home alone.

And probably the worst thing about it is this: if Miss Stairs can't meet
someone and get married, how can I ever expect a better result for
myself? Everybody around here seems to like Miss Stairs. At the store
I see people standing and chatting with her all the time — even if
they're holding up the line. After church my mother and I will almost
always have to interrupt a conversation to say goodbye to her. She's
a good cook, which I know from eating her sweets. And, most
importantly, as far as I can tell, no one thinks she's strange. She's a
regular, nice lady who somehow missed out on whatever coincidence
or string of coincidences it takes to end up with a husband.

As much as I like to have Miss Stairs around, sometimes she's just
a grim reminder of my potential future.

In the house Percy is waiting at the kitchen table with his bottle ready.
He's rolling it back and forth with the palm of his hand and the rocks
inside are jingling. He gets up, assuming we're going right away. His
interpretation of "When I get back from the store" is the second my
foot hits the doormat. My mother's coming with us today to take
Percy's picture. But her going doesn't mean that I can stay home
instead. It's not that he needs someone — anyone — for company, but
I have become a necessary part of his ritual. It's almost like I'm his
good luck charm — if he believed in that sort of thing.

My mother gets her camera and we go. She's been taking a lot of pictures lately. She still hasn't started painting again, but she claims that's what some of the photographs are for: inspiration. Maybe. I envision something more like an album labelled "Before." My mother used to only paint from her imagination or memory.

As we walk my mother trails behind us and takes a picture of Percy and me. Then when he's on the bridge, she tries three or four shots at different angles. Percy pays no attention to her whatsoever and stays at the bridge rail for twenty minutes watching his bottle. It's exactly the same as always and besides the weather, the temperature, and the wind, could be switched with any other Saturday.

Still no letters have come back from his messages, so that hasn't changed either. And he knows our house isn't moving, and that our address will stay the same. Maybe he's decided that a bottle could indeed make it through a turbine in the new dam, survive the plunge, and float merrily away. Maybe in the school library he's been doing some reading. If he has any nervousness about what's ahead, he sure isn't showing it.

Back at home, I work on my woodcarving until supper. I've got twelve of the thirty-two figures of my project done and now my father's seen some of my progress. I showed him one night a few weeks ago and he nodded after carefully examining each piece — as if of course he'd known all along. "I always figured I made a good choice," he said. Then he shook his head and smiled. It made me remember that Percy was still only five when I found that wooden owl in the river. Even back then my father must have felt safe enough giving his own father's woodcarving tools not to his only son but to his only daughter.

Today I put a new piece of driftwood in the drawer (this afternoon as Percy was putting something in the river, I was taking something out), then I work and work until my mother calls me for dinner. I clean up and carefully brush every trace of sawdust off my blouse and

pants. I even shake my hair out in case there are some stray wood
shavings or flakes. I always do this regardless of whether or not I'm
leaving the house. There's no sense chancing anything that might
further endorse, cement, or propel in perpetuity my status as an outcast. No one ever wants to be an outcast. Just ask anyone in Have Not
Town since we've been collectively cast out by the province.

~

Percy's not going to the burning of Wesley Ball's house. My mother's
staying home with him. My father volunteered to babysit, which is a
rare occurrence, but my mother says it isn't something she needs to
see. She gives me her camera and I put it in my school bag along with
the dreaded marshmallows. I hope Mr. Ball hasn't told people to bring
roasting sticks. I think I can feel the imaginary jabs of them already.

My father and I walk, which is just as well since the cars are parked
on both sides of the road leading to the Balls' house. Then there's the
fire truck and two RCMP cars — plus about a dozen other vehicles
on the lawn. Some people are sitting on the hoods and lots more are
standing on each side of the cars.

There's the sound of chainsaws as two men cut the trees and shrubs
in the backyard. There's also the sound of rocks hitting the front of
the house, and an occasional crash as boys hit the windows. They're
taking turns standing on a board (the chipboard sign that had been
at the end of the driveway) to aim. They have a big pile of rocks to go
through. It looks like a game set up in advance — probably by the
entertainment director Mr. Ball. People are watching, talking,
sometimes cheering when a boy manages to take out part of a window.
I click a picture. Caption: *The festivities have begun.*

It's very close to six o'clock and as my father and I walk the rest
of the way down the long driveway, the chainsaws stop. The men pull
the small trees they've cut onto the porch. Mr. Ball goes to his pickup,

which is parked well behind the fire truck. Mrs. Ball and Rhona follow. He flips down the tailgate and in the back are three large red gas cans. One for each of them. It gets quieter as other people notice this too. The Balls head into their house for the last time, gas cans in hand. My father and I walk to the edge of the semicircle of people. We say hello to the minister and his wife.

Linda Small, her brothers, and her parents are nearby. Linda looks at me like I've already ruined everything just by showing up. Even from this distance it looks like her nostrils are flared. I can think of the perfect use for two of the marshmallows. Linda is with her parents because June is much farther down the line standing with her new boyfriend. My father says hello to Mr. Small, who only nods in response. My father doesn't get any reply at all when he says hello to the other man behind us. It's Leonard Black.

The Balls come out and walk to the front of the crowd. A photographer from *The Daily Gleaner* takes their picture. A reporter with a tape recorder crouches down in front of them and holds out a microphone.

"I can't say a man knows exactly what to say at a time like this," Mr. Ball starts. "But just thanks to you all for coming. I tell you I never thought I'd see the day." He pauses and looks at the ground for a few seconds. He puts his arm around his wife. She puts her arm around Rhona. Rhona wipes tears from her eyes.

"We're all good people," Mr. Ball says. "And I must say as I'm sure you all well know, a man can go crazy asking himself why, but I guess if this was God's plan, then so be it."

There are some whistles and cheers.

Mr. Ball seems pleased with the response and nods several times before he goes to his truck for a bottle. It's a pop bottle with liquid inside — gas — and a twisted white piece of rag stuck in the neck as a wick. It makes me think of Percy.

"Well," Mr. Ball says, "so I guess this is what you came for." He holds the bottle in one hand and the pack of matches I saw him buy in the store in the other.

"You can do it Wes!" someone yells. "Light 'er up!"

"Send 'er all to hell!"

Our minister grimaces.

"Wes-ley! Wes-ley!" someone chants. Then more people join in. Then more. "Wes-ley! Wes-ley!"

Mr. Ball lights the rag and tosses the bottle through a downstairs window. There's a crash and an explosion of flames.

Everyone cheers. I applaud too. The reporter waves the micro-phone madly, capturing the intensity of the sound. I look down the row of people and everyone is smiling. There are at least three men giving Mr. Ball a thumbs-up. Am I the only one who finds this odd? It's getting harder and harder all the time to tell what's normal or acceptable around here.

The reporter looks around and probably because we're at the edge of the crowd, he makes his way over to my father.

"Sir, may I have a few minutes to ask you a few questions?"

I can tell everyone is listening, all the chatter around us instantly stops.

"I suppose," my father says. "But I can't guarantee any good answers."

The reporter smiles. "We're just looking for some crowd reaction. I'm from CFNB Radio. Now—"

But a loud voice interrupts from behind us.

"Christ, you're talking to the wrong man if you want some reaction." It's Leonard Black. "His house ain't going nowhere. And if you're wondering how he feels about 'er all, well hell, it seems you picked out the one man here who had a pretty good jump on all of us finding out. He's had a damn good long time to come up with what you'd call a reaction."

Leonard Black is very close behind me now and I can smell the alcohol on his breath.

The minister starts to say, "Leonard," and I look at my father. The reporter, Mr. Small, Linda, and everyone else around seems to be looking at him too.

"Now Leonard," my father says. "Yes, my house is above the flood plain and you're right I can't relate to you on that. But it's sat there longer than either you or I have lived and the fact that the water won't reach it has absolutely nothing to do with me.

"And as to me knowing anything before anybody else, well, with the minister of our church standing here as my witness, I'm telling you, I didn't. So I suggest you and anyone else who can hear me," my father pauses and looks around, knowing he has an audience, "should quit listening to any fool who says different."

My father turns to the reporter. "And now sir, if you do want a good story, I suggest you interview Mr. Black here. He's likely the most strong-willed man in our community. Leonard?" My father extends his hand to Leonard Black and probably only because of the crowd, Leonard shakes it.

Then my father puts his arm around me and says it's time to go.

I take two more pictures for my mother, but it'll never be the same as being here. You can feel the heat of the flames now — and hear the cracking, shifting, breaking. Smell the smoke strong with every breath. Then I remember something. I take the marshmallows from my bag and pass them to the minister's wife. Everyone will think they're an ingenious treat coming from her.

When I was six and Percy was still a baby, there was another fire I'll always remember. It happened in December, just a week before

Christmas. Our church's outdoor nativity went up in flames. The minister woke up on a Sunday morning and out the rectory window all he could see of the Christmas display was charred remains.

The nativity had been beautiful, with every person, animal and angel from the story of Jesus' birth made from plywood in true size. The whole congregation had worked on it for months. The men cut out the shapes and the women and children painted them. My mother, because of her artistic ability, got to do all the faces. (She told me it was our little secret that one of the angels looked like me and the baby Jesus had curly blond hair just like Percy's.) I remember painting white circle after white circle on a lamb to make it look woolly.

The cause of the fire was never known for sure, but the light bulb placed just beneath the hay, giving a special glow to the baby, was highly suspicious. All that hard work was ruined, and it was too late to make another.

But my father had an idea. On the first day of his Christmas holidays he spent hours cutting miniature figures out of flat wood panelling, each just about a foot high, and arranged them to look like the original display had. When it was dark he took me to the church. He set the little nativity up in the yard and plugged a large outdoor light in behind it. Giant life-sized shadows of every detail appeared on the white clapboard. I know it was a long time ago, almost Percy's whole stress-inducing lifetime ago, but being here tonight, seeing him have to set everyone straight, it's like the water that isn't even here yet has already washed people's memories away.

∼

It's been a week since Wesley Ball's house burned and today is my parents' wedding anniversary. For a celebration supper they go to the Pokiok Lodge. My mother cooked a stew for Percy and me, and after we eat we sit at the kitchen table and play chess. I'm always black and

Percy's always white. I've never beaten him, but sometimes I can keep him going for an hour or more. Percy loves chess, although looking at him you'd never know. He doesn't talk to me while we're playing and he always reads at the same time. Tonight he has a book from the school library on outer space. I move, say, "Your turn," and he puts his finger on his place on the page. He assesses the board for I'm sure ten seconds tops, moves, then continues reading. Even if he captures one of my pieces he doesn't say anything, but just lifts it quietly and sets it off to the side in a line. There's always a line.

The phone rings and I figure it's my mother, who said she'd call to check in with us between the main course and dessert. But instead it's a man asking for my father.

"I'm sorry," I say. "He isn't here right now, may I take a message?"

"Mrs. Carson," the man says. This has happened more and more the past couple of years. He thinks I'm my mother.

"Could you —" he says.

"Sir," I interrupt, attempting to clarify the situation.

"I'm afraid there's been —"

"Sir, Mrs. Carson is my mother. This is Ruby Carson," I say.

"Oh, I see." A pause. "Well, is she available?"

"No, I'm sorry, may I take a message?"

There's another pause as if the man is debating what to say.

"It's Robert Comeau. From the RVAC."

I wonder if he figures I don't know what that stands for. Or if I don't remember him. The River Valley Assessment Committee is the official name no one uses. Also known as The Four Horsemen of the Apocalypse, of whom now there are only three.

"Will you tell your father to expect my call later in the week, please?" he asks.

"Certainly," I say. I wonder what he wants with my father that he can't pass on through me.

Chapter 8

~

Miss MacFarlane, Mr. Cole's regular housekeeper, is the next to leave, so I get to start my summer job early. My only concern was the annoyance that is Tommy, but he's staying back at his cabin and only stops in to Mr. Cole's to use his barn for storage as part of his latest scheme. Tommy figures there's money to be made with all this clearing out of houses. He took four truckloads from Mr. Ball's place, even crowbarring the banister and newel post off the stairs. He sold what he could to an antique dealer in Fredericton. Now he's got a sign at the store (written on the back of a Schooner beer box top) offering the rest as firewood or "kinlin." I felt like ripping it down to protect Percy from the crushing impact of Tommy's horrible spelling, but ever since the map went up in the window, Percy never looks at the bulletin board.

School's still in for another month, so for now I will go to Mr. Cole's after supper on Wednesdays and first thing in the morning on Saturdays. It's been a long time since I've been to his house — the last time was when my mother and I visited just after Christmas. I've been seeing him each week at church though, and I suppose he's still looking well. Or as well as he can, considering the latest development.

Mr. Cole's farm has been chosen as the location for the new town. The very bottom of his huge acreage (where his house is) will be flooded out, but everything above it will be taken by the government too. It will all be surveyed and cleared, dug up and bulldozed, gravelled and paved. His fields will be chopped up into little squares. Mr. Cole's property will make up more than three-quarters of the whole town and will eventually be home to hundreds of people. Miss Stairs said that he was told he had first choice of a new lot. My father said that whoever told him is lucky Mr. Cole is such a gentleman.

The work on his property has already started and as I walk down Mr. Cole's driveway for my first Wednesday evening, I can hear chainsaws in the distance. Most of his land is open fields, but there are several lines of huge old trees. Pines that weren't any taller than me when Mr. Cole's great-grandfather was alive have to be cut down. It's past six o'clock and men are still working. I think that's the first indication of how long and hard a job it is to turn a farm into a whole town.

Mr. Cole's just finishing his supper when I arrive. He's having tea and offers me some.

"So why don't we just sit awhile," he says. "There's not a single thing in here that can't wait until Saturday."

The kitchen is very neat — and emptier than I remember it looking, almost as if some things are missing.

"Are you sure?" I ask. "I mean, that's what I came for."

"No, no it's fine. Just keep an old fella company."

He tells me some stories, about his farm and his family. He tells me about a narrow miss once with a skunk in the barn that he mistook for his old black-and-white cat, The Daily News. He tells me about his father grafting the crabapple tree. He tells me how his mother kept his brother Albert, Tommy Cole's grandfather, warm as a baby by letting him sleep in a little bed made from an old wooden Rankine's biscuit box set right by the woodstove.

Then he tells me how he met his wife Rita.

It was winter. He was in this house that we are in. His parents were alive. Mr. Cole was thirteen and Albert was ten. He stops to think for a bit. This would have been either 1899 or 1900, he says. His father worked on the farm and his mother was one of two women in the area who helped out as midwives. There was a lady his mother didn't know who lived about twenty miles away. She was pregnant, but the day she went into labour, the other midwife had a death in the family so she was called away. Mr. Cole's mother got the news that she had to go to this woman's side as soon as possible. Mr. Cole's father was off buying supplies so Mr. Cole had to drive her in the sleigh.

At first he wanted to wait outside the woman's house, but it was cold and his mother insisted he go in. He waited in the kitchen while the woman wailed in the parlour. It was awful, he says. He thought for sure the poor woman was dying. She was wailing. Wailing. Wailing. But eventually the wailing stopped and he heard a baby cry. His mother came to the kitchen to get more water and said the woman had a little girl. The woman called him in to see her.

Mr. Cole says he will never forget how happy the woman looked. He had heard her wailing for hours, but now with the baby in her arms it was like she'd already forgotten everything. She was smiling and crying tears of joy. There was something Mr. Cole felt in that room, something special or different that could have only arrived with the baby. When he saw that little baby girl, she looked up at him. He saw possibility. He saw wonderful things ahead of him, he says. He saw things that would be worth the wait. He'd wait.

He looks at me and smiles.

He says that baby girl was Rita.

And he did wait. He waited for her until he was thirty and she was seventeen.

"Thirteen years older than her, all that time," he says. He looks up. "But still she went home before me."

He shakes his head. "But if there's any small blessing, at least she's not here to see all this. My, how it'd be hard on her to see our beautiful farm taken away."

We're both silent for several seconds. "Have you decided what you're going to do yet?" I ask.

"Not yet. The house is likely too big to move, and after all this space, I can't see living up on a postage stamp in the new town — living up on one little speck of my own field. Pretty hard for an old fella like me to change my ways." A pause. "But enough," he says and smiles. "So do you think the Queen might be watching us now?"

"Should we go out and give her a wave?" I ask. This is complete silliness, but I'm simply following Mr. Cole's lead.

"After you," he says and grins.

We stand side by side on the porch and wave our hands as if there's a passing parade. If anyone saw us they'd wonder what on Earth we were doing.

Or maybe not. It would look like we were saying goodbye to the river.

We go back inside and I volunteer again to clean something, but Mr. Cole repeats there isn't anything that can't wait. I suggest watering the plants or maybe baking him a treat, but he smiles and shakes his head.

I phone my father to come get me and in the meantime Mr. Cole takes me into the parlour. He has a large box filled with books. He says he's started to clean out a few things for the move. I wonder if it was Tommy's idea.

"I thought maybe Percy would like some. He's quite the reader, isn't he? So why don't you take a look through and see if there's anything there he might want."

There are about thirty books. Some look quite old. Some have brown or dark red covers decorated with gold. Percy likes facts much more than made-up stories so I hope there's something along those lines. There are books on hunting and fishing, which are possibilities. There's one called *The Compleat Angler* that I consider, but then I notice a book on sea life of the Atlantic Ocean. I take it and another called *The Way to Game Abundance*, which looks like it's about moose and deer. As I'm thanking Mr. Cole, I hear my father pull in the driveway.

I'm almost positive that Percy will like the ocean book. Once at the big library in Fredericton he read an article in a special science magazine on waves. He talked about it for weeks. There's a pattern to them, he said. Every seventh wave is bigger than the little ones leading up to it. He said I should remember that if we ever went swimming in the ocean. You always had six small waves to get ready.

Before we get out of the car, my father says that Mr. Comeau phoned back when I was gone. We might have to move our driveway, my father says, because there was a slight miscalculation and the water will be a little closer than they first thought. For now our driveway is on the downhill side of our house, curving slightly out and away from it, but it will have to be moved to the top.

"That's it?" I ask.

My father nods.

~

Everyone at school is excited about the big farewell dance. It's this Saturday. The principal decided to have it now rather than at the end of the school year so it wouldn't distract from graduation. Plus, I suppose it's best to spread out the happy times as much as you can around here. The dance is for the students who will be moving over the summer. There are eight leaving that I know of. Adele "Jelly Jam" Stanley is going, but no luck with June or Linda. Everyone who is moving far away from the area seems to want to get it over with rather than wait another year. Most people who are moving their houses locally or maybe buying or building in the new town are hanging in there.

Mr. Hogan is leaving too. There's no possibility his house can be moved the way it's built into a slope with the upper deck almost hanging over the river. He explained it all to us in class one day. The timing was actually perfect, he said — trying a bit too hard to sound positive. Mr. Hogan is going to retire. He and his wife Paulette are moving to Fredericton, closer to her work at the university. Because she likes her job she'll stay at it a few more years, then they'll travel together — maybe even buy a new camper trailer, we'll see!

They're burning their house themselves, like Mr. Ball, but are doing it privately. They're going to paddle their canoe out in the river, drink some wine, and reminisce in each other's arms while watching the flames. Mr. Hogan said this in front of the whole class, but not a single person giggled or made any sort of smart remark. It was a near miracle. I guess lately there's an unusually high tolerance for nostalgia and sentimentality.

Not where I'm concerned of course, because June and Linda say after class today that they're sorry to hear my invitation to the dance got lost. I tell them it's all right because I have a date who's taking me.

It's hilarious, the look on their faces. It's just as well they don't ask and I don't tell. Sarah's coming down to go with me.

*

Right after breakfast on Saturday, I type the message for Percy's bottle, and then he insists I type his thank-you note to Mr. Cole. Percy's already read both books I brought home (twice) and when my mother told him he should send a thank-you note, it became so important that simple printing wouldn't do. The note is in Percy's typical official-sounding style, but I think it will make Mr. Cole smile. Percy also insists that I use the full Mr. Ellis Cole in the salutation rather than just Mr. Cole. It's so there's no confusion that he could mean Tommy.

I type:

> To: Mr. Ellis Cole,
> Thank you for the two books entitled *Sea Life of the Atlantic Ocean* and *The Way to Game Abundance.* I have received them from my sister, Ruby Carson, who has informed me that they were sent by you. I have completed reading both volumes but plan to study them further in the future. I have learned a great deal from their contents.
> From: Percy Carson.

I type the envelope, then deliver it. As I suspected, Mr. Cole looks pleased. I tell him Percy composed it, but I think he already knows.

There isn't much cleaning to do. Mr. Cole only uses a few rooms in the giant old house — master bedroom, kitchen, bathroom, and parlour. He's been sorting through things again in the parlour so when I go in there to dust, he tells me not to bother. I make our lunch and finish everything by one o'clock. I head home and take Percy for his bottle launch. Then it's just a matter of doing a little wood-carving while we wait for Sarah, Aunt Patty, and Uncle Kent to come for supper.

Sarah and I eat quickly so we can get ready for the dance. We excuse ourselves before dessert and look at the dresses Sarah brought. Aunt Patty bought them at a dress shop across the line in Houlton. Sarah's is purple and mine is turquoise. They're both fancy with tulle on the shoulders over satin and look like they were expensive. Sarah convinced Aunt Patty to get mine as an early gift for my fifteenth birthday — which is next week. Running my hand over the smooth skirt I feel a twinge in my chest that I remember is excitement. I hug Sarah to thank her.

Since this is a special occasion my mother's letting me try some of her pink lipstick. Sarah puts some on too. She asks me about Colin Moore, the boy she used to like, and wonders if we will see him. I say probably — with June Crouse. Sarah shrugs this off as if it's nothing. She thinks her dress and her lipstick make her look pretty enough to stir up some jealousy. She must have picked up this confidence from her new friends in Woodstock, because if confidence is a family trait it sure wasn't passed on to me.

The gym is decorated with big bunches of balloons in every colour and banners saying, "Goodbye" in different languages. There are "Au Revoir," "Adios," "Auf Wiedersehen," and "Ciao" as if the students leaving are going on vacation to exotic places rather than moving to Fredericton or Florenceville or Saint John. The banners are painted red and green and along the edges are handprints, I suppose to look like waving. There are three long tables at the side of the gym draped in yellow tablecloths. One has punch and cups, one has snacks, and the last one has a white-and-blue farewell cake.

Mr. Hogan's standing at the door.

"Well hello Ruby Persimmon Carson, Sarah Rose Carson. Good to see you again!" he says. "So, please, please, come in, welcome. There's lots of food and be sure to sign my memory book by the cake. It's just a guest book so don't be shy, but if you want you can write me a little message." He gestures to the side of the gym.

There are a lot of people already here. The dance floor has probably twenty-five or thirty people dancing and more are standing along the outside walls or near the tables. It's warm even though the back doors are propped open. The music is loud.

We head over to the punch first and each get a glass. We sign Mr. Hogan's book. Most people have written at least a line or two. The favourite themes seem to be "We'll miss you," "Enjoy your retirement," and "Thanks for being a great teacher." Sarah goes with the retirement option. I'm not sure what to put, so I write, "Merry Christmas, Mr. Hogan" and I sign with all three names.

Sarah and I take our punch and stand under a banner that says, "Sayonara." I'm curious to see if anyone will come talk to Sarah or if they'll be deterred by the fact that she's with me. Three songs play and in this time a girl walks by and waves. I tell Sarah I don't mind if she goes and talks to her, so Sarah says just for a minute or two and takes our empty cups back.

While she's gone I try my hardest to look relaxed as if she's only gone to get us a snack and will imminently return. I lean slightly against the wall. The principal sees me alone and comes and talks to me, which is pretty much the kiss of death. Dancing with him would be the only thing worse. I limit my responses to one word each — "yes," "yes," "thanks," "no" — and he moves on. I pretend to be looking around the gym at the banners with great interest. Perhaps I'm wondering about studying each of the languages in the future. I adjust the tulle on the shoulders of my dress. I take off my rhinestone necklace as if there's something wrong with it. I check it over and put it back. I do the same thing with my bracelet. I wish I was wearing earrings. Or had a hair clip to adjust. I pretend there's a little rock I have to shake out of each shoe.

Finally I see Sarah headed toward me, then the music switches to a slow song and a boy steps into her path. He leads her onto the dance floor. There are dozens and dozens of couples dancing. Even Mr. Hogan is out there with his wife. It's very hard to fight the urge to be fidgety. Necklace. Check. Bracelet. Check. I wonder if it would look too desperate to pretend I lost both earrings. The song is long, verse after torturous verse. It must be something new because I don't recognize it. The whooo-ahhh, whooo is getting to me. I'm not really sure that coming here was the best idea. But then the song ends and I know that after a bit of polite chit-chat with the boy, Sarah will come back to me.

June Louse and Linda Smells beat her to it. All of a sudden they're right in front of me. Linda's wearing a dress the colour of spat-out cough syrup and June's wearing something familiar-looking in grey. They both have on full makeup, not just lipstick like me. They obviously shared the same eyeshadow. It accentuates the mean look in their eyes, sparkling bluish-green.

"What're you doing here?" Linda asks.

"Just came to say farewell, same as everyone else. But I must say I was disappointed when I found out you weren't one of the ones leaving." I'm quite good at this now.

"Next year," Linda says. "Unless we can find a place to move our house. We don't all have fathers who can call in favours."

"June's not going anywhere either," I say. "How come you don't have a problem with her?" It's something I've wanted to ask for a while.

"June lives way back in the woods."

It's the truth, but I see June wince, as if she's just been put down by her best friend.

"So did you get lost on your way to a wedding?" June asks rather than letting Linda and me continue. "That's one ugly bridesmaid dress."

I think about letting it go as I'm sure Sarah will come along soon, but over June's shoulder I can see that Sarah's still talking to the boy.

"Well, we all have our opinions," I say. "Because I was just thinking that your dress looked much better on the minister's wife when she wore it to church last year."

June stares at me. She's silent. She's trying to think of something to say when her date and Linda's come up behind them and simultaneously tickle their waists. Both girls giggle exaggeratedly. They smile and flip their ponytails, then turn to the boys as if I'm no longer here. Maybe I shouldn't have said what I said, but their dates, their laughter, their togetherness, is the best comeback. June's perfect reply is her glorious exit, leaving me alone again.

Maybe when I'm finished high school, I'll be a maid. That's what I think as I lie in bed. I seem to be pretty decent at cleaning Mr. Cole's house and it's something I can do alone. I was going to be a teacher. I was going to be the type of teacher who got really excited about smart kids like Percy. I figure that Mrs. Poole, who he has now, is scared and suspicious of him. She told him he isn't to correct her — ever — even though, according to Percy, her grammar is atrocious (his word) and at least once a day she writes something out wrong on the blackboard. Percy fixes it as he copies it down in his notebook, then breathes in and out really fast over and over. Mrs. Poole always notices and says, "Enough, Mr. Carson." Mr. Carson, instead of Percy, because I'm sure she knows it bothers him.

But now I don't see any need to extend my years in the school system. Sure I'd be older than my students by the time I was a teacher, but if this weird of mine never wears off, who needs a lifetime of generation after generation of teenagers laughing at me? Why set myself up when I could just be alone in some rich person's dining room polishing silver?

Or maybe I could be an eccentric woodcarver selling figurines. My mother told me once about a woman from Nova Scotia who paints pictures on boards using leftover boat paint. She has a sign outside her little shack that says, "Paintings For Sale." Tourists from the States and Ontario stop in and buy them. My specialty would be driftwood owls.

～

My mother's waiting on the side of the road for Percy and me when we get off the school bus. She's wearing a yellow blouse and pedal pushers and her hair is shining in the sun. The bus driver says hello to her. He smiles and lingers with the door open as if he'd chat much longer if he didn't have his job to do.

"Mother, what are you doing here?" Percy asks before he even says hello.

"It's Ruby's birthday today, Percy. You remember, right?" She touches him gently on top of his head. "We're all going to walk down to the store together and get some film for my camera. And you can both get a treat."

"Did anything arrive in the mail for me today?" he asks.

"No, sorry, not today. But you'll come to the store with us?"

He doesn't look thrilled. At all. Her being here is a surprise.

"Is the film to document what Ruby looks like today at fifteen years of age?" Percy asks.

"Yes, I suppose." My mother smiles at me. "And I want to get a picture of her blowing out the candles on her cake."

"Okay," he says.

"Here, Percy," I say. "Give me your lunchbox and I'll run it down to the —"

My mother interrupts me. "No, no, that's all right. We'll just go," she says. "I'll carry it."

"No, Mother," Percy says.

My mother should know the presentation of any sort of new or unusual idea to Percy is often the prelude to problems.

"I can go," I say. "I'll be really fast. I'll be right back."

My mother looks at me like she's making a very hard decision. I wonder if there's some sort of birthday surprise in the house that she's scared I'll ruin.

"Just put them in the porch," she says.

I start to run, but when I round the little curve in the driveway at the end of our hedge, I see my father's car and stop. It's only three-thirty in the afternoon. There's another car as well, and it takes me a minute to recall whose it is. I drop our things on the lawn and turn back.

As I head out to the road I see my mother with a careful but sad half-smile on her face, watching me. Percy is turned, looking toward the river. I take my index finger from each hand and touch the tips to form a triangle in front of me. I trace down at an angle on each side making a roof, next two straight lines for walls, and finally I bring my fingers in toward each other to touch again for the floor — the shape of a house. I take my right hand and push this imaginary tracing off to the side, move it away as easy as shooing a fly. My mother nods slowly and closes her eyes.

Chapter 9

～

My parents say they'll take the summer to decide what to do. As far as I know we have the same options for our house as anyone else. It's a closed subject for now (and a secret from Percy), although I'm sure it's what my parents whisper about when I'm in bed — or the reason my mother and Miss Stairs always seem to be talking about the weather now when we come home from school.

I've thought about it a lot in the past week, and really at this point I figure my weirdness will just follow me whether I stay or go. It's like some secret high-pitched signal I emit, tweaked to the ears of teenaged girls. At least around here I know what I'm dealing with. It's amazing what you can get used to. June and Linda are almost predictable. Yes, our house will be flooded out like everyone else's, but I'm sure it's too late for us to be considered equals. Now they'll probably just say that my father somehow stalled things and got us all those extra months to make plans.

*

Miss Stairs tells us that the Fosters' house will be moved on Friday afternoon. They have a huge piece of land so it will stay on their property, just farther back. Miss Stairs has been helping Mrs. Foster pack. I thought the whole house would have to be empty to be moved, but not according to Miss Stairs. The pictures have to come off the walls and the dishes and breakables need to be packed away. But once that's done, it can all stay in boxes in the house. The clothes can stay hanging in the closets. The kitchen chairs can stay around the table. The stool can stay at the piano. The curtains can stay in the windows.

"We could even sit in there safe, just like this," Miss Stairs says, gesturing across to my mother and me at our kitchen table. "We might feel a little lift, but there shouldn't be any sliding or shifting."

I'm not so sure. I'll be going to see this miracle take place with my own eyes like everyone else. I'll be waiting to see the piano slide across the floor and smash through the wall, or the medicine cabinet come flying out the window.

My mother tells Miss Stairs that when it's time to pack up her house, we'll help.

Miss Stairs seems surprised.

"Oh," she says. "Oh, well oh my soul, I suppose, thank you." It's almost like she hasn't let herself think that far ahead. Except I know she has. Miss Stairs has already decided she's moving to the new town. She's even talked about buying one of the pre-fabricated houses they're bringing in. She said it was one of the hardest decisions she's ever had to make, but if she's going to start again, it may as well be with a completely different house — all nice and empty and new.

On Wednesday evening when I walk to Mr. Cole's, I look across his fields and wonder where Miss Stairs's new house will be. It's hard to figure out what will end up being yards and building lots, but there are more and more orange-tipped survey stakes. They're spotted across the whole area like a spreading rash. Three backhoes are still working, digging a long trench, maybe for pipes. There are lots of giant holes next to big mounds of dirt. A few roads are roughed in with gravel. They have deep tire tracks in them from heavy machines. The whole place looks like a sandbox after about a hundred three-year-olds have been playing in it. It's a great big mess.

The last time I was at Mr. Cole's he told me that he walks up his driveway at the end of each day. He looks across his fields like I am now, then closes his eyes. He conjures up in his mind how it was before, like a test, to be sure he doesn't forget. He says it's a way of exercising his old brain, building the strength of his memories. Sometimes the sound of a machine backing up will break his concentration for a second, but once he has the old picture focused in his head, nothing can take it away.

Tonight at Mr. Cole's the only room that needs cleaning is the kitchen. Mr. Cole has always been neat, but especially so lately. I think he's been cleaning some himself as he goes through and sorts things. He's sitting at the table while I wash the supper dishes. He's telling me about a beautiful white deer he saw years ago when the phone rings. He excuses himself but doesn't go far. The phone's mounted on the wall beside the fridge.

It's impossible not to hear his side of the conversation.

"Oh, good enough," he says. "Oh, no, no." A pause. "Oh, no, that's all right." A pause again. "There's lots of time yet."

Then Mr. Cole is quiet while the other person talks.

"No," he finally says sounding annoyed. "They gave me a year. I've told you that before. They gave me a year in my own house. The house your grandfather and I were born in, mind you, so I'll be damned if I don't take it."

Mr. Cole talks a bit longer and his voice goes back to normal. As I finish drying the last dish he hangs up.

On the way home I think of Tommy on the phone with Mr. Cole and wonder what he was saying. It's no secret around here that Tommy's worried about Mr. Cole selling away what he figures is his inheritance. If everything is turned to cash now while Mr. Cole is still alive, it can certainly be spent or given away. Everyone thinks it's probably a lot of money. Even with the low government assessments it should be a lot simply based on how much land Mr. Cole has. Really, how much would you have to pay to buy a whole town?

I wonder what Tommy's trying to convince Mr. Cole to do. He must have some plan. Tommy's no genius and he's generally lazy, but he's not completely stupid. My father says the most dangerous thing about Tommy is that he's one of those people who think they're a lot smarter than they actually are.

And he's also one of those people who only seems to see things as being worth something. Like I bet he looks at apples and really does see them as money growing on trees. He didn't seem to care what people thought when he stripped Mr. Ball's house clean. Mr. Ball told people to take what they wanted — that was all Tommy needed. Tommy's always coming and going from Mr. Cole's barn, moving around the things he's salvaged. He's always taking Mr. Cole's truck (I haven't seen him use his own car for months), running up the miles, taking things to Fredericton to sell. I wonder too if Mr. Cole's house seems emptier because he's been giving things to Tommy. I wonder if Tommy knows about the books Mr. Cole gave Percy or the rhinestone jewellery he's started sending home with me. Mr. Cole seems so pleased to give me shiny little pieces that had belonged to his wife Rita. I tried to refuse at first, but my mother says it's all right as long as it's nothing too valuable — since it seems to make Mr. Cole happy. Tonight he gave me a sparkling red-and-pink butterfly.

*

On Friday after school Percy is sitting on the edge of his seat for the whole bus ride home. My mother said he could watch the Fosters' house being moved and he's so excited I can almost feel an electric hum coming from him. At first my mother had considered not letting him go, the same as he hadn't gone to Mr. Ball's house burning. Then came the news that our house would be going underwater too and that changed things. Even if Percy doesn't know about our house yet, my father thinks this is a good way to ease him into reality. Plus he's a boy fascinated with logistics, and calculations, and how things work, and making him miss something like this could almost be considered mental cruelty.

My mother warned him the house may already be off the basement and jacked up by the time he gets there, but that she hopes he can see it put on the truck and hauled away. Percy has his arm across the front of his face with his watch about an inch from his glasses. As we ride along he's watching the seconds tick away. The moving of the house is all he's been talking about lately. He says that if it's done correctly, then Miss Stairs is right and nothing should move or slide. It'll be just like a waitress carrying a tray.

The bus slows for our stop and Percy gets up while it's still moving. He's on the inside by the window and I can tell he wants to jump right over me. My mother's about halfway down the driveway. Percy drops his lunchbox in my lap because I told him I'd take it, then I swing my legs aside and out he goes. I hear laughter coming from the Crouses at the back. Percy's already to my mother before I'm even off the bus. She takes his hand and he begins to drag her along as he runs.

I don't rush and when I arrive well after my mother and Percy, the house is already on the truck. Some of the white clapboard around the bottom right-hand side is broken and pulled off, but other than that it looks no different than it did yesterday. It seems so nice and neat on the flatbed that you could almost convince yourself it's just been popped off the basement temporarily. No windows are smashed and all three upstairs ones have the curtains neatly tied back. The front door is closed. The step leading to it is still attached.

Percy and my mother are standing with Miss Stairs at the edge of the crowd. Percy's stretched the maximum distance possible from my mother while still holding her hand — like a dog straining on a leash. I see other boys Percy's age running around loose, their mothers completely ignoring them, chatting with each other, maybe gossiping and laughing about my mother and him. But I know my mother's keeping Percy with her because his curiosity and potential for absolute engrossment in things completely distorts his sense of danger. Percy would've been right over standing beside the men working the jacks, leaning in, almost under the house while it lifted.

My mother learned a long time ago to be extra careful with Percy. One time he shook loose of my mother's hand and ran toward a moving car in the parking lot of Foster's Store. He was four and had just learned to count to a thousand. He was fascinated by numbers and wanted a closer look at the car's licence plate. My mother turned pale the only time I heard her tell that story. Maybe it's logical Percy has no common sense because nothing else is common about him anyway.

I know for sure we won't be leaving until the truck with the house pulls away, so I take my time working my way over to them. I take two pictures with my mother's camera. I walk along behind everyone, trying to get the perfect location for one more photo — a long shot of the whole scene. I need a bit of distance so I head back to the road. There are cars and trucks all along the shoulder. They'll probably have to move for the house to fit through. I look at the width of the roadway left clear and turn around again to look at the house on the truck. And then because I'm walking, and turning back and forth, and not paying attention, I bump right into someone.

"Oh, whoa," he says.

Please, please, please don't let it be someone who's going to make a big scene out of me being clumsy.

"Oh, sorry," I say. "Really. Sorry." But it's someone I've never seen before. It's a boy about my age. He's tall and has light brown hair and is very tanned. He has the bluest eyes I've ever seen. I feel like the rhinestone brooch I'm wearing, the butterfly Mr. Cole gave me, has fluttered down my throat and is asphyxiating me.

"Are you all right?" he asks.

I can't speak, but I manage a nod. And although I wait for some smart comment, or for June or some other girl to rush toward him giggling, this doesn't happen and he smiles at me.

My eyes drop like I have to check right this second if my shoelaces are untied. Except my shoes don't have any.

"Well, I don't want to keep you then, since you seem to be in a hurry," he says. I'm not looking at him, but his voice still sounds friendly.

"Okay," I say. I feel my face blush. Okay? I know I don't exactly have practice at these things, and part of me is still suspicious it's a trick, but it would have been nice to say something better — or at least find out who he was — before he walked away.

On the way home in Miss Stairs's car I ask her if she's heard of any new families moving in. She says she hasn't. Then she starts talking about her shopping trip to Fredericton yesterday and everything she bought, even though so many other people around here seem to be focused on packing up, sorting, and giving things away. I stare out the window and think of the boy. His eyes really were as blue as the river. I don't dare hope, so I limit myself to wondering. I wonder if I'll see him again.

The next day as I walk down Mr. Cole's driveway I see that the men and machines are up and at it early, even though it's Saturday, working away trying to conjure a whole town from nothing. The crushed-rock streets are stretching farther and farther, linking and crossing in the distance. Now it looks like they've moved beyond the land that belongs to Mr. Cole, and the yard that used to belong to my grandparents, where my mother grew up, will soon be under there somewhere. The new town has reached the main road on the far side, so it's obvious to everyone around here — something that can be seen every day coming and going. Although it may be easy to temporarily let yourself forget a dam is being built, since it's fifteen miles downriver, no one can pretend nothing's happening here.

As I come to the end of Mr. Cole's driveway and start to round the corner of his house, I see him standing on the shore looking across the water. The sun is strong and bright and he's a silhouette with the golden river in the background. It's like a picture that would be on a calendar hanging downstairs in the church kitchen with a Bible quote as a caption. I stop for a few seconds, but then when I walk toward him, he turns and heads back in as if he could sense me coming. I wait on the section of grass he keeps mown and he walks through the path in the taller part. The path looks well worn. The grass is really trampled down.

"Ruby," he says. "Come in. I don't think there's anything to clean today, but we'll have tea."

"Oh. Well I'm sure there must be something." It seems wrong that I hardly do any work, but he still insists I come and pays me fully.

We end up sitting on the porch with our tea. I grab the broom and sweep it off first. Today Mr. Cole is telling more stories about his old black-and-white cat, The Daily News. He's saying Rita thought it was The Daily Mews, like a clever pun, for years. After a while I realize that I could tell Mr. Cole the story about Quilty and the drywall, but

I decide not to because the punchline is Tommy's idiocy. Mr. Cole has more stories anyway, and I'm happy to listen. If only I could transform him into a fifteen-year-old girl.

We chat until we hear a vehicle drive down the driveway. A man comes around the side of the house and up the stairs toward us. Mr. Cole stands as he reaches the top and extends his hand. The man is probably the same age as my father. He's tall and has dark blond hair. He shakes Mr. Cole's hand and says his name is Ed Rutherford. He's an antique dealer from Ontario down buying in the area. He's wondering if Mr. Cole has anything old to sell. Mr. Cole is kind and friendly to the man and talks with him awhile. When Mr. Cole says he'll have to think about it, the man passes him a business card and says he'll be around for the summer except for quick trips to take loads back. If Mr. Cole wants to call him, he's staying at the Pokiok Lodge.

Mr. Rutherford turns to go, but then Mr. Cole remembers something. He says there are some old things in the barn — they aren't his to sell, but he could certainly pass the word along if there was any interest.

Mr. Cole asks the man to wait and turns to me. He says again there's nothing to clean and on a nice day like this he doesn't want to keep me. Then he goes in the house to get a bag. Inside is a book on trees of New Brunswick for Percy and two rhinestone brooches — one for my mother and one for me. Mine is a beautiful tiny ice-blue snowflake. Mr. Cole takes out the one for my mother and holds it flat in the palm of his hand. It's a large flower, white and amber. He asks if I know what type of flower it is. I nod and he winks. It's a lily. Plus there are two sealed envelopes in the bag addressed to my father. One is large and thick. The other is the size of a letter.

Mr. Cole and Mr. Rutherford head off to the barn as I start the walk home. Mr. Rutherford's truck is backed into the driveway and is already half full with furniture piled high and tied every which way. It's pretty precarious looking. There must be some trick to it.

When I'm almost to the front of the truck I notice a face in the side-view mirror watching me. It's the boy I saw yesterday.

The truck door starts to open just as a call of "Troy!" comes from the direction of the barn.

"Well if it isn't the prettiest girl in all New Brunswick," the boy says. He smiles, then runs to help.

I can hardly believe it. I have the urge to look over my shoulder, but I'm sure there's no one else nearby.

He was definitely talking to me.

Chapter 10

~

After church, as everyone's milling around, I look for him. I don't know why he'd be here, but I don't want to miss an opportunity. It's no less likely he'd be here than anywhere I hoped to run into him yesterday — on the Hawkshaw Bridge watching Percy's bottle launch, in our front yard, or during my trip to Foster's Store (which wasn't entirely necessary). It's likely best he wasn't any of those places though, or here today, because I have no idea what I'd say to him. I think the first step may be simply to look him in the eyes rather than to act like a shy three-year-old — or like Percy.

He and his father have been making the rounds in the area. Since we arrived at church today, they've come up in conversation again and again. No one can believe Mr. Rutherford's generous offers for what most people are calling old junk. People whose houses he hasn't been to claim to be crossing their fingers and waiting patiently. As I listen along I realize that for once I may know something no one else does. It's a small fact, but as people drop the tidbits of information they've gathered — Mr. Rutherford is staying at the Pokiok Lodge, he's staying all summer, his truck is grey, he carries a huge wad of cash, hundreds and hundreds of dollars — no one mentions that his son's name is Troy. Troy Rutherford called me the prettiest girl in New Brunswick.

The other thing I hear while I'm waiting for my parents is chatter about the announcement the minister made today. The church will be moved. As soon as the site is ready it will be relocated to Mr. Cole's field, also known as the new town. There are a few final details to be worked out, but it should be there by the end of the summer. The minister asked that we pray it goes smoothly.

My mother and Percy are talking to Mr. Cole, and my father walks over to join them. My mother touches the rhinestone lily brooch she has on her collar, then hugs Mr. Cole and kisses him on the cheek. Mr. Cole smiles, says something they laugh at (except Percy of course), and my mother hugs and kisses him again. This hug is longer, but as soon as she is finished she and Percy head toward me, leaving my father to talk to him. My father says something, squeezes Mr. Cole on the shoulder and shakes his hand.

My mother says if I'm not too starving for lunch we can go for a little drive and see some of the recent changes. I tell her it sounds like a great idea. I'll be watching for a grey truck with Ontario plates and a tangle of furniture — with a boy sitting in the passenger seat.

No such luck. Even as we go by the Pokiok Lodge the truck isn't in the parking lot. There's plenty to see though. We drive by the site of what will be the new mill, see part of the new highway, and what we can of the town. There are people walking along the gravel roads. This is the only day the men and machines rest — the only day to be nosy without getting in the way. There are a couple of men who do security, which means that they take turns sitting on the tailgate of a pickup and smoking, then go for a quick spin around the place every hour to see that none of us locals have decided to do anything destructive. A few nights ago, a bunch of boys from school had bike races down the main hill for an hour before the security guard thought maybe he should tell them to scram. I haven't had any desire to do more than see what I can when I walk down Mr. Cole's driveway. I feel like any more interest in it than that would seem like a betrayal to him.

We drive by the Fosters' house, safe and sound on its new basement. We see that the charred remains of the Balls' house have been bulldozed and kind of flattened. We see a house with a sign offering it for sale to anyone who wants to have it moved. It's the McShanes' place and my mother says they're leaving the area. We see the giant spray-painted signs all along the edge of Leonard Black's lawn — "Private Property," "Do Not Enter," "No Trespassing," and "If You're From the Government, Go Away!"

I sit in the backseat with Percy and look over at him from time to time, wondering what he's thinking. We see some of this from the school bus every day, but I figure this grand tour is more of the "easing him in" that I hear my parents talk about at night. Percy isn't saying anything, but he doesn't have a book with him, so he's forced to look out the window. Maybe their plan is working. I know it's working on me. As we drive around now I realize that nothing seems too shocking anymore. I hope I can feel this way when our house is on the back of a truck or going up in flames.

~

On Wednesday, Tommy's sitting alone on Mr. Cole's porch steps when I come around the corner. He's smoking a cigarette. It's like he's been waiting.

"Ruby Carson," he says.

"Hi Tommy." I'm hoping I can go right up the stairs past him.

"Now, what's the rush?" Tommy asks. "Uncle Ellis is just in there drinking his tea. Why don't you sit and talk to me a minute?" He takes a long last draw of his cigarette, then butts it out on his boot.

"I should let him know I'm here," I say.

"He'll be able to hear enough to know you're out here. Be a good girl now and sit and keep me company a minute." He pats the step beside him.

I sit down on the far side of the same step as Tommy, as close to the railing as possible.

"Nice night," Tommy says.

I nod.

"Pretty view."

I nod again.

"Gonna be a lot of houses up in the new town all sharin' this nice view soon."

"I suppose."

"I wonder where good old Uncle Ellis will end up. He could prob-ably have a nice little house up there somewhere too." Tommy looks off in the distance and nods slowly. "Sure would be nice for him to live simple and easy and carefree the rest of his years. No more big lonely house, all those rooms to keep neat and clean and care for, no more giant yard to keep up — lots of neighbours to talk to." Tommy nods again as if he's convincing himself of this as he speaks. If it was anyone else I might almost believe it, but from him it sounds like a practised speech.

"So what do you think, Ruby?" he asks. "Don't you think that sounds nice?"

"I don't know, maybe," I say. I don't want to be rude and annoy him, but it's the best he's going to get from me.

"Well I hope he's considering it, God love him," Tommy says. "I sure do want what's best for him."

I nod but don't say anything and get up. I guess Tommy's done with the message he wanted to give me.

I go into the house and wash Mr. Cole's supper dishes. Then I sweep the floor even though he says it doesn't need it. For a house Tommy claims is hard to care for, I sure never have much to do.

Friday's the last day of school. I finished first in my class, but considering the circumstances that allowed me to dedicate so much time to my studies, it's no big thrill. I'm just glad it's done. And that I don't have to hear the whole Crouse family, collectively the Octo-Crouse, make watery gargling sounds each time I get on the school bus, or the hissing that I finally figured out was supposed to be a splash each time I get off. As Percy and I ride along on the bus, I keep reminding myself I've got two full months of Crouse-free summer ahead.

When we get home Miss Stairs is in the kitchen with my mother. On the table there's a cake decorated with a bright yellow sun and two wrapped gifts. Percy asks my mother if anything arrived in the mail for him (it didn't) before sitting in his chair. Miss Stairs congratulates us on another completed school year, then my mother says we can open our presents. Percy looks disappointed when he sees that his is a baseball mitt. It had to be my father's idea. But Miss Stairs says she brought him a special wooden pop crate from the store to keep his bottles in. She points at it in the corner and he runs over as if it's a pirate's treasure chest. My gift is a beautiful lilac sweater set and matching gauzy scarf.

My mother serves the cake and asks me to pour the tea. When I get up, I notice a business card tucked under a magnet on the fridge. I see the *ford* of *Rutherford* and the full word *Antiques*. I take it down and sure enough on the back in handwriting is *Pokiok Lodge*, the phone number and *Cabin 7*.

He was at my own house and I missed him!

"I think this is the same man who stopped in at Mr. Cole's when I was there the other day," I say, trying to sound calm, waving the card.

"It could be," Miss Stairs says. "He stopped by the store today and said he was down for the summer buying."

"And he came by here today?" I ask my mother.

She shakes her head. "Vergie brought the card."

"So do we have any antiques to sell?" I ask. "What about some of the furniture that came from Gramma and Grandfather's?"

My mother looks surprised. "Those are special things, Ruby. For you and Percy when you get older."

"Oh, no." I feel my face flush. "I just meant as an example. Like an example of what an antique is. I didn't mean to sell those things."

My mother nods, then goes back to serving the cake. "I'm not sure if we have anything," she says. "I doubt it, but I thought I'd mention it to your father."

I put the card back. It's definitely best to stop talking now. I don't need a compliment from a boy I've seen for a grand total of about forty-five seconds making my mother think I'm overly zealous about selling our family heirlooms.

Cabin seven. I think of it as I fall asleep. I can picture the slant of the roof, the white gingerbread trim, the little shutters, and the miniature porch. It seems to me that cabin seven is one of the ones closest to the river near the base of the falls. That's where Troy Rutherford is right now. With his father, but for the sake of my imagination I'll let his father be out driving around, or up in the restaurant, or by the water having a smoke. I see Troy alone on the little porch, in the ladderback rocking chair I know is there, his feet on the rail.

On Saturday morning when I walk to Mr. Cole's, I see that the town workers are creeping closer. The last strip of trees that is only about three hundred feet behind Mr. Cole's house is being cut. One man is running a chainsaw and seven or eight others are standing watching — I suppose staying out of the way. Two giant pines are already down. They're so huge that lying on the ground they make the nearby bulldozers and trucks look like toys beside a knocked-over Christmas tree. I wish they could have left them a little longer. I know they were the only thing saving Mr. Cole from having a constant view of the construction (or destruction). He said as long as those trees were there he was able to forget, at least temporarily, everything going on.

The trees had helped keep the noise out too, because as I walk down the driveway I realize the work is not only closer, but louder. In Mr. Cole's house the noise used to seem like a distant rumble and hum, no worse than the occasional big truck rolling down the roadway. Even with the windows open it wasn't too bad. Now I wonder how Mr. Cole can stand it.

I can also smell gas and exhaust. And smoke — from men's cigarettes and a little brush fire. There are puffs and wisps of dirty air. I walk faster.

Mr. Cole's standing on the shore when I round the corner of the house, but even with the noise he seems to sense or hear me. He turns and waves and I sit on the porch and wait. It's overcast and there's no sparkle to the river today. It's dark. It looks like it would swallow a thrown rock without even a ripple. Mr. Cole lingers for what seems a long time. Then he turns quickly and smiles and heads in toward me.

Mr. Cole has a lot of work planned. He has a list and we go through the house room by room. Many of the chores are simple, like changing two light bulbs, but he also asks me to clean all the windows and mop the stairwell and main hall. I figure he must have company coming. I hope it's someone better than Tommy.

I eat lunch with Mr. Cole at noon, then take another forty-five minutes to wash the dishes and do the windows in the kitchen. I check to make sure the stairwell and hallway have dried okay and don't look streaky. I run a damp cloth down the handrail and over the newel post as a finishing touch. Mr. Cole's in the parlour reading.

"All done," I say.

"Wonderful Ruby, thank you. You've done an excellent job today. The house looks just as it should be." He looks around the parlour even though all I did in here was water a couple of plants, and then he nods approvingly.

"So I'll see you Monday," I say. Now that school is out I'll be coming every other day.

"But just a minute first," he says and sets his book aside. I see a small box that was underneath it on his lap.

"There's something I want to give you," he says. "I've been going through more things and I've found something special."

"But you've already given me the brooches."

"Yes, but this is nicer. And please oblige an old man and tell me you'll accept it. You'll see in a minute why it has to be yours."

"I'm not — " I start, but Mr. Cole interrupts me.

"We can call it a gift for grading if you want," he says. "And if your dear mother thinks I've lost my old mind giving away all my treasures, you can tell her I promised it's the last thing and I was insistent." He smiles and nods as if this solves everything.

He holds the box in one hand and lifts off the cover with the other, not looking down but looking at me. Inside is a gold heart-shaped locket that's engraved with "R.C."

Mr. Cole lifts it by the long chain and it starts to spin. On the back, in the middle at the top, is a tiny red stone.

"A ruby," I say.

"It's perfect, isn't it?" he says smiling. "You see why you have to have it now. Not only do you have the same initials, but her birthstone was a ruby."

Her. I turn the heart over in my hands. Rita Cole. I swallow and take a quick breath.

"Open it," he says.

Inside are two old black-and-white pictures of a man and woman.

"Back when I was handsome," he says and laughs. "And my dearest Rita of course. You can take them out, but I wanted you to see us first, back in our glory."

"I won't take them out," I say.

"Oh you never know. I'm sure you'll meet your own beau someday."

"Thank you so much. I love it," I say.

Mr. Cole smiles and nods. "You're most welcome, Ruby. But now I don't want to keep you."

"See you Monday," I say.

He raises his hand in a wave as I walk away.

I'm wearing the locket, but it's hanging inside my blouse so it doesn't bounce and swing. Every few minutes I check to make sure it hasn't fallen off. I think of the miniature pictures of Mr. Cole and his wife inside it. I think of all the years Mr. Cole waited for her to marry him and how he must have had so much faith all that time that she'd say yes. I remember too how Mr. Cole told me once he felt like the lucky one. It was the same day he said my father was the man he respected the most around here. He said he had to be a good man because my mother chose him.

Percy's waiting at the end of the driveway with his bottle.

"Ruby, our mother says we will be leaving for Fredericton immediately after I put my bottle in the river. Our mother and father will be picking us up at the bridge. If you need anything from the house you are to retrieve it now."

Right.

Percy's bottle launch is the same as always. He counts out to the middle of the bridge. He drops the bottle. It plunges and bobs. He watches it. I watch him. The only difference is that my parents pull up after ten minutes and I wait out the rest of the time in the car with them. We're parked on the shoulder at the end of the bridge.

"How was Mr. Cole's today?" my mother asks, turning in her seat.

"I think I cleaned every room in his house," I say. "And he gave me something. And I know maybe I shouldn't just accept something so valuable, but he was insistent, and he said it was for passing school this year too and it's the last —"

"What is it?" my father asks, interrupting me.

I take the locket from my neck and pass it to my mother.

My mother turns it over in her hands and my father looks down at it too.

"It was Rita's," she says.

"Yes, see the initials. Rita Cole, or," I emphasize, "Ruby Carson." I lean ahead in my seat. "And see the little ruby on the back. See why Mr. Cole wanted me to have it."

My mother nods. "It is perfect. Isn't it Jack?"

"Keep it in a safe place," my father says. "If you ever lost something like that it would be impossible to replace."

In Fredericton we go shopping. We go to Simpsons-Sears and Levine's. My mother buys a new light green dress for church and a pair of matching shoes. She buys Percy a package of white T-shirts. I choose two pairs of shorts. Then we eat in a restaurant downtown, a special treat for finishing school.

Before we head home my father suggests a drive around. Percy doesn't love the idea because he's scared we won't be home for his bedtime. My father says we won't take too long and we only drive ten or twelve streets. My parents don't give any special reason for this, but I notice we go a little slower past the houses with For Sale signs.

~

The Pokiok Lodge isn't far from our house and on Sunday afternoon I'm tempted to walk there. It's across the river, but only five minutes up from the bridge once you get to the other side. I doubt Troy Rutherford and his father are out doing business on a Sunday, so maybe if I just happened to want a little look at the falls I'd find him there. I have nothing else to do. Percy's in his room reading. My father's in the sunroom reading. My mother has finally begun a new painting.

Troy doesn't even know my name, so unless I rely completely on chance, my only other choice is to find him. But I know that's not what I'm supposed to do. Even though I've never played before, I still know the rules of the game. I ask my mother if it's all right to phone Sarah. She'll have an idea. But she's not home.

I sit outside in the sun for a while. I make a special thank-you card for Mr. Cole using some of my mother's art supplies. I work a little on my woodcarving, but I don't have my usual concentration so I almost slit my thumb. I weed our flower garden. I eat supper and then after six, I try Sarah again. There's still no answer. I've barely set the receiver down when the phone rings.

A voice asks for me.

"Speaking," I say.

"Hello, my name is Troy. Troy Rutherford. My father's an antique dealer and I met you at a Mr. Ellis Cole's home when we were out buying things."

"Yes," I say. It's the best I can do.

"I was wondering if you'd like to meet me at Foster's Store tomorrow? Is that near you? Maybe we could sit and talk — have an ice cream. Is there any chance you'd like to meet me at about two?"

"Yes," I say. I'm a real chatterbox sometimes — and to think I've ever said anything mean about Percy and his one-word answers.

I manage to sputter out a goodbye and then sit at the kitchen table. It must have been Mr. Cole who told Troy my name. And after all the wondering and hoping, he called me. But just so I don't go overboard I remind myself it's only a phone call and that maybe he'd been waiting until he knew our school was out for the summer. There's coincidence and fate and then there's simply good timing.

I want to be at Mr. Cole's right at nine so I'll have lots of time to clean, go back home, eat lunch, change my clothes, and walk to the store before two. As I hurry down Mr. Cole's driveway, I can see the whole back of his house for the first time. Every single tree has been cleared. Even the stumps are gone now and the whole area is flattened as if they were never there to begin with. It's strange to be able to see Mr. Cole's house from here, and stranger still how it's now the thing that looks out of place.

I round the corner of the house and look to the shore of the river, but Mr. Cole isn't out today. Then up on the porch both the screen door and the inner one are closed. I knock twice and turn the knob to go in, but it's locked. I knock again and wait.

I sit in the porch rocker. I flick at the corner of his thank-you card with a fingernail. Today is the first day of my new summer schedule, the first time in almost a year that I've been here on a Monday, so maybe he's forgotten. His truck isn't in the driveway, although I know most of the time lately Tommy has it. I wait maybe ten more minutes, then tuck the thank-you card under one of the slats in the screen door. I walk home.

*

I'm able to calm myself enough to carve without amputating any
fingers, and this is what I do until almost five minutes to two. I figure by
the time I arrive at the store, I will even be a little late. I walk quickly;
my legs just seem to motor right along like a wind-up toy, and it's hot,
so I worry I'll sweat. I sprayed on the tiniest mist of my mother's
perfume and I hope there's a lingering scent left. As I get close to the
store, I see Troy standing out front. He's turned, looking at the map,
so I can walk without worrying about how I look. He's wearing jeans
and a white T-shirt, but the effect is completely different than on Percy.
I'm wearing a pink striped top and one of my new pairs of shorts.

When he hears me on the steps he turns around.

"Well if it isn't Miss Saint John River Valley," he says.

"I'm Ruby," I manage.

"I'm Troy," he says. "Shall we?" He points at the bench and we sit
down.

Then a pause.

Two seconds. Three.

Now that he seems to have used up his practised opening lines,
here we are. Silent. I can't believe that in all the time I spent anticipating this moment I didn't consider what I might say.

"So do you work in a sawmill or are you a woodcarver?" he asks.

I can't even imagine the look on my face. I look around, behind
me, then across the parking lot as if maybe I'll see someone holding
up a sign providing Troy this information.

I turn back and he's grinning.

It's a set-up. I should have known. I'm the joke again.

"On the bottom of your shirt," he says.

"On your shirt," he repeats. Sure enough, there's a good-sized
patch of sawdust and wood shavings stuck to me.

I jump up and brush my blouse frantically with the back of my hand. From a distance you'd maybe think I was on fire — or being attacked by poisonous insects.

Troy stands too.

"I was kidding," he says. "Honest, it's no big deal. Don't worry about it."

I'm still checking to make sure I haven't missed any spots.

"Okay, don't answer just yet then. But let me show you something and maybe I'll be able to tell for myself. My dad says if I want to go into the antique business someday I should practise trying to read people."

Troy reaches into the front pocket of his jeans. He pulls out a small wooden chain. It's about six inches long and on the end is a tiny wooden ball trapped in a miniature cage. He passes it to me.

"I never leave home without it," he says. "My father got it four or five years ago out of this old guy's estate. He lived to be a hundred, this guy who made it. So now it's like my good luck charm. See if some of his good luck, living that long life, will pass on to me."

I've never seen anything like it. It's so simple yet intricate. The ball has just enough space to completely rotate in place. The first link of the chain comes from the corner of the cage so it hangs at an angle like a pendant. It must have been made so carefully.

"Carved from one piece of wood," I say.

Troy nods. "Amazing, isn't it? My dad says it would have taken a lot of skill to do that."

"And patience." I hand it back to him.

"So I'm going to say yes, then," Troy says. "That you carve wood."

"I try not to advertise it."

"So is that what all the girls down here in New Brunswick do for fun?"

I shake my head. "Not exactly."

"Well I'm impressed," Troy says.

We talk a little longer about (and I can hardly believe it) wood-carving. For now at least I don't mention my project, I just describe some of the contents of the kindling bin. Troy seems interested, but to stay on the safe side, I take the first opportunity to change the subject. He buys me an ice cream and afterwards we talk about the map. He asks where my house is and when he seems pleased, saying it looks like we're safe from the flood waters, I explain the discrepancy. He says he's sorry to hear it. It's the first time anyone's said that.

Troy's fifteen too. His school in Kingston, Ontario, got out a little earlier than ours. We eat our ice cream and talk for almost an hour before I tell him it's time for me to go. I'm sure my mother and Percy are back from Woodstock. I also know that the longer I sit here, the greater the chance someone will come along and wreck things. With each car that pulls up I expect someone from school to hop out, rush over, and set Troy straight — ask him what on Earth he's thinking.

I realize he's what my mother and Miss Stairs call a sweet talker with his snappy lines. But I don't understand why he's chosen to be sweet to me. Ontario is gigantic compared to here. I'm sure he knows dozens of girls and has probably seen hundreds more. Yet here he is sitting in front of me. Spending his money to buy me an ice cream. Smiling. I'll have to ask Percy the population of Kingston.

Troy offers to walk me home, but I politely refuse and say I have to stop somewhere first. It's almost the truth as I might go see if Mr. Cole's home. It's more because if Troy is going back over to the Pokiok Lodge, then I know our house is on the way — and that might mean running into Percy. I just don't want to ruin this one happy day. Troy asks me to meet him again tomorrow and I agree. I tell him I have to go in the store for a minute so he leaves. I don't tell him the reason I'm in here is so he doesn't see me with what I bet is a goofy smile, as I stand back from the window in shadow and watch him walk away.

Chapter 11

One summer day two years ago, I found one of Percy's bottles lodged in some driftwood along the shore. I was at the back of Doyle's orchard when I saw it glint in the sun. I knew right away that it was one of his bottles rather than garbage. Even though it was stuck, it was floating with its weighted base and the white of the note was obvious behind what I could read of *Nesbitt's*. I picked the bottle up and threw it overhand as far as I could into the river. I watched to see that it started downstream rather than get swept back in toward me.

I didn't mention it to Percy because I thought it would either upset him, or he'd want a complex description of my exact location, species of driftwood, position and condition of bottle, throwing technique, estimated distance thrown — and other answers I probably couldn't give him. Maybe when we're older, and if Percy ever somehow grows out of the way he is, I can tell him and we'll laugh about it. But for now I'm glad I put that bottle back in circulation. Percy's launched 109 bottles to date so that means he still has 109 possibilities. He wonders every day if any replies will come, but even with none, I have yet to see him disappointed. Once the bottles are launched he has no control over what happens to them, but he can control his expectations. If they haven't been found, then nothing has changed and they must be still out there floating.

If anything, Percy could teach you a thing or two about eternal optimism.

So I'm trying only to be hopeful and happy about today. I'm not going to think of what could go wrong with meeting Troy — just that I'm meeting him. I spent the morning baking cookies and watching my mother work on her painting. She said the finished project will be a surprise, but I can already see the river across the bottom of the canvas. It's back to its usual lilac colour. Miss Stairs stops in for a few minutes to drop off my mother's sunglasses, which she had forgotten in Miss Stairs's car. Miss Stairs went shopping yesterday while Percy and my mother visited Aunt Patty. That's how I knew she wouldn't be working at Foster's Store when I met Troy, and she won't be there again today. It's not that I'm hiding anything, but before I mention him to my mother, I want to be sure there's something to tell.

Perhaps it's my own fault then that after lunch, when I'm getting ready to go, my mother asks me to take Percy. He wants to buy more stamps for his envelopes in the bottles, and if I'm going then my mother can stay home and paint. I volunteer to buy the stamps and bring them back, but I already know better. The buying of the stamps is part of the whole process for Percy, and he has to witness the transaction taking place. It's already a stretch asking Percy to be tolerant of the fact that it will be me rather than my mother buying them.

I should have at least hinted about Troy to my mother because I know she would have understood. Percy's sitting at the kitchen table waiting. His hands are folded in front of him like a sweet little boy in a storybook illustration. The picture of patience. I wonder how much awareness he has that it will work out for him. If I say no, then all it means is that both he and my mother will show up while Troy and I are sitting out front.

"I was planning on getting an ice cream," I say. "So I might be a while." This won't make any difference, but I'll let them know what to expect.

"Oh, well here," my mother says and goes to the Ganong's candy tin where my parents keep their spare change. "I'll give you enough for the stamps and a cone for both of you. Would you like to get an ice cream, Percy?" she asks.

"Yes, thank you, Mother. I would like to study the map at the store as well during this outing, so I can eat the ice cream while I'm looking at it."

"That sounds good, Percy," my mother says.

Percy's eating his vanilla ice cream cone, staring at the map, while I sit on the bench on the opposite side of the step and wait. I know I can't completely ignore Percy, but after a quick introduction I figure he should be calm and quiet and he'll just go back to studying the local geography.

I see Troy coming down the road. I start to dig my fingernails into my palms to stay calm. Percy is leaning in close to the window with his face about three inches from the map. Maybe I'll tell Troy he needs new glasses. That seems reasonable enough. Troy's coming up the steps now. I raise my hand to wave.

"The lovely Ruby," he says.

Out of the corner of my eye I see Percy turn when he hears my name. This is it.

"Troy—" I start to say, but he talks at the same time.

"Hey," he says. "Percy, just Percy, not short for Percival, Carson, it's good to see you again today. How are you?"

"I am fine, thank you, Troy Rutherford," Percy says, then looks again at the map.

"I met Percy yesterday," Troy says to me. "It turns out I walked by your house and he was in the driveway. So I asked him to explain the mysterious phenomenon of the trail of bread along the roadway."

I try to imagine Troy walking by our house and calling out to Percy. Percy would be wary, but if there's any way to engage him it's to ask for something to be explained. Plus the way Troy talks, especially using the word *phenomenon*, well, that would be right up Percy's alley.

"I also liked his chosen ensemble, which I see you're sporting again today."

Percy looks down and nods. He has on his white T-shirt and jeans (as always), just like Troy had on yesterday.

Even when Troy asks Percy for his permission to talk to me and Percy says that only our parents have such a power and responsibility, Troy smiles and winks at me.

I believe I may have just witnessed a miracle take place. So I remind myself to be positive. Enough with expecting imminent disaster. Maybe my time for happiness has finally come. We talk for half an hour while Percy stares at different sections of the map.

Then I tell Troy I have to go because once again everything has been unimaginably fine and I don't want to push my luck. Sitting here I felt like my old self (pre-skating disaster), and even with Percy hovering nearby, I was comfortable. Troy asks to meet me Thursday because he has to help his father tomorrow. He goes into the store to call his father to pick him up.

When he comes back out, Troy goes over to Percy to say goodbye.

"So have you picked out where you'd like to move to?" he asks. "Ruby told me your parents haven't decided yet."

Percy turns and looks at Troy's chin just as I'm registering what Troy has said.

"I do not understand your question," Percy says. "Our house is indicated by this square." Percy touches it.

"I mean after the flooding," Troy says. "When that square's underwater." Troy taps the map. "Where would you like to be?"

Everything seems to slow down around me as if even the dust floating in the air has stopped.

"Percy," I say as Percy says, "Ruby."

His little shoulders begin to curl and rise. He looks at the map again, at the square that is our house, sitting in the yellow area, in safety above the danger zones of blue and green. The map is absolute, you see, and if I know anything about Percy, part of the problem even before the bigger realization hits, is that what Troy's saying can't be true, as the map, this all-important document, hasn't been updated. It hasn't changed. The map doesn't indicate this new truth, so how can it be?

Percy starts the little whimpers and fast breathing that are always a predecessor of worse to come.

"I'm sorry," Troy says, clearly confused. "Am I wrong?"

I can tell that Percy is waiting to hear my answer too.

It feels like a chunk of river ice fills my stomach. I feel badly for Troy because he didn't know any better, angry at my parents for not telling Percy and setting this up to happen, bad for myself because now I have to deal with it, but most of all, I feel an overwhelming compassion for the confusion going on in Percy.

"No," I say. "There was a miscalculation." I pause. "They just figured it out lately," I say — as if this makes any difference.

Percy starts to cry. Loud. Really loud. So loudly that Mrs. Foster comes out of the store, but when she sees who it is she goes back in again.

Troy's father pulls up at the same time and beeps the horn.

"Is he going to be okay?" Troy asks. He seems unsure. He's taken a few steps back from Percy and is staring. "Should we get my dad to drive him home?"

"Thanks," I say. "But I think it'll be better if we sit a bit."

At that Troy hurries away and as he leaves I wave. I figure it will be the last time I see him.

I smooth Percy's hair over and over. He cries and cries.

Really by now I should know better than to even try. I think maybe my whole life is one big miscalculation.

Percy sobs, with his shoulders shaking and his chest heaving, for what feels like hours, but is maybe fifteen minutes. Then just when I think he's calm enough to walk home, Miss Stairs drives in with my mother in the passenger seat. Mrs. Foster must have called her. Considering the noise Percy was making it's no surprise, but who knows if it was out of concern for him, or concern that we were scaring customers away. My mother rushes over to us and all I say is, "The house. He knows." Seeing her, Percy starts up again and cries the whole way home.

He goes to his room and stays there until my father insists he comes out for supper. Percy sits in his chair and doesn't say a word. He's completely quiet all night and silently puts himself to bed at eight o'clock.

When Percy was small, a fourteen-month-old baby, he learned to talk, but then somehow his little brain forgot. According to my mother, there were seventeen words my brother once spoke: ball, cup, dog, water, book, cow, baby, car, truck, milk, bird, boat, river, bear, cat, door, and deer. I can't remember hearing him say them myself, but I've seen them on a sheet of paper folded up in my mother's jewellery box. The words are listed in my mother's perfect printing. The way they're written so neatly I've always thought they looked important — like they were items to be distributed in a will. They are there as proof, I suppose. Or so my mother could recall them all. So she'd have some way to make her mind listen for the echo of Percy's tiny baby voice saying "baa" for "ball" all those years ago. She'll sometimes look at them when she finds the paper while digging for a pair of earrings. I've seen her read the list and get this little smile. I sometimes wonder if even back when she wrote it my mother knew Percy would always be a mystery she was trying to solve. I wonder if she knew the list would become evidence — really one of her very first clues. But she'll fold it again carefully and put it back with her opal earrings, pearl necklace, bracelets, brooches, and my grandmother's diamond ring. She keeps it prized and safe with her gold and silver, as if it's a map to a treasure and not just a list of a baby's babbling.

I don't know if this quieting of my brother happened in a second, like mid-sentence, or in a minute, an hour, a day, but somehow all those words he had known just faded away. My mother took him to the doctor. We drove to Fredericton with Percy sitting silent on my knee. But there was nothing the doctor could do except tell my mother to try not to worry, and to wait and see. Percy hadn't turned deaf as Miss Stairs thought, and he still cried and pointed and played. He had no wax in his ears. He had no tie in his tongue. My mother took him home again and then one afternoon six months later when she turned from his high chair to go to the kitchen sink, Percy said, "Bye" to her, plain as day.

Which for another four months was the only thing he'd say. He said "bye" to me when I went to bed at night, "bye" to cars and trucks that drove by. He used "bye" to mean "no" and "stop" and "don't" and "go away." It was "bye" to sweet potatoes he didn't want, "bye" when he saw my mother coming with a diaper, knowing he was going to be changed. "Bye" to loud noises. "Bye" to the bath. "Bye" to the minister's wife when she made faces and cooed at him ridiculously.

He learned to use "bye" as a language all its own, and it's funny how everyone thought he was so cute and smart back then — being so versatile with the only word he could say. He was every bit as cute and smart as Lori Lynn Lowe, who tried to pee standing up like her daddy, or Carla Doyle, who could match up socks when her mother was folding laundry, or Jasper Saunders, who could hum "Jesus Loves Me." My brother could be the main character in anyone's after-church story — oh what a sharp little sweetie that Carson boy — because then he was still young enough, simple enough, and innocent enough, and not yet hinting to anyone (except maybe my mother) just how truly, almost incomprehensibly intelligent he'd be one day. He was publicly allowed to be smart because really it was only those silly delightful baby smarts, something all babies have in one way or another, some little habit, quirk, action, sound, facial expression for people to comment on, compliment the mother on, and everyone knows a baby really can't be smarter than you or me!

Back then, as near as I can remember, everyone loved Percy. He was safe then. He didn't live in a complex world of his own.

Percyville. Population: 1.

It didn't last. As if to make up for lost time, he spoke a full baby sentence "River water wet, Mommy" as we drove across the Hawkshaw Bridge one day. My mother turned in shock to look at him sitting in my lap, and when the car veered a little he said, "Careful, Mommy." He had just turned two. It was like someone had flicked a switch. It was like he'd always been listening, secretly learning, but saving it until then. Even though he had never responded to what seemed like hours of my mother's coaxing, maybe he had been aware the whole time. My mother's early theory was that he was quiet all those months because he was concentrating. She said if you're thinking really hard, trying to figure something out, then you're probably not distracting yourself by talking at the same time. My early theory was that he was tricking us and it was all some joke. But it wasn't. To this day, as smart as he is, Percy doesn't understand jokes.

So I know now he's not kidding around, teasing us, thinking it's funny to hold a grudge, or giving us the silent treatment. Percy only reacts rather than plans to act in a certain way. We all figured it would upset him to learn of this one big change, the flooding of our house, but we didn't know just what the magnitude of the upset would be. Maybe it's what my mother thought all those years ago and Percy is being quiet so he can concentrate and not distract himself while he figures things out. My mother thinks a good night's sleep will help. All we can do is wait.

As I lie in bed I listen for Percy in his room. I listen for crying, or bottles clinking together, his globe spinning, or the sound of him flipping the pages of his notebook. I wonder if he's in there awake, trying to memorize his room. Even though we've known about the flood for so long, it really is hard to grasp that someday there will be water where you lay your head at night. Your room will be the river and the river will be what was once your room. The air will be wet. This air you are breathing will be drowned and gone. A fish could be swimming in front of you now. See it there? See it? These are the things you think. Or the things I think. I can only imagine when it comes to Percy.

I lie awake longer and try to think only of him. I think of him as that silent baby, thoughts and observations all the while churning in his head. I wonder what it must be like to be my mother, his mother, always dealing with this. I remember how distraught she looked at the store today seeing him. And how scared. I wonder about me too. I wonder if I looked anywhere near as awful as I felt. But then this reminds me of Troy, so I think of something else. I try to concentrate on my mother's most recent painting, conjure up the image of what she's done so far, and try to guess what it must be.

*

I'm halfway down Mr. Cole's driveway before I remember that he wasn't home on Monday. It hasn't exactly been at the top of my mind considering the recent drama. Percy still hasn't said anything and he only came to breakfast this morning because my father went up to his room and carried him. It was a big scene. My father was annoyed that Percy wouldn't hold on and he's pretty heavy. Percy's legs dangled and his feet made a pinging sound as they hit each spindle on the railing. My father left for work once Percy was sitting at the kitchen table eating a banana. He was in the same spot reading a book when I left for Mr. Cole's forty-five minutes later.

I'm looking forward to some nice straight-ahead dusting and scrubbing. Maybe I'll volunteer to mop the kitchen floor too if Mr. Cole doesn't have a lot of other things planned.

My thank-you card is gone from the screen door. The main door is closed like it was before. I knock and wait.

Knock and wait. Once again no one's answering.

I go to the back door. Knock and wait.

I'd like to peek in a window, but all the curtains are closed. Were they on Monday? I check both the back and front doors and they're locked. I sit on the porch and wait a little while just in case. I stare across the blue river — which reminds me of someone's eyes.

It's quiet when I arrive home, and I figure it was this way the whole time I was gone. My mother is sitting by the kitchen window in the good light painting, and she says Percy's in his room. I explain to her about Mr. Cole and she looks a little concerned. She sets her paintbrush down and goes to the phone. She asks the operator to ring Tommy. I'm glad that she's checking about Mr. Cole, and I'm also glad that she'll be the one talking to Tommy and not me. I wonder if she'll call him Tommy or Thomas. I like to think she uses Thomas not to be formal or respectful but because it annoys him. There's no answer. She tries once more just after lunch, but then says she'll have my father try to track Tommy down after work.

Miss Stairs stops by about three o'clock. She brings gingersnaps, which would normally be a temptation for Percy, but today my mother doesn't call him from his room. I check on him before we have tea and he's lying on his bed looking at the book on sea life of the Atlantic Ocean. This is an improvement over him staring at the ceiling, which is what he was doing the last time I looked in — except I wonder if it's the best thing for him to be reading. Percy seems to live in a logical, literal world without fantasy, but I hope now that he knows what's happening to our house he doesn't think we could stay and live underwater — like in the sea. I ask him if he's doing okay and he looks up and puts his finger on his place on the page. He doesn't speak but stares at my chin. I nod and close the door again.

Back downstairs I walk in halfway through an update of Miss Stairs's latest news headlines. She talks about Leonard Black's continued standoff, all the problems the Fosters have been having getting the power and phone lines hooked up at their house, and how the Johnsons are trying to have Uncle Kent and Aunt Patty's old house moved. Men from the moving company are going to check if it can be done.

"They're coming from Fredericton on Friday and they're going to have a look at a few other places too, I've heard," Miss Stairs says. "Have you made a decision yet? Maybe you could have them stop in here."

My mother sets her teacup down and scans the kitchen as if she's considering it. Then she turns and looks out the window.

"We just don't know yet," she says. "It would be wonderful to keep the house, but it would be so strange to be anywhere but here."

Miss Stairs looks at me and smiles slightly, then turns back to my mother.

"I know your situation's different," Miss Stairs says and points her finger at the ceiling, referring to Percy in his bedroom upstairs.

"Yes, it is," my mother says. She looks back out the window. "It is," she says again after a long pause.

One summer night a few years ago, my mother got locked out of the house. She and Miss Stairs had gone to Woodstock to celebrate Miss Stairs's birthday. They ate at the Connell Park Restaurant, then went to a movie. My father stayed home with Percy and me. After supper my father took out his cards and taught us to play Crazy Eights. Percy was reluctant at first because he had a book on African animals he was reading, but my father was insistent.

My father got us to sit at the kitchen table, and as he explained the rules I could tell he'd already thought about what he was going to say. He had the cards all sorted and held up the eights, jacks, twos, and the queen of spades, noting the significance of each. It was for Percy's benefit. Percy was nodding and my father was smiling. I expected the cards being shuffled to cause some problem. I was just waiting for Percy to realize how truly random and unpredictable the whole game was, but it was fine and we began to play.

It didn't last. Who knows if Percy has the ability to count and track a whole deck of cards (although it wouldn't surprise me), but suddenly he stopped playing. He looked around the table and then over to the counter where the cards were before we started. A card had been left behind there. My father must have missed it when he was sorting the deck into his demonstration piles.

Percy put down his hand of cards. Then his head went down too. That was the end of the game. Percy was so upset you would've thought we were playing for cash and he'd just lost his life savings. I felt sorry for my father as he'd tried really hard. He swore and left the kitchen. After that I know the only eight my father was crazy about was eight o'clock when Percy put himself to bed.

When my mother came home, Percy was sound asleep — along with my father, who'd drifted off in a chair in the sunroom. I was awake in my bed and Miss Stairs's car headlights flashed across the screen of my open window. I heard my mother and Miss Stairs talk and laugh a while before the sound of a car door closing. I heard Miss Stairs's car back out of the driveway, but I didn't hear my mother come into the house. After a few minutes I got up to look out my window. It was a clear summer night with a full moon and about a million stars. My mother was walking around the backyard. I watched her for a few minutes then saw her go to our storage shed for an old picnic blanket to spread on the ground. She lay down on it and stared at the sky.

The next morning I heard her joking with my father that it was a good thing it wasn't winter considering he'd locked her out. She said she had to climb in the kitchen window. My father was saying she should've pounded on the door, but she claimed she didn't want to wake Percy and me. I didn't say anything, but I hadn't even heard her knock. Or try the knob. I looked at Percy, who was sitting at the table eating a banana, dividing the pack of cards into the four suits. Maybe my mother just hadn't wanted her fun away from us to end. Maybe she wanted her break to last a little longer. I remembered the problem with Percy and the card game and considered how it would compare to a nice supper in a restaurant followed by a funny movie.

I've overheard my mother tease Miss Stairs before about the joyous freedom of her single life, but I wonder if my mother's ever jealous. I wonder if she ever stops to think about what her life would be like without us.

I wish I knew how long my mother stayed outside staring at the moonlit sky. It may have been all night. When she beckoned me over to kiss me good morning, her hair still smelled strong of the must of the old picnic blanket.

*

After supper my father calls Mr. Cole's house. I'm sitting at the kitchen table hoping I'll suddenly hear him say, "Oh, Ellis, good, good. We were just wondering," but he's silent. Then he phones Tommy, who picks up right away. His voice is so loud on the line it's impossible not to hear his "Yello." My father identifies himself and Tommy asks, "For what do I owe the honour?"

My father briefly explains. There's a long pause before Tommy says, "Oh, yes, yes, I do remember something now." Then there's another pause before Tommy says, "It was a private family matter. Monday, you say, why yes. He left Sunday and I expect he will be gone until late Friday or the weekend." My father asks if he's sure and again Tommy talks like he's the school librarian, so calm and careful. "Yes, thank you for your concern though, Jack. And please give my best regards to Lily and the children."

When my father hangs up he repeats the conversation to my mother and me. Tommy said Mr. Cole had been gone since Sunday so I tell my father about the missing thank-you card. When I explain how I left it tucked in the screen door, I realize as soon as I say it that it could easily have blown away.

But my father surprises me and says, "Let's go check. If Ellis is away it won't hurt to make sure everything's all right down there." It's like it's just the excuse he was waiting for.

It's a warm clear night. The sun is getting lower in the sky, but it will be at least two hours until it sets. My father parks at the very end of Mr. Cole's driveway, right near the house. Mr. Cole's crabapple tree is glowing in the light. It's no longer in bloom, but its leaves are a deep burgundy. A sparrow lands on one of its lowest branches as we round the corner of the porch. I look down at the grass as we go, scanning for the white rectangle of the card, but my father is looking at the windows of the house.

We're almost to the steps when we hear the loud sound of tires speeding down the driveway. Two doors slam and as my father and I turn he takes a few steps ahead of me. First comes Tommy, then Alton Crouse.

"Well now, Jack Carson, fancy meeting you here," Tommy says. "What're you up to? Sure wouldn't look good if I called the cops now, would it? You down here trespassing just after I tell you on the phone no one's home at old Ellis's house."

"Seems to me I was the one who told you no one was home, Tommy. You seemed to have a little trouble remembering where Ellis was, but I figured you were just drunk." My father looks from Tommy to Alton to Tommy again. "Now I must say seeing you here I'm not so apt to believe you. Timing seems a little off if what I said wasn't new information. I'm a little worried. I find myself wondering if you didn't make it all up."

"I'd be careful there, Jack." Tommy looks at Alton and smiles. "Didn't you think it just maybe wasn't any of your business?"

"No one's digging for secrets here, Tommy. Seems to me it was a simple enough question — out of concern for an old family friend."

"Well, I can't say I recall anyone appointing you old Ellis's keeper, but I suggest right now you get it through your head, I'm the only one who needs to be concerned here. All your call did was remind me with Ellis being away, it might be a nice little courtesy if me and Alton here came down, did a check on things."

"Don't let me stop you then," my father says. "That's all Ruby and I were doing." He steps back and puts his arm around me. "Be our guest."

My father sits on the porch steps and I sit beside him. I can tell now that Tommy isn't sure. I wonder what Tommy and Alton were planning on doing, but I know from conversations with Mr. Cole that Tommy doesn't have a key to the house.

"Don't mind us," my father says. "Since you're behind us in the driveway we'll just wait it out."

"I can move the truck," Alton says. And I wonder now if Tommy told him why they were coming. I wonder if it matters that my father and I are here, or if he just came along to escape his wife and eight kids, go for a little joyride. "Tommy, throw me the keys," he says.

Tommy seems like he's considering it, but looks at us and smiles. It's a standoff.

"That's all right," Tommy says. "Jack and pretty Ruby here can wait."

Tommy saunters as slowly as possible over to the barn and starts to circle it.

"Nice night," my father says to Alton.

Alton half nods.

Tommy comes back from the barn.

"All clear so far?" my father asks.

"So far so good," Tommy says. "But I want to be thorough now. Big grounds. Wouldn't want to miss anything."

"Indeed," my father says.

It's a game. They're talking as friendly and nice and courteous as Mr. Cole himself. Except I have this odd feeling there's more than dislike they're hiding from each other.

When Tommy finally comes back after a bit too long behind the house, it's Alton who gives in. "I figure you're good there, Tommy," he says. "That's a real nice little check you did for old Ellis."

Tommy looks at Alton, then my father. He nods several times as if he's pleased with himself.

"So, after you, Jack," Tommy says.

My father nods and gets up. I stand too.

"Goodnight then, boys," my father says.

Tommy moves the truck out of the way of our car. As my father and I back past him down the driveway, Tommy smiles at me.

Chapter 12

~

On Thursday afternoon I walk to the store. I figure it's just to torture myself. Troy had asked me to meet him today, but that was back before the big Percy scene. Which I'm sure the whole of Haventon knows about by now. It'd been a while since Percy had lived up to his reputation so publicly and delivered that volume of wails, sobs, and screams. Troy and I hadn't decided when to meet before the dramatic finale started, and he hasn't called to say anything about it, but our usual time, if twice before counts as usual, is two.

From a distance I can see that he isn't sitting on either of the benches out front. There's a couple on the one near the map and the other one is empty. I'm tempted to keep walking, or go back home, but it's hot in the sun and I'm sure I'd be angry at myself later if I didn't give in to the part of me that's saying you never know. I figure I'll buy a Nesbitt's Orange, drink it, then take the bottle home. Sitting by myself is no big deal. People are used to seeing me alone.

As I get closer I can tell that the couple on the bench is Linda Small and the boy she had with her at the dance, Wade Hill, who's maybe her boyfriend now. She's smiling, talking, and laughing while Wade slouches and scans the parking lot, seemingly oblivious to her presence. He rubs the top of his summer brush cut with his hand, turns and nods at her, then looks back to the road.

Wade notices me before Linda does and watches me walk to the steps. Linda's angled in toward him and for a second I dare think she may be so involved in whatever enthralling tale she's telling that I can slip by undiscovered. She turns around as soon as my foot hits the first step. As usual she looks like she's allergic to even the thought of the memory of the reality of my existence. I smile at her subtly as if my being here the same time as her was cleverly orchestrated and a part of my master plan. She quickly turns back to the boy, her ponytail swinging so fast it causes a little breeze. I sit on the bench.

After the grand total of maybe a minute, Linda turns and looks at me. Another few seconds pass and she looks again. Then she turns a third time and I know she's about to say something when the door of the store swings open.

"The lovely Ruby," Troy says.

My face flushes so warmly I feel my eyes water.

"Your choice," he says and holds out two open pop bottles — a Pepsi and a Nesbitt's Orange. "I was figuring maybe we could go for a little walk today."

I thank him. We head down the stairs. I move quickly and ignore Linda. I'm counting on her total shock being enough to allow us a clean escape.

But Wade calls after us.

"Hey, Troy," he says. "Will we see you tomorrow night?"

"As long as I can convince Ruby to go," Troy says, turning slightly.

"We need him there, Ruby," Wade calls. "Breathe some fresh air into this place."

I turn when he says my name. Linda looks stunned. She looks like a bird trying to puff up her feathers in a defensive manoeuvre, but she's just realized that they're all stuck together.

"We'll see," I say. I wish I'd worn my hair in a ponytail too, so I could swing it exaggeratedly behind me.

Troy and I cross the parking lot. I'm trying to simultaneously walk, talk, drink my pop, and somehow process everything that's happened. We talk about Friday night, which Troy says means going to the bonfire, and I agree as long as it's all right with my parents. Troy just met Linda and Wade while he was waiting for me. Troy says Linda seems a bit flitty but okay, he supposes.

He does most of the talking. Troy says his father's been buying so many antiques that they'll be taking a load home next week. He talks about the Pokiok Lodge and how kind the people who run it have been. He mentions his little cottage by the river and how it's a shame that next year at this time it'll be gone.

We walk along and then Troy says all of a sudden, "Oh, hey, I should've asked before. How's Percy?"

"Percy?"

"You know, your little brother," he says and smiles.

"He calmed down eventually," I say. "It's just really hard with everything going on." I hope this sounds forthcoming and is enough. I look at Troy.

"He seemed so upset," he says. "I wish I could've helped or something."

"It's okay," I say. "Or not okay that he was upset, I mean. But it happens a lot. With him. I just mean it's okay because you probably couldn't have done anything anyway." It's strange to talk about Percy with someone besides family. No one ever asks.

"It's just that Percy's a little different," I say. "But a good different — I mean, he's only ten, but I'm already positive he's the smartest person I'll ever know."

I look at Troy. He's nodding.

"So what subject is he good at?" Troy asks.

"Pretty much everything. But he really likes math. I swear he can add anything in his head in about two seconds —"

I stop talking when a vehicle beeps twice behind us.

I turn around. Oh joy of my existence. Wade's driving what must be his father's truck. He pulls it across from the other lane and stops with a jolt, then skids dangerously close beside us. I feel the Nesbitt's Orange form a citrus tidal wave in my stomach. Here we go.

"You just get your licence?" Troy asks.

"Two weeks."

Linda's in the passenger seat and I notice her roll her eyes, then reposition them in a glare at me.

"Any verdict on the bonfire yet?" Wade asks.

"We're good," Troy says. "But it's going to be up to Ruby's parents."

Wade nods, but Linda pipes up, "Are your parents strict, Ruby? Is that why I never see you out anywhere?"

"I think they'll be okay with it," I manage.

Linda smirks at me while Troy wipes the sweat from his face onto his sleeve.

"So see you then," Wade says. He puts the idling truck back in gear. "But Troy, watch this!"

Troy puts his arm across the front of me and moves us both back from the truck. The engine revs and the tires spin. I see Linda lurch when it finally surges ahead.

"That girl doesn't like you much, does she?" Troy says as the truck rolls down the road.

"Linda," I say, stalling.

"Is it just her problem, or are you some secret psycho or something?"

It feels like my stomach falls to my feet. Did he say psychic or psycho? And why is he smiling?

"I'm kidding," Troy says. "Really. Wow, you look like I just accused you of murder." He laughs.

I don't know what to say. I move my legs forward. Maybe something will come to me.

"Hey," Troy says. He catches up to me. "Ruby, what's going on?"

I wonder how fast I can think this through. I wonder if Linda said anything to him before at the store. I'm so out of practice at normal conversation that I can't even catch a joke anymore.

Troy steps in front of me.

"It's just that it was so easy for you to talk to them," I start, "even though you'd never met them before, but me, well, it's different, and yes, Linda obviously doesn't like me, and actually it's not just her—"

I'm rambling, but Troy only seems to be half paying attention before he cuts me off.

"You know back home there's lots of morons who give me a hard time saying Dad's some junk dealer garbage picker," he blurts.

"I never would've thought that."

"Because I seem so confident?"

I nod.

"I work hard on that, you know. Real hard. It takes a lot of practice."

"That I believe," I say.

Troy shrugs. We're both quiet for a few seconds.

"But listen, does it matter that they think that?" Troy asks.

I shake my head.

"So you know, Ruby, I don't care if that girl doesn't like you." Troy wipes sweat from his face again. "Let's call it even and pretend I didn't ask. I like you, and that's all that matters."

We take a few steps down the road in silence.

"You really are pretty smooth," I say.

"I'm just trying to impress you."

"It might be working. But I will say that I thought calling me Miss Saint John River Valley the other day was a bit much."

"Huh," he says. And at first it seems like that's his only response, but then he says, "Okay, so you're demoted to First Princess."

He reaches over to hold my hand.

My mother already knows about Troy when I mention him. I should've figured as much considering that Miss Stairs is her best friend. My mother has this little smile as she pretends to be concentrating on her painting. She's painting something very small and bright red, pinching her brush tight, right up by the bristles, leaning in close. I'm lucky that she already knows who Troy is or I doubt I would have been allowed to go to the bonfire with him. But my mother doesn't wait long enough to blink, breathe, or even think before she says yes. She doesn't even say she'll have to check with my father. She dips her brush back in the dob of red paint to get a little more. It's as if finally here I am with the good news she's been waiting for.

I wish Percy would talk again. As annoying as he can sometimes be, I miss hearing his wise little comments. He still hasn't spoken a word, but at least now he communicates with gestures, nods, taps, and pokes. My mother says maybe he's just taking a break, perhaps once he stopped talking he realized how nice the quiet was. To me it sounds a bit too hopeful. My mother's been asking him more questions than usual, waiting for that first verbal response. My father's annoyed by it all and has dealt with Percy's silence by being nearly silent himself.

As for me, I've certainly tried to get him going again. This morning at breakfast I told him I saw a cloud shaped like Africa out the kitchen window. (Percy never seems to notice rabbits or dinosaurs in the sky,

but for years he's pointed out white fluffy geography.) Percy just
shrugged. Then I told him I heard they were having a sale at Foster's
Store with a whole display of items for $2.99 — which is his favourite
price. To that he nodded. I tried once more, my absolute best effort,
by asking if he knew of any meteor showers coming any time soon. I
thought I saw the tiniest start of a smile on his face before he shoved
a piece of banana into his mouth. But maybe I was wrong. Percy is
horrible at hiding any sort of emotion. Once he was chewing, he shook
his head no. Maybe he really is done with us all.

Two summers ago I watched a meteor shower with Percy. He set his
alarm and woke me at three in the morning because he'd read an
article in the newspaper saying that was the peak period to see. He
came to my bedside fully dressed in his white T-shirt and jeans, with
his hair combed and his breath smelling like toothpaste.

"Ruby, you must wake up now. The prime viewing window is about
to commence."

I reluctantly rolled out of bed in my pyjamas and wrapped myself
tightly in my purple-and-white quilt.

As with anything science-related that could be researched ahead of
time, Percy was well prepared for the meteors. He had two books on
space, each with a page that he had read again and again. Living where
we did, we had a perfect wide-open sky for viewing. Percy claimed there
would be no man-made light interference and as long as the weather
was clear, which it was, we should experience the full display.

We went to the backyard. The grass was already a bit dewy, so I spread
out the quilt for us to lie on. I was still tired and closed my eyes.

Percy noticed. "Ruby, this is an infrequent and spectacular event
that is not to be missed."

I opened one eye, then the other. I'd agreed I'd come out with him
so that my parents could sleep.

Suddenly a streak of light came from behind us, seemed to skim the roof of the house, and shot across the sky above the river.

I sat straight up and I heard Percy suck in a breath.

Then another meteor, somehow even bigger, brighter, and lower than the first flew above the top of Miss Stairs's house, almost touching the chimney.

I had never seen anything like it. Percy quickly turned in my direction and smiled.

We sat in silence for the next hour staring at the awesome sky. Percy gave no additional information or analysis of what was happening, and for me there was really nothing to say. I watched the meteors and I watched Percy. After a while I remembered that you could make a wish when you saw a shooting star, but that night I didn't bother. Right then I wouldn't have wanted anything different.

My mother takes Miss Stairs's suggestion, and the men from the moving company stop by on Friday afternoon. They greet my mother at the door, then walk around the outside of the house. I watch from the kitchen window and see them look at the cement of the basement, stop where the sunroom attaches, talk to each other, and point. Percy's out on the lawn wearing his baseball mitt on the wrong hand. I'm sure he's only there to listen to them. He looks up or down as they do. Percy follows at a distance, staying far enough back that they don't say anything to him.

When the men come inside, Percy does too. They ask my mother some questions as he sits with me at the kitchen table. When my mother follows the men outside again Percy goes to the window and leans right up against it so he can hear. I wonder what they're saying too, but I stay at the table. It's only when my mother talks to them from the step that I know.

"Well, thank you so much for coming," she says. "That's certainly good news. Now we'll just have to see if we can find a place to put it."

~

It may be wrong to call it "the bonfire" as if it's a huge special event that only happens once, because it takes place three or four times a summer and has for years. Lots of people have bonfire stories and bonfire memories. Many now-married couples in our area will talk about a bonfire being their first date.

There's a nice flat area of rock not far from the bridge called Fire Flat. There are four huge cedar logs someone dragged there years ago for seating. They're placed in a large square around the permanently blackened patch where the fire always is.

Burning material shows up by anonymous donation. People drop off driftwood they've gathered while out for a walk. Sometimes wood from an old shed will be piled there, or an old rusty-coloured dried-out Christmas tree that wasn't taken to the dump or burned at home. Once, years ago, someone secretly lugged an old pump organ down. To this day no one knows who it was. It made a spooky, sad, almost howling sound as it burned. Another time someone dropped off a big long antique couch. Kids took turns sitting on the end that wasn't burning, seeing who could stand the heat the longest. There's always something there to make a nice big fire. Or so I've heard. I've never gone before.

Troy comes to pick me up at dark. Percy's in bed. My mother's in the sunroom reading. My father comes to the door and shakes Troy's hand. Troy calls my father "Sir" when he greets him, which my father seems to like.

As soon as we leave the driveway, Troy reaches for my hand. He says he could see the fire going when he came across the bridge. There are already a lot of people there. I hope we can find a seat and I don't have to stand around feeling self-conscious.

When we arrive, two boys are making quite a production out of carrying two giggling and screaming girls into the water. The boys have only waded to their knees but are threatening to throw the girls, clothes and all, out farther. This goes on for about ten minutes, but in the end it doesn't happen. It's the perfect distraction for Troy and me to wander in mostly unnoticed. We sit on one of the cedar logs.

I quickly locate June and Linda and their boyfriends, who are a safe distance away on the far side. Troy may say he doesn't care about anyone else's opinion of me, but I see no need to test him with some big embarrassing scene. June's two favourite things to tease me about — drowning myself or burning at the stake — should be pretty much at the top of her mind. I mean here I am sitting beside the river in front of a big fire.

Linda's boyfriend Wade has a guitar, which he's starting to play. He begins to sing The Beatles "All My Loving" and it's pretty painful, the mistakes and slow chords lagging behind his seagull-squawk singing. Linda's smiling as if he's Paul McCartney himself sitting right there beside her, sending out a personal dedication. She and June put their arms around each other's shoulders and start swaying back and forth. After the first verse Troy puts his arm around me.

We sit for three songs, talking a bit and watching the fire burn. The biggest piece of wood in the flames is a No Trespassing sign, likely stolen, since people are getting a little tired of Leonard Black. Troy doesn't seem to notice or care in the least that no one's come to talk to me. He's sitting here like he's lived just down the road his whole life and was baptized (like many of us) right in the river.

Wade takes a break from the guitar and notices Troy. He pokes June's boyfriend Colin and they head our way. Troy moves his arm from my back to shake Wade's hand. He introduces Colin and Troy shakes his hand too. I'm just waiting for Wade to ask Troy to join them and then watch some awkward disaster unfold. I can feel Linda's and June's eye beams on me now, warmer than the flames.

"Those were some nice tunes," Troy says.

Wade looks pleased.

"I just got the guitar for Christmas," he says. This explains a lot. "Still practising but gettin' better."

Troy nods. "You know any Dylan?"

Wade doesn't respond.

"You know," Troy says, and starts to sing the chorus from "The Times They Are a-Changin'." Troy's singing is beyond awful. I hate to think it, but he makes Wade sound like a soloist in an angels' choir. Troy's confidence is clearly not an act. You'd have to be confident to even hum sounding like that.

Not a second too soon, Wade says, "Nope" and cuts Troy off.

The three of them talk about music for a few minutes until June calls Colin back. Wade goes too.

Troy and I listen to four more songs and then he asks me if I want to leave. We walk down along the water's edge. It's a clear bright night with a half-moon. The river is almost still with just the gentlest lapping at the shore. Troy doesn't talk as we walk the five minutes to the bridge. I start to worry that something is wrong. He's holding my hand though and he finally leads me up the slope. We stop. He takes my other hand. Then with the fire only a small orange glow in the distance, and the river black and calm below us, Troy leans in and kisses me.

Today I wonder if I can find the exact spot again. I'm out with Percy for his bottle launch and I'm on the hill searching. The warm sun reminds me of Troy, so close to me. I stop looking after a while and sit down and think back — to how he stroked my cheek with his fingers, then ran them through my hair. It seemed to happen so fast and yet last forever.

I'm not sure how long I daydream, but when I look over to the bridge again, Percy hasn't moved. He's still standing there in the middle, leaning slightly on the rail. His bottle must be almost out of sight now, floating downstream, so I walk to get him.

Percy still isn't talking. This morning when I typed his note he poked me and pointed when I struck a wrong key and had to start again. I was distracted so it happened four times. Once I even made a mistake in the second-to-last word. Percy looked like he was going to cry. Normally I would have found it very annoying, but today it doesn't seem like much will bother me.

As I get closer to the bridge I can see that Percy isn't looking toward the water but seems to be scanning the shore much farther downstream. His bottle must be gone, which means we should be able to head straight home. He doesn't turn as I approach, so rather than call to him, I want to see what he's looking at. He's concentrating as if he's watching something happen. I wonder if someone's started cutting the trees and brush along the shore, like I've heard has to be done. Twenty-five-foot trees can't be growing in the middle of the river, which is what the shore will be once the flood waters come.

But it's men Percy's watching. There are two of them, small and distant, not far from the giant old pine tree that marks the edge of Mr. Cole's property. They're walking along the shore with something in their hands, sticks of some sort, swinging them now and then, bending down sections of the tall grass. I watch with Percy, as silent as he's been for days now, while the men stop to talk to each other and then head in toward Mr. Cole's house. The men are dressed in dark pants with a yellow stripe down each leg. Even though Percy doesn't say so I'm sure he knows who they are as well as me. The men are from the RCMP.

Chapter 13

~

The police come to our house after lunch. Percy jumps up and runs to the kitchen window as soon as the cruiser pulls in. I can't say I share his excitement. Unless it's the Canada Day parade, seeing their car usually doesn't mean anything good. The two constables come to the door and ask for my father. My mother says she'll leave them to talk, and she takes Percy and me outside.

The police are in with my father a long time. My mother and I sit on the edge of the lawn. I pick a dandelion and pull at bits of it. I start, "He loves me, he loves me not," but I'm so desperately curious about what the police want with my father I keep losing track. Percy's in the driveway. He's looking for tiny rocks to put in the bottom of his bottles. Every so often my mother glances to the kitchen window. Every so often she turns to me and smiles. There's not much to say. I haven't exactly been a conversationalist either while we've been out here. I look at Percy. That makes three of us.

Finally one of the constables comes to the door and I figure they're done. But instead he asks for me.

I get a chill.

"It's okay, Ruby," my mother says. "Go ahead. Your father's still in there too."

I look toward the door but not right at the policeman. I focus my eyes on his neck like Percy would. It probably makes me look guilty of something, but I can't help it.

"Ruby?" the officer repeats. "We just want to ask you a few questions."

We go to the kitchen and sit at the table with my father and the other officer. He has a notebook open with several things written down.

"They just want to ask you a few things about the last time you saw Mr. Cole," my father says.

"You're fifteen, Ruby?" the constable sitting closest to me asks.

I nod.

"So you work for Ellis Cole? You do some housekeeping for him?"

I nod again and shift a little in my chair. I slide my hands under my knees.

"You're doing fine, Ruby," my father says.

"Yes," the policeman says. "This won't take long. When was the last time you were at Ellis Cole's home?"

"With him there too?" I ask. I want to be sure I answer right. I wonder if my father already told him about checking the house and Tommy showing up.

"Yes," he says.

"Last Saturday." Then I add, "Afternoon."

"And did he tell you when you left that he'd be going away, that he wouldn't need you to come by for a week?"

"No."

"And what did you do at his house last Saturday, just the usual cleaning?"

"I cleaned. But it was a lot more than usual. He wanted the whole house to be clean."

The officer asking me questions looks at the other and subtly nods.

"And was there anything else unusual about that day? Anything special or different? Something he hadn't done before or maybe he said something?"

"He gave me a locket," I say. "He had given me other things, but this was the nicest thing. It was a gift for grading."

"And he had given you other things, you say?"

"Some rhinestone jewellery and some books for my brother. He was going through his house sorting things for his move."

The constable asking the questions again turns to the other one.

He thanks me and says they have to finish up with my father so I should please go back outside. I'm at the door before the policeman who was taking notes calls to me and says he has one more quick question.

"How would you describe Ellis Cole's relationship with his great-nephew, Thomas Cole? Was Thomas ever at the house when you were there?"

"A few times," I say.

"Did they get along, in your opinion?"

I don't answer right away. I think very specifically about each word of his question. It's the police that I'm talking to. My personal view of Tommy doesn't count.

"I think so," I say. Then, as if I need supporting evidence, "He lets him use his truck and store things in his barn."

I look at my father. He's been quiet, listening as I answered each question. I notice now that he has the two envelopes Mr. Cole had sent home with me in front of him on the table.

"Tell your mother we won't be too much longer," he says.

I nod. I look again at the envelopes. They have both been opened.

*

My parents don't talk about the police visit or Mr. Cole's disappearance while Percy and I are awake, but I can hear them as I lie in bed. My mother's been crying and saying she should have somehow done things different.

"It's the damn government's fault," my father says. "Playing God with people's lives."

They're quiet after this, as if the reality of it needs to sink in. Then my mother starts crying again and I put my pillow over my head to block out the sound. Today was supposed to be my good day. Mr. Cole could be on a train back home. He could be eating a late supper with distant family or friends. He could be unlocking his front door and marvelling at how clean his house is, thinking what an excellent job I did. He could be having a tour of Buckingham Palace, looking for my mother's painting of his house. He could be anywhere in the world, trying to find a wonderful new place to live.

I'm not going to accept my mother's sadness and listen to her cry. Because my mother is a woman who believed she could catch a bird in her hand, was sure she could pull it out of the whole endless sky.

After church, the disappearance of Mr. Cole is all anyone is talking about. No one seems to care that a date has been chosen for the church to be moved, and that the graves in the cemetery are also going to higher ground. Tommy's at the church alone, the first time without Mr. Cole. I've seen men who've probably never said a nice thing about Tommy in their lives go up and shake his hand. The minister and his wife are standing with him now.

Maybe it's because we're in a church, but like me, I overhear many hopeful others who think Mr. Cole will come home safe and sound. It seems to be a well-known fact that he told Tommy he was going away and is perhaps only late to return. Everyone seems aware too that it was Tommy who phoned the police. He's been saying it again and again in a loud voice. Tommy declared he "wanted to be on the safe side," but I wonder about the safe side of what. The safe side of looking good before my father beat him to it? The police checked Mr. Cole's house and grounds — but as of yet there's no search party.

I look at Tommy. His hair's slicked back and he's wearing an only semi-wrinkled white dress shirt. He found a tie somewhere. He even shaved. Tommy's face is a perfect balance of concern and hope.

A day passes. And then another. Mr. Cole's still missing. Not dead, maybe not even missing if you think about it, but to us his whereabouts are unknown. Am I missing, I wonder, if I don't tell anyone where I am? Will Troy be missing when he goes to Ontario? I'd love to hear Percy's take on this because these seem like the type of questions he might wonder about — but he's still not talking. I do know that missing is a feeling. I miss my friend Mr. Cole.

With each day the speculation of Mr. Cole's fate darkens. When Miss Stairs visits, I hear how some people think Mr. Cole could've got confused and wandered off. He could have got lost. He could have fallen walking in the night. He may have collapsed from a heart attack or stroke. He may now be buried in a muddy basement hole dug in what were once his back fields. And, now that no one is standing within the divine buffer of the church, there's speculation about Tommy. Does he know something? Why doesn't he know where Mr. Cole went? Has he looked, or is he looking for him? Then, the last thing I allow myself to listen to before I leave the kitchen is something Miss Stairs whispers. I bet it was whispered too when it was repeated to her. Maybe Tommy killed him.

*

I walk to the store. It's overcast and before I leave my mother offers me her umbrella, but I refuse so I don't have to carry anything. It doesn't look like it's going to rain any time soon. The sky is blue-grey in the parts that peek through and the clouds seem undecided, maybe like they're just stalled before passing by.

I'm going to meet Troy. It'll be the first time I've seen him since the night of the bonfire. I've talked to him on the phone once and I know he's been helping his father get ready for their trip to Ontario. Troy's been helping to pack all the small fragile items like glass and china. Troy says he's never seen his father buy so much. I'm not supposed to tell people, but he's almost out of money. Mr. Rutherford will probably have a special sale as soon as he returns to Kingston to make back his investment. Then he'll come buy more. I guess our area, our situation, is an antique dealer's dream come true.

Troy's sitting on the bench in front of the map when I arrive. His father dropped him off, and we only have about twenty minutes until he comes back from gassing up at the garage, and they leave on their trip home. Troy offers to buy me an ice cream, but I refuse so we can spend our little time sitting together. Twenty minutes seems like two minutes before his father's truck is again in the parking lot.

His father beeps the horn as he pulls off to the side of the road.

"You're not going to elope with anyone while I'm gone are you?" Troy asks.

"Two weeks at the most, right? I'll try to be patient."

He smiles. "I still haven't seen any of your carvings."

"First thing when you come back."

"So my dad's here," he says.

We're in front of the store, so I'm not expecting the same type of kiss as the other night, but Troy hugs me and then sneaks a little kiss right on my lips. For that split second I feel light enough to defy gravity.

He steps back.

"Ruby Carson," he says. "To think you were down here in New Brunswick all this time."

Yes, to think. I say goodbye and wave to his father.

Troy gets in the truck and his father beeps the horn as they start off. The way the truck is loaded is almost comical, tables and chairs and chests painted every colour, probably ten times fuller than the first time I saw it at Mr. Cole's, a spider's web of furniture all piled and tied and angled. It's amazing how everything stays perfectly in place as Mr. Rutherford picks up speed. Not a thing sways, slides, or shifts. I watch as they drive into the distance. I wonder if Troy is looking in the side-view mirror trying to get a glimpse of me. I watch until a few seconds before they round a bend and I won't be able to see them anymore. My grandmother always said you should never watch someone drive completely out of sight or it will be the last time you see them. I know it's just a superstition, but I'm not taking any chances.

The sky's a little more grey. I walk as slowly as possible and I realize even though he's not more than five miles down the road, I'm already trying to put in the time until Troy's return. I decide to go to Mr. Cole's. Maybe he'll be there. I'll tell him about Troy.

They've made a lot of progress on the new town. It's small, tiny even, not like coming over a hill and discovering a hidden city, but it can still throw me off seeing it, knowing that what in my memory was a field is now divided into a whole grid of straight little streets and lots for houses. The development follows the slope of the valley, down to Mr. Cole's big old house, which I can see in the distance. His driveway now looks like a crooked mistake. It twists and turns like a squiggle, unlike all the new streets, which seem as if they were drawn in with a ruler. Mr. Cole's big old house looks lonely and out of place, hovering on the edge of everything, beside the river. It's easy to see because there's hardly a tree anywhere.

I can smell the dirt. And it's loud with the sound of bulldozers and backhoes digging and trucks dumping out gravel. There are some long metal poles lying in a big pile, which I'm guessing will be streetlights. Along the new main street that runs down the hill through the middle of town, the basement for our church is ready, and across the street the basement is dug for the new high school. Surveyors are out at the high school site and men in hard hats are everywhere. They're talking, and pointing and unloading supplies.

At Mr. Cole's I knock on the door, but I can already tell that nothing is any different. I knock again and when no one answers I sit in the porch rocker. There's a cool breeze here, closer to the river. The patch of grass that Mr. Cole kept mowed is starting to catch up in length to the patch he left. I remember the police laying down the tall grass with their sticks. Wherever they were, you can't tell now. Even the path that Mr. Cole made to the river is starting to fill in.

I walk down to the water. I'll stay for a few minutes, maybe see if there's any interesting driftwood for carving, then head home.

I make my way through the tall grass to Mr. Cole's pine tree.

But something happens. There's a pause it seems.

In the air.

In time.

I see Mr. Cole's clothes folded and set in on the lowest branch. It's the coat from his best suit, the one he always wears to church, and his shoes with his socks rolled inside. His hat is on top. They're in the exact place he showed Percy the day of his birthday picnic. They're up and hidden out of the way and not anywhere the police would have thought to look. They're in the place he puts his shoes and socks whenever he goes in wading.

I might sit down.

I might fall.

My head feels first heavy and foggy, then light and clear. It's as if every thought, observation, overheard statement, rumour, opinion, and conclusion about the coming flood and what it's already caused converges in my head at once.

So let me say this:

If ever you wake one day and the people who run your little province tell you they're going to drown the valley you lived your whole life in, the valley your parents were born in, the valley your ancestors thought was as good as a gift from God when they sailed to this New World and were given a piece of it to start their lives over again (and that's why it's called God's country), if men who live in a city of planted elms on squares as big as half your front lawn, and work in buildings from which they should be able to see the same river as you (but somehow you just know they don't see it the same way), if those men decide for you that a tidal wave is coming to wash your whole life away — well then know that there will be at least one, maybe some, who will love that beautiful land so much they won't ever want to see it different, won't ever have it turned into only a memory, and would rather become one with it than let it go.

Let me say now if this happens, there will be casualties. I knew it, had known it, but didn't want to, didn't let myself. If someone you know starts talking only about the past and not the future, and gives away the things they have owned, touched, sentimentalized, given meaning to in this life, says goodbye to people, but then leaves without telling, has you clean their whole house so at least that won't tarnish their memory — something bad is coming.

I decide to think of Mr. Cole floating gently downstream, asleep and dreaming, the sun on his face. He's like one of Percy's bottles, always with endless possibility. I know he's gone forever, but he hasn't sunk to the bottom. The river hasn't swallowed and taken him. The water is blue and shiny, reflecting the sky wherever Mr. Cole is. It is Saint John who the river is named for after all. How can your spirit not be safe and happy and free if you're with a saint?

I weep.

Chapter 14

~

My father joins the search for Mr. Cole's body. Men from our church congregation gather after work and look until it's too dark to see. They walk along the shore, both sides, for a stretch of about five miles from Mr. Cole's house downstream. They check near every rock and low-hanging tree branch. But my father comes home and solemnly shakes his head. I'm just as glad. Not that I don't want his body recovered, but I know Mr. Cole wouldn't want my father to see him the way I haven't been able to stop myself from thinking of him: wrinkled and waterlogged, his pant leg snagged on a piece of driftwood.

Tommy didn't find him either, but as to whether I think Mr. Cole would or wouldn't have wanted him too, it doesn't matter because Tommy wasn't even looking. Over the next few days, as the police and volunteers from other communities expand the search downriver, this fact is repeated. People are sad for Tommy, but with Mr. Cole gone, the only reason anyone had to be nice to Tommy is gone too. I think

Tommy chose wrong by deciding to be too distraught to look. Mr. Cole would have looked for Tommy, people are saying. And I know that's true. Already some people are saying that Tommy's just sitting back waiting for a cheque.

Miss Stairs doesn't mention it when she comes to visit, and it isn't that she hasn't heard, but as a sign of respect. Instead she tells us the Johnsons have decided to move Uncle Kent and Aunt Patty's old house to a new lot in the town. They're hoping to get one of the lowest-lying lots so the house will still have a nice view of the water. My mother smiles when she hears this. Miss Stairs also mentions that they're pouring the foundations for the new elementary and junior high schools, and some expensive silver maple trees from a big nursery in Fredericton have been planted at the back of the lot for the church.

Miss Stairs brought cookies made with dots of her own strawberry jam in the middle, which we're having with tea. She stops talking for a minute to eat a few bites, then gets a little twinkle in her eye and asks about Troy. Thankfully, at almost the exact same time she says his name, there's a knock on the door.

My mother gets up. Miss Stairs stands too and takes her teacup to the stove to refill it. I know she's only doing it to look out the kitchen window. I ask who it is, but she says it isn't anyone she recognizes, then as an afterthought, she mentions he's handsome though.

My mother talks to the man for several minutes before she calls for Percy. She calls for us too. Percy doesn't come right away so my mother goes to get him.

The man introduces himself as Hazen Howard to Miss Stairs and me, but he doesn't say what brought him. He's a nice-enough-looking man I guess, probably about my father's age, tall with auburn hair. He has a brown paper bag in one hand and in the other is a folded piece of paper. I'm wondering what he wants when my mother and Percy show up. Percy looks both puzzled and slightly nervous. He's standing very close to my mother. I hope he doesn't cry. I hope whatever this Mr. Howard wants was worth calling him down here for.

"Percy Carson," Mr. Howard says.

Percy nods suspiciously.

"I found something of yours. By the river," he says.

I watch Percy's face. He has no ability to hide or contain his emotion. I instantly know what Percy's thinking and I pray this man hasn't instead found something like an old raincoat of Percy's that he didn't even know he lost (his name on the tag) or a book he set down somewhere, or his baseball mitt.

"I found a bottle. Number 1964-11," Mr. Howard says. "I thought maybe you'd like to have it back to see how it did being out there floating all that time." He hands Percy the bag. "And I wrote down all the information you asked for." He gives him the paper.

Percy looks like he's going to explode from excitement.

"Thank you kindly, Mr. Howard, for providing me this data," Percy says and runs back to his room, presumably to read, record, and chart everything.

My mother turns to watch him go, then says my name.

"I heard," I say.

Percy is talking again.

My mother invites Mr. Howard to join us for tea, and he stays about half an hour. He's originally from Sussex but moved to the area to help with construction of the dam. He's staying in Fredericton in an apartment. He isn't married. He thought that returning Percy's bottle in person would be a good excuse to take a drive on his afternoon off and see the river valley. Miss Stairs nods and smiles at everything he says. She blushes the colour of the jam dots when he compliments her on the cookies. When Mr. Howard gets up to go she accepts his offer to walk her the two hundred and fifty yards home.

This leaves my mother and me at the kitchen table. We sit quietly. I wonder if my face looks the same as hers. I wonder if we're thinking the same thing. She's happy I know, I can see her smile, but there's also sadness. Mr. Howard found Percy's bottle while searching for Mr. Cole's body.

Percy comes downstairs when my father gets home to tell him about the bottle. My father's surprised by the sound of Percy's voice, but seems to want to confirm that his talking again isn't a momentary fluke and starts asking him questions. Percy quickly answers everything and tells us some of the information he learned from Mr. Howard's note, and some of the statistics he calculated. The bottle was launched June 20, 1964, which meant it was in the water for 775 days. It travelled approximately 17 miles. It was stopped up in driftwood in a small cove near Mactaquac. The bottle itself remained in good condition and stayed watertight. It's as if Percy's completely forgotten his period of silence. It's as if the return of the bottle was inevitable and all he was waiting for.

Perhaps seeing this as the perfect opportunity, and good timing for something they were waiting for themselves, after supper my parents tell Percy and me they've decided to move the house. It won't be until next year, and they're still hoping to buy a nice piece of land somewhere rather than go to a small lot in the new town, but they say that these walls we're in will remain.

"So what do you think?" my mother asks.

"Sounds good," I say. I've figured for a while that this is what would end up happening. (I've long given up on fantasies of a more extreme move.) I also know I'm not the one they're most concerned about.

Percy's quiet for several minutes.

"I think," he finally says, "it would be important that the house be positioned such that the angle of my bedroom windows is exactly the same in relation to the morning sun as it is currently. I think the direction the house faces should be carefully calculated and maintained. Also, I would not want any large trees near my window to block my view or cause shadows."

My mother looks at my father.

"Certainly, Percy," he says. "You're right. Those are important points."

My mother is so relieved she laughs.

~

It's been ten days since I found Mr. Cole's clothes by the shore, but there's still no body. Divers were in the water in front of Mr. Cole's house a few days ago. There was a big search downriver all around the dam construction site. Then police sent out word past Fredericton, and people have been looking along the whole length of the Saint John River all the way to the Bay of Fundy. I'm torn between wanting him to be found just to know for sure, and hoping he's escaped all this and is floating free and peaceful in the Atlantic Ocean.

At church on Sunday the minister had us pray for him to be brought home, so he could be put to rest. I have no idea what happens if he isn't, or when and how it's decided he's lost forever. There hasn't been any funeral or memorial service yet. Tommy wasn't at church on Sunday and I guess he'd be in charge of the arrangements. That in itself is a scary concept. My father went out to Tommy's place last night and was gone for over an hour. I guarantee that was the longest my father (or maybe anyone besides Alton Crouse or Mr. Cole) has managed to tolerate talking to him. I don't know what kept my father there all that time, but I know it wasn't a social visit.

I work on my carving project for a little while after lunch. I go to my bottom dresser drawer, take out my tools, then line up the completed figures on my window ledge. With the sun coming in behind them, they make little silhouettes. I have twenty-two of the thirty-two pieces finished now. I carved the easiest, repetitive ones first. Each fancy piece I do now takes longer as I carefully work on each detail and try not to chisel out a mistake that can't be corrected.

Today I'm starting a brand-new figure, so I choose a piece of driftwood and begin the tough job of roughing out the shape. I start to remember Troy's kiss as I work, but about three strokes in, and all in the matter of a second, my knife slips off the end of the wood and grazes my left wrist. I jump up, but it barely breaks the surface of my skin and doesn't bleed. It's instead a dark red line, just a bad scratch.

It's probably best to take a break from playing with sharp objects. I clean up my things and decide to walk to the store. I gather the figures from the window ledge. Then, just for fun, I slip one of them into my pocket for good luck.

It doesn't work though, because Linda Small and June Crouse are sitting on one of the benches out front. June's wearing a yellow eyelet short-sleeved blouse that used to belong to Mrs. Foster and beige pedal pushers that were my mother's. June and Linda are each eating a chocolate ice cream cone.

They start in before I even reach the steps.

"So Troy didn't last long," June says. "I heard you already scared him all the way back to Ontario."

"My," Linda says as if this is new information to her. "That was fast, wasn't it?"

"It was," June says. "But you know Ruby, maybe you could send him a postcard as a remembrance of your wonderful love affair. Send a little note — wish you were here."

I pretend not to hear them.

"If she has his address," Linda says.

June laughs.

"That's right," June goes on. "Maybe he was even scared to give her that. He probably wanted to be careful — make a clean getaway."

I go into the store to buy flour for my mother and a Nesbitt's Orange for Percy. On my way back out I'm planning to ignore them again, when June stands up and points at me.

"Goodness, Linda, look!" she says, trying to sound concerned, but obviously hiding a smile. "Now Ruby, you weren't so broken-hearted you tried to do yourself in, were you?"

It only takes me a second to realize that she's pointing to the new red mark on my wrist. She was able to see it as I pushed open the door.

Linda stands too. "Oh my," she says, looking at me. "Much more dramatic than drowning yourself. Although, I must say, it doesn't look like the best effort."

I take a deep breath. "Actually I was carving and my knife slipped and scraped my arm."

They look confused. Linda's nose wrinkles in a seriously unflattering way. It gives me a little surge of delight and I'm able to add, "But thanks for your concern."

I go down the stairs and move quickly across the parking lot, perhaps because it feels like there's a new spring in my step. Whatever June yells after me I don't have to ignore. I am far enough away I can't make it out anyway.

When I'm well down the road, I reach into my pocket and pull out the wooden figure. Maybe it did help me out. And it was a good choice of the ones I could have taken from my window ledge. The figure is a knight. It's a knight from the chess set I'm carving for Percy.

*

I manage to keep June and Linda out of my mind until I'm in bed. I don't regret what I said to them, and even if they decide to call me Paula Bunyan from here on out (I doubt they'd be more creative than that), it doesn't make any difference. I hadn't planned on telling them, but whatever little shift happened inside me at that moment, it felt natural and good to be honest.

It's what they said about Troy that I can't forget. About him leaving. In only a few days, Troy will have been gone a full two weeks. That was the longest he expected to be away, and since the second he left I've been waiting for him. I didn't need to hear them going on about his address, because beyond "Troy Rutherford, Kingston, Ontario," I don't know it. I didn't need to be reminded that if something happened and he didn't come back, I have no way of reaching him.

Then it's two and a half weeks and then three. August is creeping along now and I know if he doesn't show up soon we'll barely have any time together before he has to go back again to start school. I try to stay busy and not think about it, but without Mr. Cole's house to clean, the days stretch out long and boring before me. I carve a rook for the chess set. I look for driftwood in the river. I go to visit Sarah once in Woodstock. I watch my mother put the finishing touches on her painting, which shows both Miss Stairs's house and ours sitting above the river on the hill. I sit with them as they have tea and listen to Miss Stairs talk about the two dates she's had with Mr. Hazen Howard. I walk to the mailbox with Percy each day because now that one reply has come back, he waits anxiously for more — always limitless possibility. He doesn't receive anything, but one day I do. It's a letter from Troy.

Dearest Ruby,

    I'm so sorry to tell you this, but we won't be coming back to New Brunswick this summer. Dad found buyers for a lot of what he bought, but he still has more than he can fit into his store and our shed. He decided it's best to not buy any more until the spring. I hope I'll see you again then. I had a great time this summer. I hope you'll write to me and send me your picture. I don't want to forget your pretty face. Please give my best regards to your parents and Percy.

Yours truly,

Troy

I read the letter over and over until I have it memorized. I ask my mother for one of the pictures she took of me earlier this year down by the bridge. After supper I write back. What else can I do? Why should I have expected any different? Nothing around here goes the way it's supposed to. It's the taint, the darkness, that came with word of the flooding. We're living on borrowed time, in borrowed space. Our whole existence now is a freak of nature. The fact that Troy and his father were here, even temporarily, in our valley of change, seems like it could be a figment of my imagination.

I go to sleep and try to concentrate only on Troy, but when I wake I am thinking of flames. It's hot in my room even with the window open and I can smell smoke. That's what floated up my nose and twisted my dreams. The smell is distant and faint, but I know that's what it is. It's drifting in from outside.

    When I get up and look out, I hear the first siren. It's a police car. Then, almost right after, our one fire truck goes by. I hear my parents wake up and start to talk in their room. I listen as the sirens fade, but not too far from here downriver, the sound stops.

My father goes downstairs. My guess is that someone's decided to light up one of the two houses left empty waiting to be demolished. That's what happened to a couple of others upriver. Two more families have moved since school ended.

Another siren starts. It's farther away still but getting closer. I wonder if it's the fire truck from Meductic. If another village is helping, it has to be something big. My father must think so too, because he comes back upstairs and talks to my mother, then goes out to the car and leaves. Somehow, Percy sleeps through all of this. Good thing. For as curious as I am about what's going on, with him there'd be a multiplication factor of a thousand.

I wait and wait, trying to stay awake until my father returns. I even get out some of the chess figures to look at. Who knows when I fall asleep but soon enough I'm dreaming that I'm floating in a boat in the middle of a lilac ocean, and Quilty is rowing.

It's just as well I wasn't awake to talk to my father, because it takes two days to hear enough versions of what happened for it to make any sense. Tommy Cole and Alton Crouse burned Mr. Cole's barn and part of his house. The house was only saved because they were drunk and slow and lit the barn first. A security guard who was doing a late-night check on the heavy equipment in the new town saw flames in the barn, probably as soon as it started. Tommy had barely scorched the porch of the house before the RCMP and the first fire truck showed up. He had stayed too long trying to finish the job. Tommy finally ran away, but he'd driven Mr. Cole's truck there. It was parked in the driveway — with empty beer bottles on the floor mats.

As to why he did it, that's where the stories vary. Some people simply state the well-established fact that Tommy is an idiot. Most say that Tommy likely thought since the house was his to inherit, he'd get more from the insurance company than he would from the government. It's an odd situation though, because without Mr. Cole's body, is he officially dead? Was the house Tommy's to burn? Certainly other houses have been burned around here lately. Some people are saying that Tommy was drunk and just got some stupid idea to do it now, not realizing he had things ass-backwards, forgetting the government had to buy it first.

Maybe Tommy was stupid, or impatient, or greedy, or some combination of all those things, but there's also one piece of information that no one besides Tommy and my family know. My father told Tommy that night he went to see him and told me yesterday. Those envelopes that Mr. Cole gave my father, the two he sent home with Percy's books and the rhinestone jewellery: one of them had his will inside. My father was named sole executor. In the other envelope was a letter saying that if anything ever happened to Mr. Cole, he trusted my father to disperse things any way he saw fit. Tommy may have tried to take Mr. Cole's house from my father assuming that he'd never see a cent from it anyway. Tommy went against Mr. Cole's judgment that my father's a good man who'd see everything would be taken care of fairly. That's what I think would hurt Mr. Cole if he knew, as much as anything.

And as it turned out, Tommy tried to burn the house just two nights before the police found Mr. Cole's body. Mr. Cole had floated all the way to Westfield. Normally such an event would be big news around here, but there was already someone else on everybody's mind, someone who hadn't left people guessing for weeks, someone who had died by fire and not water. A man who had a wife and eight children burned to death on the floor of Mr. Cole's barn. It was too late for Alton Crouse when he was sprayed with water pumped from the same river.

And yes. Yes. There is something I remember. No matter how many times I've dismissed it, absolutely refused to let myself think about it, made myself forget all this time — months, a year — here it is back again.

I think of the people I saw swimming beside me, three of whom are dead.

Hello Mrs. Abernathy. Hello Mr. Cole. Hello Mr. Crouse. Hello Percy.

Spring 1967

Chapter 15

~

There's a new joke around here that everyone likes to repeat. Miss Stairs uses it as a permanent opening line at the store and claims it's the perfect conversation starter. She asks, "So, how are you celebrating?" We're four months into Canada's centennial year, and a week or so ago, a government brochure asking just that question showed up in everyone's mailbox. Percy and I both read our copy before my father quickly skimmed it, shook his head, and threw it in the garbage.

The brochure had lots of information and suggestions for "embracing our heritage" and "remembering and memorializing our local history." Plus, the thing that really, really annoyed everybody, and absolutely confirmed that we weren't invited to our own country's big birthday bash, was a form at the back. It could be filled out if you had a hundred-year-old building that you wanted to mark with a historical plaque. Special centennial markers would be given to the owners of century homes so they could permanently display their significance. Mr. Foster said he doubted the plaques were waterproof. And several people said they were tempted to order a precious plaque so they could hammer it to their house just prior to its burning and see it melt in the flames.

But at least there is one thing that makes it seem like the celebrations and the flood do have pretty good timing. There's a new historical village being assembled as the province's centennial project. It will be a tourist attraction located downriver not far from the dam. The houses used in the village will be some of those rescued from the flooding. They will be restored to look like they did when they were first built. It's considered a great honour to be included and a way to secure a family's history for evermore. Houses will be referred to in the historical village by their family names.

Only one house from Haventon was chosen. That house was Mr. Cole's.

We watched it be hauled down the ice of the river on Groundhog Day. Although there had been at least a million measurements, calculations, checks, and double checks, I know that everyone standing on the shore was saying a little prayer. I was digging my fingernails into my palms, and I could tell that even Percy held his breath for a while. There was a puff of white fog from his mouth when he finally let it go. There'd been a service for Mr. Cole in the fall, but that day was as much a memorial as anything. People stayed and talked about him as the house slowly slid out of sight. The blackened porch was there as a reminder, but no one mentioned it. For now Tommy's in jail. People remembered only the best of Mr. Cole as his house followed the same path he had taken down the river. Then when we turned around to leave we had a clear view of the new town.

The streets are paved now, and are all finished with curbs and even sidewalks. The town is linked at the top and bottom of the hill to roads that used to only bypass fields. Most people have gone in and had a drive around. My parents took Percy and me last Sunday afternoon.

I don't know how to describe it, except that it reminds me of a table all set for a special dinner that no one remembered to come to. The strangeness has yet to wear off and it's even eerier at night. There are streetlights lining every block, dozens of lights in a grid surrounded by darkness. My mother says it looks like a full jar of fireflies set in the middle of an empty black room. Driving along the new Trans-Canada Highway on the other side of the river you'd probably think it looks like a decent-sized place to stop. But I tell you now if you drove over you'd be in for a surprise. You'd figure for sure there had been an alien abduction, or that something evil lives in the forest or water and scared everyone away.

There are only eleven houses moved in so far. Our church is there, and the schools are almost done, but that's it. The Johnsons moved Uncle Kent and Aunt Patty's old house in. Two other families also moved their houses. One local family bought a new prefab. The other seven bungalows belong to men who came to work on building the mill. More than two hundred lots are empty. The streets lead past square after square of dirt. If the pavement wasn't so new and perfect, you'd think the whole place was old and deserted. I've heard comments that the historical village downriver may not be the only tourist attraction nearby worth charging admission for. Right here we've got our own modern ghost town.

It will fill in with time, people say. I think a lot of families are still holding out for a piece of land elsewhere. They are hoping some nice farmer will decide to sell off a few acres. Some are still considering moving farther inland to places like Millville or Temperance Vale. Except time is beginning to run out. The dam will soon be done, the flood will soon come. My father says that everyone feels they're already giving up so much just by moving, they don't want to also be told where to go. Plus the lots are small, shockingly so, and no one can convince anyone otherwise. The prefab houses all look the same. There are only a few trees, no grass yet, and so many lights at night that a person could forget all about a full moon. No one even calls the place by its name. It's only the new town. The government's new town. As in, "Christ, I'll be damned if I get stuck moving to that new town." Moving to the new town is definitely a last resort. Who wants to be anonymous in a place with no name?

Miss Stairs too has been more and more wary of it. Maybe she's been influenced by everybody else, hearing so much bad always said about it at the store. It's odd though because that never seemed to matter until lately. But this year as the purchase and delivery date for her new home came closer and closer, she got cold feet. She moved the delivery date back two weeks and then a few days later moved it back another. She told my mother that she simply wasn't ready yet, that she hadn't got everything sorted, packed, and organized. My mother says she understands because Miss Stairs's house is the one she grew up in, and no matter how much she tries to make it sound exciting to start fresh, it's hard to leave. Some people say Miss Stairs is holding out for a marriage proposal from Mr. Hazen Howard, who she's been dating since last summer. Why buy a house alone when you can buy something twice as nice together? My mother says that isn't it.

But the speculation should end soon because this Saturday my mother and I are going to help Miss Stairs pack. My mother's been offering our help for months. Miss Stairs has been almost stubbornly reluctant, but she finally gave in. I'm really looking forward to it. I think my mother is too. Neither of us has been in Miss Stairs's place for years.

The days at school seem long. It's only the end of April, but already you can tell that everyone's waiting for it to end. Outside the school walls, the whole area's in motion. Now that it's warm, and the snow's finally all melted, the scenery can change between the bus ride in the morning and the one home again. Who wants to sit in a chair in a classroom when everything else is on the move?

Men have begun cutting trees along the shoreline. Foundations are being poured for houses that'll be moved or built, and wells are being dug. In the distance there's the continued construction of the mill and the finishing touches on the new Trans-Canada Highway. A bypass is being built to link part of the old secondary highway to the main road leading to the new town.

And, to Percy's fascination, they really are finally building a new bridge.

As for me, I'll be glad when school is over, just because I'm tired of being ignored. No one actively teases me anymore (the woodcarving didn't even make it into the mix), but it's like I've been out of the loop for so long, no one can be bothered to get to know me again. Once June stopped her badmouthing, Linda and then everyone else did too. In the beginning it was probably as much about not upsetting June as anything to do with me. People were very careful around June in the months following her father's death. I know a lot of parents were whispering that her family was probably better off without Alton Crouse, and maybe everyone at school was scared that if they talked to her, that would be the one thing they'd accidentally say.

People felt sorry for the Crouses. If my father hadn't given them what was rumoured to be a small fortune (though only a portion of what Mr. Cole left for him to distribute), this pity might have gone on endlessly. As it was, one day June showed up in a brand-new outfit, the same one as on the model on the cover of the Simpsons-Sears catalogue, and whether her mother forbade her, or there was an unspoken truce, she never suggested I should drown again. She still pretends I don't exist, although I guess that's an upgrade. For anyone who says that money changes people, I've come to realize the results can be subtle.

But for all the mean things that June ever said to me, and Ronnie ever said to Percy, I know that my father did the right thing.

June's mother was pregnant with her ninth child when Alton Crouse burned to death. The baby was born a month after my father gave them Mr. Cole's money. The baby's official name is Alton Jack Ellis Crouse. June's mother phoned my father to tell him. I know this and June knows this. At school June told everyone the baby was simply named A.J.

Percy has a new after-school ritual. He gets off the school bus, runs inside to ask my mother if anything came in the mail, and then asks to see the progress on the new bridge. He's always allowed to go, this he knows, but he asks because he's not allowed to go alone. So I have a new after-school ritual too.

Today we walk toward the old Hawkshaw Bridge, then just before we reach it we walk across the slope following the shore. The new bridge is upriver, close to Pokiok Falls. Only a part of it has been completed so far, but already people are calling it "The Big Green Monster." It's a pale, sickly mint green and it's shockingly tall — high above the water. Its construction is taking into account the level of the river after the flood. One of the piers is on dry land and quite a ways in from the shore. If anyone is having trouble visualizing what is to come, one look at the bridge and they'd wonder no more. There's a roughed-out gravel road leading to it, which ends high up the hill in huge barricades. Percy always wants to go up onto that road for a really good view of things, but I only take us halfway up the slope, no farther.

It's Friday afternoon and by the time we arrive, the men have already left early for the weekend. Percy doesn't seem to mind and for ten minutes he sits on a rock and stares. I ask him what looks different from yesterday and try to sound interested. I hover close to be sure he doesn't take off. The feeling I've had a lot lately, a twinge of nervous dread that can suddenly sneak up on me, comes back. It's my job to keep Percy safe. He's my brother. My little brother. He's the one person still alive that I saw swimming beside me when I fell and hit my head and absorbed the freezing river.

～

I wake early on Saturday morning. Miss Stairs warned my mother that sorting and packing up her whole house would be a big, big job that may take all weekend, so we leave at eight. The sun is shining as we walk down the road together. My mother's hair glows with a hint of red. We both have our hair pulled back to keep it out of the way as we work. I can feel a bit of breeze blowing my ponytail behind me.

Miss Stairs is sitting on her porch. Piled beside her are at least twenty empty boxes from the store and I see more in the backseat of her car. She has an apron on over her clothes and a kerchief covering her hair. She doesn't look happy at all to see us — especially considering that we're free help.

"Good morning Vergie," my mother calls and I raise my hand in a wave.

Miss Stairs stands up, then grabs the porch rail as if she's going to fall over. My mother hurries closer.

"Vergie?" she says.

Miss Stairs's face is pale with the slightest hint of purple. She looks like she might throw up.

"Are you all right?" my mother asks.

Miss Stairs nods.

"You're my good, good friend, right, Lily?" she says quietly.

"Of course," my mother says.

"Well, let's just get it over with," Miss Stairs says. She points at the door.

My mother looks confused, but then seems to realize something.

"Ruby, you just wait here a second with Vergie, okay?"

"It can't be that bad," my mother says, but Miss Stairs doesn't reply. My mother goes inside and stays a long time. I sit on the porch steps and wait. I braid little pieces of my ponytail. Miss Stairs doesn't talk to me. She paces.

When my mother comes back she pauses in the doorway just long enough that Miss Stairs looks up and starts crying.

"It's so horrible," Miss Stairs says. "I just didn't know where to start, Lily. It's just such an awful, awful job. I feel so embarrassed."

"It's okay," my mother is saying. "It's okay. Really. We can do it. It doesn't matter how long it takes."

I get up as my mother hugs Miss Stairs. I figured there'd be some reminiscing and tearful memories as we went through old stuff of her parents, but I wasn't expecting so much upset before we'd even left the porch. From what's been said, it's got to be a pretty bad mess in there, but I still don't see why that's a big deal. I mean, you'd think she'd have to figure we'd wonder about something like that, when for so many years we hadn't been asked to visit. I know my mother has said before to my father that never being invited down is a little odd, but Miss Stairs is her friend and she respected it.

"You won't tell anyone?" Miss Stairs says.

"Absolutely not," my mother says. "Not even Jack. And don't worry, we can do it. We can get through it all."

"Ruby?" Miss Stairs says. She lets go of my mother and they both step to the side of the door so I can see in. "Ruby, you won't tell anyone either, will you?" she asks.

I stand staring.

I shake my head.

There's no way I'm telling because even if I wanted to, I don't know how I'd ever come up with a proper description.

*

But here goes. Imagine every single thing you ever owned or touched in your life — every piece of mail, every Christmas and birthday present, every piece of clothing that fit or didn't fit, every toaster that broke, every single unmatched earring, every empty shopping bag, every book, every tablecloth with a stain, every lamp, every spoon, every empty shortening tin, every chipped dish — you kept. Then imagine that you loved to go shopping and shopped all the time, always wanting one more thing — to have some fun, or to match something else new you bought, or to replace something else you already owned but couldn't find. Imagine all this piled in one house. Imagine a department store's worth of things mounded so high that they're hiding a pump organ, a china cabinet, and a couch.

This has to be the reason that The Four Horsemen of the Apocalypse weren't allowed in for Miss Stairs's house assessment. They wouldn't have been able to see what it was they were supposed to assess. They would have had to wade through all this stuff, probably wondering if it was the house itself or the contents that had more worth.

As we go into the house together, I don't think it will take all weekend. It will probably take a month. I'm carrying a cardboard box from the porch and Miss Stairs goes to the kitchen for a garbage bag. My mother asks where we should start and when Miss Stairs starts to cry again, I leave them and walk the narrow path between piles to the parlour.

I wonder how long it's been like this. I wonder how much it's gotten worse over the years. I really don't know how Miss Stairs didn't walk out the front door one day and never come back. She must truly know what dread feels like — knowing that something had to be done before the water comes.

Somehow, somewhere, we find a place to start, and then work all day except for lunch and a break when I take Percy for his bottle launch. By suppertime Miss Stairs's car is loaded with six garbage bags and four boxes to take to the dump. My mother has three bags of clothes to give to the church, but it makes so little difference you can't even tell what we've done. On the way out the door my shoulder brushes against a pile and with just the few things we moved from it missing, it begins to fall. I know it isn't for me to decide, but if it was I would be tempted to burn the house as is — contents and all.

On Sunday after church we work again and then my mother keeps helping every day for a week. Miss Stairs drives carloads of donations to the Salvation Army in both Fredericton and Woodstock so that she can keep her secret. She goes to the dump after dark. She keeps an almost constant fire of Simpson-Sears and Eaton's catalogues, *Farmer's Almanacs* and folded paper grocery bags going in her woodstove. She returns some recent purchases to stores — those things sitting unworn in shopping bags with the original receipts.

She and my mother work and work and after Miss Stairs says she can't possibly accept any more help or she'll be indebted to my mother forever, she continues on her own. She gathers and sorts and packs and sweeps. She cleans and organizes the whole house until the only thing left is the question why.

My mother says she thinks it's something Miss Stairs already had in her, like part of her personality, but the way her life worked out, all the sadness and disappointment, made it worse. Maybe when her parents died and year after year went by with her alone and not married, buying and gathering things made her feel good. Then the feeling wore off and she needed something else — and something else.

When my mother tells me this in our sunroom one evening, she shrugs when she's finished and begins to rock in her chair. It sounds reasonable enough I suppose, and as good an interpretation as any. With Percy the way he is I know my mother's spent a lot of time thinking about his behaviour and trying to reason it all out. As far as Miss Stairs goes, my mother says lots of people have little hidden things about themselves, like an unseen birthmark, that you'd never know is there until something happens and the quirk expresses itself. Tragedy, sickness, death, accidents, you just never know. My mother also says the stress of the flood coming probably made Miss Stairs's situation worse — but at least it gave her a reason to seek help. You never know what some people are capable of, she says, until they are given a test, for better or worse. Unexpected problems bring unexpected results.

I wonder if hitting your head and having a vision of the future counts?

Chapter 16

~

After all this waiting and knowing for so long that things had to be done, the time has come. A second church is moving to the new town today, and this morning the school bus had to sit on the shoulder while four halves of prefab houses passed us. The Legion was moved last week and the gas station closed. The store will be burned and the Fosters will retire. Everyone is hoping that we'll somehow end up with a fancy supermarket in the new town.

Leonard Black finally gave up on his standoff, and whether it was out of disgust or embarrassment at having to let the government win, he's moved away. The big news before he left was that for a proper grand exit, he put a homemade nail belt across his driveway — rusty spikes sticking up through old leather reins — then called Mr. Comeau and said The Horsemen could finally come do his house assessment. The nails were well hidden in the tall weeds growing in the gravel, and Mr. Comeau sped so anxiously down the driveway that all four tires of the government's Buick Skylark blew out. Leonard Black said he had a good laugh, then phoned the tow truck. Mr. Comeau was swearing and furious, but really what could he do? A lot of people commented that it was pretty damn juvenile on Leonard's part while trying to hide their smiles. My father said everyone knew it was what he'd been reduced to. If Leonard Black had done anything more dramatic like destroy his own house, he would only have been helping the government out.

This Friday night the school will have the farewell dance to end all farewell dances. Our minister and his wife have moved the rectory to the town not far from the church. They invited everyone to see it in its new location last Sunday. The Pokiok Lodge and cottages have closed for good. They served the final meal in the restaurant last week and aren't taking any more guests. Obviously Miss Stairs won't get to fulfill her wedding fantasy. They're having an auction of the contents of the Lodge this Saturday.

Miss Stairs finally took Mr. Hazen Howard to her house for the first time, if only for the romantic task of moving boxes. Then yesterday when we went to school, she walked out her front door, got in her car, and drove to visit him in Fredericton. While she was gone, men who she had hired came and burned her house to the ground. Percy ran so fast to the smouldering debris when we got off the bus, I could barely keep up with him. I was expecting a volcano eruption of upset, but he simply stopped, looked, circled it once, then went back to our house. I was still trying to figure out how I felt when Percy returned and asked me to take him to the bridge. I didn't say anything, so in a few seconds he spoke again.

"Ruby, I am also glad our parents have decided to have our house relocated rather than burned," he said.

I turned. There was Percy in his white T-shirt and jeans, standing still with just the slightest smile and his eyes fixed on my nose. Was it observation, statement, perception, or conclusion? Was it just to get me to move and go with him, a quick way to end a conversation that never started — or could it be that he was trying to sympathize with me?

I think of it again today when we go to the bridge. Maybe Percy's way of dealing with all the change around here is by making sure it doesn't change him. Small variances in routine have always bothered Percy — all the little unexpected disturbances in life — but maybe the magnitude of everything happening around us is so great he has to accept it. It's been such a long process, almost two years out of a boy's life that has lasted barely eleven, that maybe he gradually realized he had to make do. Haventon is changing, that's a reality. It's a continuous, everyday, ongoing occurrence, and perhaps he decided this is his new standard of normal.

Maybe Percy finally changed in his own subtle way — if only by altering his expectations. His day-to-day is the same. His emotions are the same. I think he's making all this work in his favour. Percy and I heard on the school bus today that they're blowing up the old Hawkshaw Bridge at the end of the summer. Percy wasn't upset, only excited about the coming explosion. He's not stuck in the past but looking to the future.

I think sometimes I'm just as bad as anyone for judging Percy. I always thought his personality seemed so unusual and fixed that Percy was destined to be only Percy as-is forever. Maybe that's so, but I really think I need to give him the benefit of the doubt. I think of how grown adults — Mr. Cole, Miss Stairs, Tommy Cole, Leonard Black — dealt with our situation and then here is Percy, calm and seemingly happy beside me. He's fine. Isn't he?

Except Percy's often fooled and confused us in the past. Thinking you have him figured out, even temporarily, isn't a good idea. Maybe I'm giving him too much credit just so I'll have an excuse not to worry.

I guess the real test will be when they move our house. When it's broken from the foundation, lifted, and carried away. My mother's already said she doesn't want to watch, but Percy won't miss it for anything and has a calendar in his room counting down to the day.

I think about it a lot too, but I wonder more about the first night sleeping in my same room, in my same bed, yet in an entirely different place. Will I feel confused? Will my body know the difference?

Neither Percy nor I have seen the land where we're moving. My parents think it's best if it's revealed to Percy as a whole package with the house already sitting there, and I'm being kept in the dark too to keep things fair. I do know the land isn't in the new town but along the road that links to the top of it, far from the river. It's two acres once owned by Rita Cole's family. It's land we didn't know Mr. Cole had and the only thing in his will my father kept for himself.

The house will be angled exactly the way it is now for Percy's sake. My father hired surveyors for just this purpose. Our land has been cleared and levelled and a basement dug. I know in the evenings my father drives out to the place to look around. Sometimes he's gone for hours.

When Percy and I come back from the bridge, I go to my room. I take out my carving tools and a new piece of driftwood. I use the tiniest chisel to begin a deep curved line down one side of the wood. I'm not sure what it will turn out to be. I'm back to just whittling, practising, seeing what happens. After working for so long, the chess set is finally done.

For now it's in the drawer. When I finished painting the pieces black and white, I showed them to my mother and father (my secret models for the faces of the queen and king), but I haven't given them to Percy. After so much effort it seems too important to give to him without a special occasion. Even though his reaction will likely be little more than a nod or "Thank you for this gift, Ruby," I thought

I'd wait for a time when it might have more meaning. It wasn't finished before his birthday, so I'll probably save it for Christmas. Someday maybe he'll realize all the time I put into it and, corny or not, that it was carved with love from me to him. For now I'm just thankful that Percy likes chess. It made the perfect project for me. Slowly carving those thirty-two pieces, week after week, month after month, probably saved my sanity.

I whittle for a while, then write to Troy. With everything happening lately I have lots to tell him. We've written each other about every two weeks since he left last summer. I'm probably as anxious about getting a new letter from him as Percy is waiting for another reply to one of his bottles. Troy's never mentioned coming back here and I can't bring myself to ask him about it. I do worry that eventually our communication will fade away. Our brief time together already seems like a distant memory. At night I find it hard to conjure up the feeling of him kissing me.

On Friday night we go to Miss Stairs's new house for supper. It's the first time I've ever been in a brand-new house, and especially compared to her last place, the clean uncluttered plainness is startling. Everything is painted white and for now it's the type of clean that makes you feel you should check your hands — and fingernails — before even walking in. Percy's never been in a house like this either and as soon as we go through the front door he takes off and gives himself a tour. Miss Stairs laughs and says she doesn't mind a bit. She says she's just thrilled to have visitors.

Her furniture is in place and her kitchen cupboards are full, but there are still boxes piled in the hall waiting to be unpacked. There are curtains in the living room, white and filmy and as bright as the walls, and a blind in her master bedroom. Other windows are empty and no pictures are hanging yet. Miss Stairs wipes away tears when my mother gives her the painting of her old house and ours as a housewarming present.

Miss Stairs serves a full dinner of pot roast, potatoes, gravy, carrots, and squash. She's even made a double-layer chocolate cake with chocolate icing. After we finish eating she shows us what she calls the best part of her new house — the dishwasher. My mother and Miss Stairs measure all the windows without coverings. Tomorrow morning they're going to Woodstock to buy curtain rods. Miss Stairs talks to my father about planting a few trees and making a little hedge, but we don't stay too long. Tonight is the farewell dance and my mother and Miss Stairs want to be sure I have lots of time to get ready.

I'm going because I think it's something I'll regret if I don't. It's part of this story I'm telling. We're getting down to the end of all this now. There are last things to be done and remembered. This year the dance isn't only for saying goodbye to people who are leaving, but also to the school, which will be demolished after graduation. I know it's just a dance, but it feels important. I'll go and stand by the wall. In a week I'll be sixteen years old. I can do it. Somehow it's like proof that I made it through. Years from now, I want to be able to say I was there.

I wear the same dress as last year — the turquoise satin one trimmed with tulle. My mother pulls my hair back and off to one side and ties it with a beautiful sleek gold-coloured ribbon that she saved from one of the dozens of shopping bags at Miss Stairs's. I put on the locket Mr. Cole gave me and the heart shines the same colour as the ribbon. The pictures of him and Rita are still inside. My mother lets me use a bit of plum-coloured lipstick and she lightly brushes my cheeks with blush. She gets her camera and takes some pictures. She takes three inside and then one of me in the middle of the lawn. This fourth picture I know is not just to remember how I look standing here at this time in this place, but also the house.

At the dance the decorations are as extensive as last year, but this time they're focused on the theme "Sail Away." There's a giant banner taking up most of the back wall of the gym with these words at the top. The bottom two-thirds of the banner is turquoise blue water and above that are blended bands of yellow, orange, pink, and red. A sailboat is painted in the upper-right corner floating in the distance. It all looks peaceful and pretty. The dance is a time for happy celebration after all. By now everyone is so aware of what's coming, no one needs to be reminded.

There are balloons everywhere, mostly shades of blue to match the painted water, but a few red and yellow ones are mixed in. Streamers are hanging in doorways, windows, and off the stage. There are four food tables and one with punch. Old yearbook photos dating from the entire history of the school are taped to the wall in a big display.

The gym is full. I think every student and teacher turned out. Most people are dancing, but others are near the food or milling around. I get a glass of punch and take up my position by the wall. I'm an island against the painted banner of blue. I stand for a while, and for all I know I may be in the exact place I was a year ago when I came with Sarah, but I don't feel the same. I'm not going to lie and say it's thrilling to be here alone, but I'm not yet counting the seconds until I can leave. I don't miss Sarah like I used to. She's still my friend and I look forward to our times together, but it seems her leaving is now a long, long way back, at the bottom of a whole list of things that have changed.

I stay in my spot for five songs, and then when a waltz plays I head for the picture display. I'd say there are hundreds of photos, and I scan all of them. I sip my punch as three or four more songs start and finish. I find an old photograph of my father standing near a giant stegosaurus snow sculpture for winter carnival. I see a picture of Uncle Kent playing basketball, and Miss Stairs working at a bake sale. There are newer pictures too. I see our class photo, and then one of me alone — that I don't remember being taken. I'm painting something. A banner? I step closer. It's really a picture of my mother — my unquestionably beautiful mother.

I finish my punch, then go back to my spot along the wall. I watch the dancing couples. June Crouse glances at me briefly, lifting her head from the shoulder of Colin Moore. Linda and Wade Hill are beside them. I scan the whole gym once more, taking in the entire scene — the people, the decorations, the dimmed lighting, the loud music, the slightest smell of sweat and perfume. There. I did it. I leave.

I could call my father to come get me, but it's a warm night so I decide to walk. My parents won't be expecting me any time soon. The sky is clear and bright. The moon is almost full, and is shining off the windshields of the cars in the parking lot and highlighting the little ripples in the river. I don't have to go too far before the music from the dance fades. Now it's quiet. Besides me, the road is empty. I can hear a little echo coming from each of my footsteps.

Soon enough I regret my choice. As nice a night as it is, my dress shoes weren't made for a cross-country trek. I sit on the shoulder in the tall grass. I tuck my dress beneath me and my hand brushes against a square of something — a slice of stale bread. I take off my shoes and rub my feet a little, wiggle my toes. A bat flies above me. I see the Big Dipper beyond it. A breeze blows.

It's all fine until I hear a vehicle heading in my direction. I quickly put my shoes back on and stand.

I start to walk again as a truck gets closer. Even with the glare of the headlights, something about it seems familiar. A chill comes over me as I think it could be Tommy in Mr. Cole's truck. But then I remember.

I raise my hand to wave and hope, hope they don't stop. But sure enough the truck slows and pulls up beside me. I should have called my father. The headlights are so bright they're blinding me. I fake a smile and try to look comfortable, like wandering down the main drag of Haventon, in the dark, in a satin dress and fancy shoes, is my usual weekend thing.

The driver turns off the lights and the ignition and leans across the passenger seat to the unrolled window.

"Well if it isn't Miss Saint John River Valley."

I'm not imagining it. I reach for the side-view mirror to be sure I'm standing perfectly steady.

"Troy?" I say.

"At your service. May I drive you home?"

I think I nod before opening the door of the truck and climbing in.

"Pretty good surprise, eh?" Troy says.

"You drive?" Out of everything this is what comes out of my mouth first.

"I turned sixteen."

I smooth my skirt for a few seconds before I turn to meet his blue eyes.

"I can't believe it," I say.

Troy smiles. "Then I would say it's a pretty good surprise."

As it turns out his reappearance is not so magical but simply the result of good timing. Troy says that the owners of the Pokiok Lodge phoned to tell his father about the auction being held tomorrow. They're selling the old furniture, paintings, dishes — everything. Mr. Rutherford came down to buy what he can — both because it's a good opportunity for some inexpensive inventory and because the people at the Lodge had been so nice to him last year. Troy and his father drove since seven this morning and are going back home as soon as the auction is over.

We pull into the driveway.

"Your parents know it's us," Troy says. "I was already here."

"Can you come in for a while?"

Troy shakes his head. He and his father are staying at a hotel up in Meductic and he has to get back.

"But you'll come to the auction tomorrow?" he says.

"Definitely." I reach up to the heart on my necklace and rub it with my thumb. I can feel Troy looking at me.

"You know, you look so nice, Ruby. I think I forgot how pretty you are."

"Thanks," I say. And for maybe the first time, I feel like I really believe him. I don't blush but smile.

"So would it be okay if I kissed you?" Troy asks.

How could I ever say no?

~

Miss Stairs drops me off across the river at the Pokiok Lodge at eight-forty when she and my mother are on their way to Woodstock. My mother's given me her camera to take some pictures of the auction in progress, but it might have more to do with her offhand comment that maybe I could get someone to take one of me and Troy.

Troy's already here, sitting on the tailgate of his father's truck in the parking lot. He looks so good. He's already a bit tanned and his hair is a little longer than last year. Troy takes my hand and we walk down to the falls until the auction starts. We sit on a big flat rock at the base of the falls and talk. The sun is shining bright on the water as it gurgles and plunges. We could be a picture in a postcard. There are people looking at the contents of the cottages in the woods behind us and occasionally someone will come over to look at the falls too.

More than one person has said to us they can't believe how the flooding river will almost completely swallow the falls. Troy's so kind and understanding talking to everyone. People smile and nod when they speak with him. I almost wish someone from school would come along and see us, but it's also fun knowing that Troy is my own secret surprise that I don't need to share.

Way, way too soon, the auction starts and we head back up to the parking lot. The auctioneer is fast and all his words seem to run together. He's got a rhythm going and without really thinking about it, I can feel my foot tapping along. It's like "five lookin' for ten — thank you — ten and need twenty — twenty and —" People are following him and obviously understanding what he's saying because he's pointing out bidders. Mr. Rutherford is buyer number fourteen and even now, only twenty minutes in, I've heard it probably ten times. Troy and I are sitting on the tailgate of the truck well behind the buyers, but Troy has said that after a while he'll have to help his father and load some things.

I recognize a lot of people at the sale. I see Mr. Foster and Linda's father, Mr. Small, Colin Moore's parents, our minister, a few teachers including a new couple, Mr. and Mrs. Givan, who I've heard will be starting at the big school in the fall. The Johnsons are here with their two-year-old daughter, Wade Hill is here with his mother. I see the Doyles, the Brewers, and Miss Stairs's boyfriend, Mr. Hazen Howard. As time goes on, I realize that I haven't seen any of the local people bidding, except our minister, who bought a painting. They're probably only here out of curiosity. With everyone packing up, moving, and trying to lighten their own load in the process, who needs more things?

Mr. Rutherford buys and buys and Troy's spending most of the time running and loading. Suddenly I hear the auctioneer say, "Well, that's it for inside, folks. Thanks to all my good bidders so far. Now, if you'll just excuse me for a moment, nature calls, but then we'll get on to the big real estate." People laugh and I don't know what he means by big real estate, but I see Mr. Rutherford fold his bidding card and reach for his wallet.

Troy's heading back toward me when he suddenly U-turns because his father beckons him over. Mr. Foster joins them and shakes Mr. Rutherford's hand. Groan. Talking to Mr. Foster always takes a while.

The auctioneer comes back and it turns out the big real estate is the cottages themselves. "They'd make you a real nice sturdy storage shed," the auctioneer says. I see some people nod in agreement. I look across the crowd to Troy. He winks. I feel better because I really can't explain it, but somehow even after sitting here watching everything being sold, the idea of those wonderful cottages turning into storage sheds has made me feel what I think is nostalgic. I feel a little disappointment like when you're all done undecorating the Christmas tree and you throw it out the back door into the snow — you know for absolute sure the season is over. The cottages don't sell for much either and I don't recognize any of their buyers except one. The last cottage, proclaimed by the auctioneer to be in the best condition, is bought by Mr. Hazen Howard.

I see Mr. Rutherford pay at the desk and then he and Troy come over to me.

"Ruby," Mr. Rutherford says. "It seems about the only thing that hasn't changed around here is your lovely face."

"It's good to see you."

"I must say I'd have thought I was having some strange dream if I hadn't known what was going on down here. I've mentioned it at home and people think it's just crazy — craziness — they figure you've got to be one tough bunch to deal with it."

Troy puts his arm around me. "Give us ten minutes?" he asks his father.

"Absolutely," he says, "I'm sorry we can't stay longer, Ruby, but I'd like to get in as many miles as we can before dark."

"I understand. Drive carefully," I say.

Troy takes me by the hand and we hurry back down to the falls. Now that the auction is over, everyone else is up in the parking lot and we're alone.

We sit very close facing each other.

"It's right what he said, you know," Troy says. "With all this going on, not everyone could keep it together."

I shrug. It's strange to hear. It's something I think about every day, but at the same time not at all. Really, in all this time, the flood has been almost the least of my worries.

"You get used to it, I guess," I say. "But what's harder is it seems I just barely got to see you and now you're leaving again."

Troy has a look on his face that I haven't seen before, and I wonder if I shouldn't have said what I said. His coming was the best surprise I've ever had, and I certainly don't want to sound like I'm complaining.

"I —" I start, but he interrupts me.

"I'll come back again, Ruby. It may be a while, since for now it's not something I can control myself, but you'll see. You're different from any girl I've ever met. And I mean that in the best possible way. It doesn't matter how much everything else changes down here, it's not going to change what I think."

I know it's okay if I don't say anything. He kisses me, then we walk back to the road. I look down on the beautiful falls and the shining water. And then I think about what Troy said. It's something I've probably known for a while. I think I'm fine and it's just the people in this place that distort me, like a reflection in the river, altering my image.

Sometimes different is a good thing.

Chapter 17

～

My grandmother had a ghost story she used to tell when I was little. She claimed that the house she grew up in was haunted. The ghost, a woman named Charlotte, would appear in her bedroom at night. My grandmother would wake up to the sound of her chamber pot being stirred with a wooden spoon. It was always clean, my grandmother would say each time, making Sarah and me giggle, but the rest of what she said was strange enough anyway. She'd see transparent pale-blue Charlotte cradling the chamber pot to her chest like a mixing bowl. Charlotte would stir for a while, pace back and forth, then I suppose when her otherworldly concoction was done, she'd leave. My grandmother said she found out eventually that Charlotte had lived in the house decades before. When her family lived there, my grandmother's bedroom was the kitchen. Charlotte died while mixing a cake, suddenly collapsed from a stroke with the bowl in her hand. My grandmother said she returned again and again to finish that cake. Maybe, she thought, it was something special, like for guests or a birthday.

Charlotte never went into my grandmother's kitchen, only her bedroom, which was the scene of her death. The chamber pot was the best thing for a mixing bowl that she could find. She was tied to that space, my grandmother said, because in her life, in her memory, it was something else. The surroundings changed, but the place on Earth that it was hadn't. The exact physical location counts with ghosts. That's what's the most important. My grandmother always said that the passage of time and life changing and moving on once they're dead is confusing to ghosts. That's why ghosts are usually doing weird things and seem out of touch with reality. They are. Ghosts are working from memory.

It's only three nights before we move our house and that's why I remember Charlotte. I lie in my bed and think of her stuck forever in that space. Charlotte was lucky that the kitchen changing to a bedroom was all that was done. If it had been our house I'm sure she would've been in for quite a surprise conjuring herself up one night only to find it had disappeared. What would she have done then? Hung out on the lawn? Pretended a chopped-down tree stump was her oven? I think too about the ghost of Isaac Thorne, who drowned in Pokiok Falls and is said to haunt our river. What's he going to do with so much extra water? I think of all the ghosts in the cemetery that was moved. What did they do? Where are they now?

I really don't believe in ghosts, but as I lie here ghosts are easier to think about than the idea that this space I am filling, the air I am breathing, will soon be out of reach to anyone alive. It will be deep in the river. Every invisible dot in front of me now, contained in these walls called my room, will be drowned and gone.

School's been finished for a month and this afternoon they're de-molishing the place. It's one of those things that I'm sure has been many a student's fantasy, but when it comes right down to it, I think it'll be hard to watch for everyone who's graduated. The new high school in the town is finished and ready to open in the fall. It's big and students from all around who we've never met before will be bused in too. The gym is huge and there are even two science labs in addition to all the classrooms.

I'm going to the big smash and crash of course. Pay my final tribute to the school, reminisce about all the good times I had leaning against its walls by myself. I heard that this morning a bunch of kids are going to break in and graffiti the blackboards, kick down the principal's office door, have a smoke in the staffroom, pull a mooner on the gym stage, ride bikes up the halls and down the stairs — all that good stuff. I don't see the need. Just watching its windows shatter and brick walls crumble, knowing it will soon be underwater forever, is enough.

Besides, up until it's time to leave, my job is to watch Percy. He's so excited that he wants to go now and see the heavy equipment arrive. Percy was up and dressed by five-thirty this morning — earlier than Christmas. But December 25 comes around every year. How many kids in their whole life get to see a building demolished close up?

He's fascinated by the destruction potential contained within the wrecking ball. For days Percy's been experimenting using a potato threaded with a blue piece of yarn. He's been swinging it at various heights and angles into wooden blocks he hasn't touched since he was a baby, then analyzing the results.

The high school is the last public building to be destroyed. Foster's Store has been burned and every other business, church, or hall is now moved or gone. The Pokiok Lodge is gone. Everyone who bought a little cottage has plucked it from the woods. A dozen more houses have been added to the town in the past month. Most are people new to the area — the families of men who came to work on the mill — but Linda Small's family bought a prefab house so they wouldn't have to move away. Almost everything is out of the flood plain, with only the finishing touches of clearing and grading land, finishing roads and the bridge to be done. And of course moving our house. My mother said we never planned to be the grand finale, but that's how it worked out.

She and my father have a saying now that seems to come up every time I hear them talking to anyone. It's "Last to know, last to go." It always seems to get a good laugh. People believe it's true too. I can tell. People respect my father again after what he did with Mr. Cole's money. People even respect (although I don't know that anyone else would have done it) that he saved a good portion for Tommy. My father didn't know about the flood coming before anyone else. And the false suspicions are water under the bridge.

Miss Stairs comes to drive my mother, Percy, and me to the school. Cars are parked well back from the parking lot all along both sides of the road. In front of the school itself are three RCMP cars, an ambulance, and our local fire truck. Sawhorses, orange pylons, and rope make a line along the edge of the property. As we walk closer I can see a huge crowd gathered, hovering behind the makeshift barricade. Probably every teacher and student is here. There are entire families. It's obvious that quite a few men left work early. Police officers pace along the inside of the rope.

My mother is holding Percy's hand. He's old enough and tall enough now that no one mistakes him for a little boy needing guidance, but my mother's used to the judgmental looks. At first we stop near the middle of the crowd, but Percy pulls my mother along until we're at the end of the line with an unobstructed view. It's overcast and cool and even slightly foggy. Someone's put the school's New Brunswick flag at half-staff and it seems ominous.

To Percy's disappointment I'm sure, the equipment is set up on the river side of the two-storey school, far from us. I can just barely see the yellow ends of two bulldozers, and the wondrous wrecking ball is completely hidden from view. The only evidence that it's even here is the top of the crane with a dangling chain peeking above the roof.

There are three workmen not far from us on the other side of the rope (behind the pacing policemen) carrying two-way radios. I hear "Check," "All clear," "Check," "Check," "Check." Two men with hard hats come out the front door of the school and another man with a white hard hat goes in. Then all the workmen who are standing on the lawn walk around to the back of the school, to the river side. The man who was inside comes out and goes around too. They stay for probably five minutes and everyone's quiet in anticipation.

We can't see anything that's going on. I hear a machine start up and someone rev the engine. I look at Percy. He has one fist clenched and the other is squeezing my mother's hand. Even though it's cool out, his forehead is a little sweaty. The poor guy. I think of him swinging that potato over and over, until the skin wore off in spots, planning for this occasion. He's craning his neck wondering where the action is. He's on his tiptoes. I'm sure he can hardly stand that whatever they've set up is on the opposite side. I hope he doesn't cry.

A man with a hard hat comes around the front of the school and begins to walk along the crowd, telling people to be sure to stay well back. The policemen now appear to be doing the same. The top of the crane starts to move back and forth above the school as if the operator is warming up, practising his swing. The man in the hard hat turns to look at it for a second. I hear him say, "Believe me, you don't want to be anywhere near that thing."

When the man makes it all the way down to us, Percy speaks to him.

"Sir," he says. "Is it true that the demolition of the school will not take place until you return and give your word?"

The man seems surprised, probably partly by the formality of the question. Percy also isn't looking at the man, nervous that he's spoken to a stranger and as usual not making eye contact.

"Yes," the man says. "But it will be soon, don't you worry. So it's just important—" the man stops talking because at the same time he pronounces the "s" of "Yes," Percy shakes loose of my mother's hand with a single strenuous swing and twist, ducks under the rope, and takes off running. He runs about fifteen feet until the RCMP officer nearest us darts with amazing speed and grabs him.

My mother screams, "Percy!" and Miss Stairs and I gasp.

Percy cries at the touch of the policeman's hand—who knows if it's from the force of his grasp or from Percy being interrupted mid-task. Percy wails and wriggles and twists, but the policeman is too strong for him to get free. The officer has his hand squeezed tight around Percy's forearm. The man with the hard hat is now on his radio saying, "Wait! Wait! Hold on. We're going to need a few more minutes." I notice all the heads in the crowd turning in our direction, like a ripple in the river. Those who didn't witness Percy's foiled dash are now at least hearing his screaming.

The police officer brings him toward us and speaks to my mother.

"Ma'am, is this your son?"

My mother nods.

Percy is no longer squirming, but he has his head turned as far as possible from the policeman. It's turned so far he's almost looking backwards. Tears are still streaming.

"Ma'am, for everyone's safety I'm going to have to ask that you both leave. I'll walk you to your vehicle."

"Of course," my mother says. "Thank you, I'm so sorry." Her voice trails off. I'm not going to try to guess what combination of fear—for what almost happened—and embarrassment—for what did—she feels. For me the mix is about fifty-fifty.

The police officer ducks under the rope while still holding on to Percy. Percy's head is locked into position as if he'll turn to stone should he look at anyone.

"Percy," my mother says. "Percy." She reaches to touch his hair. The officer, Percy, and my mother move as a unit, and Miss Stairs and I, forgotten in this, just trail along.

We hear the bang, crash, and crumple when we're about three-quarters of the way to the car. The sound of the second crash, the wrecking ball swinging back again, is almost drowned out by the sound of Percy's renewed wailing. He wanted to look. That was it. I'm sure. For as much as things change, they stay the same.

Two more nights. It's what I lie in bed and think even before I overhear my father tell the same thing to my mother. Two more nights in this space and then we can start fresh. My mother's crying. It's because Percy shook loose of her hand and she says she didn't keep him safe. He's getting older, stronger, she says, that's why he was able to get away. My mother just wants it all over with — no more worries about fires and demolitions. No more destruction or house moving.

My father had been the angriest I'd seen him in a long, long time. My mother made Percy wait at the kitchen table for almost an hour until he came home, but Percy just read his book on sea life as if nothing had happened. Then my father arrived and yelled about fifteen questions at once. Some of the highlights were: What were you thinking? Do you know what kind of a position you put your mother in? What makes you think you're so special you can break the rules? Why the hell do you think it was roped off? Why the hell do you think everyone else was keeping back? What if the damn thing had started swinging around right then? How do you think you made your mother feel?

"Father," Percy said finally. "My mother, Ruby, and Miss Vergina

Stairs witnessed me ask a gentleman from the work crew whether the demolition was to immediately take place. I did not request my mother's assistance so I do not understand your concern for her involvement as there wasn't any. As to why I proceeded when others didn't, I cannot know, but perhaps it was not their area of interest."

"Jesus Christ," my father said. "Do you understand the word selfish, Percy? Have you looked that up lately in your goddamned dictionary? You don't live here by yourself, you know. What you do affects other people. Other people have feelings, Percy! What the hell goes on in that head of yours?"

Percy looked at him with an even expression. You'd swear Percy was a master manipulator if we didn't already have years of family research supporting the theory that he simply didn't know any different or any better. I think Percy isn't so much selfish as he is self-centred. I think selfish means putting yourself first at the expense of others — deciding to consider only yourself. But for Percy I don't know that it's ever a decision. It's just the way he is.

Percy didn't answer my father and of course that made him angrier.

"You're old enough to know better. Christ, you've got to learn to be careful. Do you know, Christ —," my father shook his head and gave up. He turned to my mother, who was looking out the kitchen window. He rubbed his hand through his hair and took a breath.

"Almost, Lil," he said. "Almost over. Pretty soon this'll all be done." He touched her on the back. "No more changes. No more turmoil. No more destruction."

"The bridge is still to be blown up once the new one is completed," Percy piped up.

I could hardly believe it. But then I could. This is what I mean. Only facts. Only information. No perception. No clue. No idea. The only thing that changed about Percy was the fact that the older he got, the more set in his ways he got. He could adapt enough for his own daily self-preservation and on his birthday declare he was upping his bedtime to eight-thirty, but that was about it.

"Well you're sure as hell not going to be anywhere near it," my father said.

Percy started to cry.

Two more days. Two more days my father is saying. Not that that will finish it all, but at least when my mother goes to the same kitchen window she'll have a new perspective. This has to be so hard on her — not just the house and all the changes everywhere, but having to deal with Percy. Even once everything is settled there's still Percy. I think of how she kept twisting piece after piece of her hair, knotting and tangling it, not saying a word, staring out the window at the river, as Miss Stairs drove us from the school home.

So that's why tonight I went to my bottom dresser drawer and ran my hands over the chess set figures. I allowed myself some of my mother's worry. Some of hers to go with my own. Even if Percy has no idea how he frightened me too when he ran. He took away my breath. He made me remember. Even if he can't change himself, he changed something in me. He made me change my mind. For now. I have to believe what I saw in my mind all that time ago is a destiny that could come true. Until the water comes and it is calm again and there's a new bigger river and a new reality and I can let it go. But until then I worry and watch. Hello Percy.

～

Miss Stairs comes over after lunch with eight cardboard boxes for packing, and we have them all filled before supper. She brought us a large stack of newspapers to use for wrapping fragile things and we also use every dishcloth, doily, and towel. My mother and Miss Stairs clear the dishes from the kitchen cupboards and I take the pictures and paintings off the walls. I take my carved driftwood owl from his perch above the coat hook. Percy's in his room packing his bottles from the windowsills.

While my mother and Miss Stairs move to the china cabinet, I take our few potted plants from their stands and put them on the floor. I take the casters off each of our beds, then help Percy box the books from his shelf. He tapes closed his desk and dresser drawers. In my room I empty the top of my dresser and shove everything in my hope chest. My mother cleans out the bathroom medicine cabinet. She and Miss Stairs lift the television, radio, and record player down off their stands. We all walk around to look for anything we may have forgotten, but that's it. We're done. Two hours and ten minutes. When my father comes home, we eat the sandwiches and cookies my mother made. Now one more sleep until the truck comes.

I lie in bed and I think the weirdest thing isn't that I can't conjure up any special memorable feeling for this moment, but that even in the darkness I'm aware that the painting my mother did for me isn't on the wall. I get it from my closet and hang it back up. I look to my little brush-stroke self on the rooftop, our house on the island. It's almost as if I'm riding the house. That's how it looks to me tonight. I'm perched on the house as if it's a parade float. With my perfect paint -dot posture and the bright colours, it all seems quite exciting. Now if only I could see where I'm going.

We get up at six. My mother puts out rolls and jam, apples and bananas for our breakfast. Percy takes a banana because he always has one in the morning. My mother and I, even my father, are too nervous to eat. My mother starts going through the house, taping closed more drawers and cupboard doors. My father looks at the row of packed cardboard boxes and pushes each one back slightly with his foot, making sure they're flush against the wall. My mother comes back to the kitchen, then they leave together and inspect everything room by room. My job is to watch Percy.

At about seven we go outside when the crew arrives to cut the power lines. (My father is paying extra for an early start to get everything done in a day.) We all get in the car and my father drives us down to park in front of what used to be Miss Stairs's place. My father goes to talk to the men. My mother gets in the backseat with Percy, and I sit in the front. She locks the doors and tells Percy to leave his seat belt on. It looks a little silly, but it's to slow him down and extend our reaction time should there be an attempted escape. I know a view from the inside of the car wasn't what Percy was dreaming of, but I think he should consider himself lucky he's here at all. My mother couldn't bring herself to deprive him of it, so she's watching too.

We wait. And wait, it seems. Two years — plus this. The sun shines bright on the house and turns the windows to bars of gold. Eventually the other trucks pull up. My mother takes a picture as a long flatbed backs across the front lawn right over our small round flower garden. The back tires are squishing a clump of pansies. She doesn't say anything. So I guess it's official. Why be concerned about some place you don't live anymore?

From here it takes hours. It's a big job. It seems to go on and on. There's no single dramatic moment like when you spring a jack-in-the box. It's slow and careful and tedious. Percy's leaning against the car door, his face out the open window (still in his seat belt), but not my mother and me. I'm braiding bits of my hair, checking out my reflection in the rear-view mirror. My mother takes a few more pictures but sometimes even leans back (her fingers securely through one of Percy's belt loops) and closes her eyes.

Eventually I do too. It's warm in the car and the sun's on my face. But unlike my mother I fall asleep.

When I wake, the house is gone.

My mother drives Percy and me to Miss Stairs's place to wait. My father went with the moving crew and told us to give them five hours. That's how long until our old house becomes our new house. I think of our house travelling too, taking the scenic route to who-knows-where.

It's after supper. My mother waited an extra half-hour to be sure. We're back in our car and my mother has two scarves borrowed from Miss Stairs for Percy and me to wear as blindfolds. Percy refuses, which she probably expected anyway, and she doesn't push the idea for fear of upset on this momentous day. I take mine and my mother ties a band of pink over my eyes. When will we ever have a chance again for silly fun like this? For just a second I remember Mr. Cole and how we waved at the Queen.

We drive and it isn't far. I can tell we drive straight up the hill on the main street through the new town, turn right, turn left, and continue just a little longer. My mother turns left again and I hear the crushed rock of our new driveway under the tires.

"We're here, Ruby," she says. "Welcome home."

I take off my blindfold. It's the strangest yet most familiar thing. It's an image I'm sure I'll remember for the rest of my life.

There's our house.

"See it, Percy?" my mother says.

I know he does. I can see him staring, still trying to establish this new reality in his mind.

My father comes out the front door. He jumps down because the front step hasn't been put in place yet, and comes toward us. We get out of the car.

My father kisses my mother on the cheek.

"It's perfect, Lil," he says. "Look, you'll hardly believe it. They put it down so good it was like angels hovered and gently lowered it into place."

"You see it, Percy," my father says. "You see your windows up there. And now," my father looks at his watch, "it's almost eight o'clock and see where the sun is setting. See how it's just passing below your first window there. Why don't you go in? You'll see it's just the same."

Percy takes off running to the house.

"There's really no damage?" my mother asks.

"Nothing you wouldn't expect. A few of the clapboards pulled off at the bottom like they said they might, and a few cracks in the drywall — one pretty good long one in the stairwell — but really it's unbelievable."

"And the furniture?"

"Not more than an inch. You, Ruby, and Vergie could've sat in there the whole time and had tea."

My mother shakes her head in disbelief. She's smiling.

My father looks at me.

"So how about you, Ruby?" he asks. "Was it worth the wait for the big reveal?"

I look all around and try to take everything in. Our new yard is bigger than our old one, and even though the house had to be angled just right for Percy, it's beautifully placed. We've driven by here lots of times before, but now the space looks so different. Our house is well back from the road and surrounded by distant trees. Our driveway is long and curves at the finish. We don't have any grass yet and no flowers or shrubs, but there's one thing I'm almost as surprised to see as the house itself.

"Is that Mr. Cole's tree?" I ask. It's a huge flowering crabapple and as unlikely as it seems I think it has to be.

"I transplanted it a month ago," my father says. "We got a backhoe to bring it up here. I wasn't expecting it to live, big old tree like that and moving it in the heat of summer, but I thought I'd try since they were going to cut it down anyway."

"It's pretty amazing, isn't it?" my mother says. "Not just the tree, but the house — everything." She pauses. "And look at our view," she says.

My mother turns around and I do too. We're just high enough to see most of the new town and the river is a skinny blue strip below it.

"A month or so," my father says, "and it'll be just like our house was never anywhere else."

"Probably," my mother says.

It seems hard to believe, but even I think it's likely true. I'm standing in front of a hundred-year-old tree that has grown new roots and a house that already seems well rested from its journey. I'm looking down on a river that had the power to move them both.

Anything is possible.

Chapter 18

～

We've been in our new old house for three weeks and this morning I remember the instant I open my eyes. It's an odd feeling to have the idea you're somewhere else when you wake in your own bed, but until today it was as if my body was suspicious and needed confirmation this was a familiar space. There's something to be said for Percy's insistence that the house have the exact same orientation, because I can go for hours, forgetting completely about the latitude and longitude part of where I am — the new air in my old room — until I catch a glimpse of the view out the window.

For anyone driving by our house who isn't familiar with the area, I think now it almost looks like it could have always been here. Our grass is still quite short and patchy, but that's really the only giveaway. My father fixed the broken clapboard siding and built us a new front step. My mother planted cedars on both sides of our front door. She laid rocks (bits of flat shale she got from where they blasted during the building of the new Trans-Canada Highway) to make a pathway from our entry to the driveway. She made a nice round rock garden and filled it with marigolds. She put our two big white Adirondack lawn chairs under Mr. Cole's crabapple tree.

Our power and phone lines were hooked up within a few days of our arrival. Our well is dug. Our mailbox is at the end of our driveway. My father painted a little sign that says "Carson" to hang from its post.

Inside things are completely back to normal too. The few cracks in the drywall have been filled and repainted. We unpacked our boxes and replenished the cupboards. We hung our pictures and paintings back up. I helped Percy with his books. Everything went back exactly where it was. Everything, that is, except Percy's bottles.

Percy's decided he only has one bottle launch left. It isn't because we now live far from the river, or he's grown bored with it, or too old, but because what he calls "the parameters of the commencement site" are changing (that is, they're destroying the Hawkshaw Bridge) so it is a logical end to this phase of the project. There's also of course the dam. Just knowing a permanent possible obstruction exists that wasn't there before changes everything. Percy's been reading the articles about its construction in the newspaper, trying to decide if a bottle could pass safely through it. Perhaps is the answer, but Percy likes things more definite.

Percy's notebook is intact though and he's verified several times with my mother that our mail will indeed be forwarded from our old address. I think he anticipates years of responses. I can't say I'm disappointed and I certainly won't miss the now thirty-five-minute walk down the hill to the river with him, and worse, back up again. My mother sees this decision on his part as a wonderful acceptance of change, but I see it more as him not having any choice. If the bridge is gone, then the sameness of his ritual is gone. Not that I'm complaining. I just don't want to get too hopeful. It still sounds like the usual Percy to me.

*

The blowing up of the Hawkshaw Bridge is now the last thing left. The buildings are gone, the graves and the trees. The whole shoreline is a carefully crafted disaster zone of holes and missing pieces. Finally everything is ready for the water to come. Sometimes I wonder if the river has picked up on these clues and is preparing too — if it could ever know what's expected of it.

The actual detonation of the bridge is set for Sunday when it's expected to cause the least interruption in daily traffic flow. Sunday also means most people will be home and around to watch. Everyone has been talking about it. Everyone except Percy.

My parents haven't changed their minds about him going and I can't say I blame them. Sure he could probably watch from far away, locked in the car, safe in his seat belt, but somehow, like me, maybe my mother has this uneasy feeling of not tempting fate. Everything is so close to being done, why set yourself up for worry? My mother's told him she's sure the television news crew will be there and he can watch it at home later.

Percy hasn't said anything about this compromise. I'm not really sure if it's the best approach. It's one thing to know something is happening and quite another to see it with your own eyes. It's almost like something all of us have earned. The idea of the Hawkshaw Bridge being replaced has been with us from the very, very beginning. We've invested so much time in all this, constantly preparing, we need to see it through. No one wants to read a whole book only to find out the last page is missing.

Plus, Percy's obsessed with the construction of the new bridge and the idea that the old one can be blown up before the new one is complete. Apparently they will be laying down planks for essential vehicles until the bridge platform is finished and paved. (For the few more days until it's ready, the rest of us will have to cross either up- or downriver.) Percy's fascinated with the idea of a fire truck driving across the river on a few boards set down on the metal beams. I figure he thinks a vehicle may need to drive over the instant the old bridge is gone and he wants to be there to see it happen. I know it tears at my mother to keep saying no and stick to her decision. But I really hope she does. I just want it to be over too. What I saw in my underwater vision is still clear in my mind, but really I have good reason for concern and am no different than my mother. It's simple. Percy is Percy. Made with the original formula. Unchanged. Forever. He ran at the school. He could run again.

I'm only letting myself worry until the water comes. That's my promise to myself. And what I repeat in my head again and again. After the flood the river will be different, soaking up bits of old land, old memories. It will be a new river we'll have to get to know all over again. It will be bigger, bolder. It will sidle up beside us like someone wanting to be our new friend.

For now though, it's still the way Mother Nature made it, and I must say I've spent so much time on its shores lately I don't think I'll have any trouble remembering the way it used to be. Percy still makes a daily check on the progress of the new bridge and it's usually me who's with him. Since we live farther away, my parents sometimes drive us, but mostly, like today, we walk. We go down the hill, through the new town, then pass by where our house used to be. Now we can walk past the empty foundation, the driveway leading to nothing, the holes from the transplanted shrubbery and not even glance sideways. The black flat charred square that was Miss Stairs's house is a distant memory.

We walk to the spot on the slope up from the river that Percy has established as his permanent lookout. Because it's Friday we came right after lunch so we don't miss the workmen. Even I can tell the new bridge is almost done. Percy's always able to point out the progress from the day before, but lately the changes are more minute.

Today the obvious difference is not with the bridge itself, but that the army is here. I heard that they came a few days early so they could use their preparations for the bridge explosion as an opportunity for training exercises. We knew they'd arrived, but hadn't seen them since they came after we finished our check yesterday. They're camped on Fire Flat right along the river shore. There are three large and ten smaller khaki canvas tents, six jeeps, two trucks, and an army ambulance. There are about a dozen men near the tents talking, walking around, doing who-knows-what. At least it gives me something else to watch while Percy spies whatever new puzzle piece has been added to the bridge.

I sit on the ground and Percy stands right beside me. I figure we'll be here at least twenty minutes so for now I lean back and tilt my face to the sun. I lay one hand off to the side so I can feel the coolness of Percy's shadow. I think he'll stay close because my parents have made it clear that if he makes any sudden movements and scares me, his final bottle launch will never come to be.

It's strange though when Percy doesn't take so much as a step. He seems nervous and I can sense that he turns several times as if it isn't me watching him but him watching me.

After maybe only ten minutes he says, "Ruby, I am ready to return home now."

"That was fast," I say. "So what's different about the bridge today?"

"I believe I notice a new support on the platform," he says.

"That's it?" I'm used to a detailed description involving materials and lengths and even once what I think was a welding technique.

"Ruby, I would like to return to our residence now," Percy says. "I would depart myself, but our parents have instructed me to stay

in immediate proximity to you at all times. I would like to leave now
if you would stand, please."

He looks up behind us to the side with the army encampment. I
realize now it's where he's been looking the whole time.

Two soldiers are probably forty feet away on the hill above us.
They weren't there when we arrived so maybe they wandered over to
see what we were doing. Maybe part of their training is to monitor
the surroundings. Maybe they were bored or curious. Maybe they're
taking a smoke break. But they're there, tall and strong and official,
and they're definitely making Percy anxious.

Sure they're strangers, but I bet it's something else. After the police
officer grabbed Percy that day he ran at the school, what bothered
him more than anything was that he could see the bruise on his arm
for a week.

~

On Saturday, I type the message for the final bottle correctly the first
time through. Percy hovers at my shoulder as usual, but he doesn't
say a thing. I watch as he fills the bottle — note, envelope, and seven
rocks selected from our old driveway (for the sake of consistency)
that he picked out yesterday on the way home. My mother seals it
with wax, and as we head out the door even my father acknowledges
this occasion by nodding at the bottle and saying, "Smooth sailing."
My mother asks Percy if she should join us, but he doesn't clue in that
she's asking because she wants to go, and he says, "Only Ruby." My
mother gives me her camera, and I know Percy has no objection to
me preserving this moment for posterity.

It's just after breakfast. The sun is out and bright and climbing in the
sky. We're going early because this is the last full day that the bridge is
open and as the day goes on we expect there will be sightseers — people

driving down for their last trip across or taking pictures like me. Plus I know Percy is nervous about the military men, and I think he just wants to go now and get it over with so he can send off the last bottle in peace.

Percy is silent as we walk. He often is, but today it's almost as if he's trying to respect this solemn occasion. The last bottle is in his hand, flashing in the sun as it swings. The last bottle.

As we get close to the bridge I let him walk ahead of me and I take his picture. The bridge is in the background, and almost as hard to believe as Percy carrying the final bottle is the fact that tomorrow the bridge will be gone. Two cars drive across it when we first arrive, but no one is parked or out walking. The soldiers aren't at their camp, but down on the shore, almost under the bridge and quite a ways from us. There's a group of about ten on our side and ten across the river. Percy looks at them but doesn't stop walking, so he must be comfortable with their distance. The men seem to be listening to instructions of some sort. An officer is standing out in front of each group talking. They are busy and, like me, Percy probably figures they have no interest in what we're doing. I tie the shoelace on Percy's glasses. I take my place on the hill and watch him count out his two hundred and seventy-three paces.

When Percy reaches the middle of the bridge he stops and looks around. There's a car driving in the lane opposite him, but no one else. He leans ahead on the rail as he always does, lifts the bottle, and lets it go. It quickly drops the twenty feet to the water, plunges then bobs, and that fast it's finally done. I'm surprised that I feel a little sob rise in my throat that I have to swallow back down. It's like I'm missing something that isn't yet gone. I think it's both relief and sadness. But it passes, and I decide to take a few more pictures for my mother.

∗

I get up and walk a little downriver to get a long shot of Percy — so you can tell he's standing in the middle of the whole bridge. He's very small but with his white T-shirt against the black rail it's obvious where he is.

I look through the camera, then back up a few more steps, trying to frame the picture perfectly. Percy hasn't noticed I've moved and he's still watching his floating bottle. I move back farther and then through the viewfinder I see him look up. I wave, hoping he'll do the same. I know he won't look away from his bottle for long so he doesn't lose track of it, but there's a chance he might see me.

He doesn't though, and he turns sideways to look along the bridge platform, first in one direction, then the other. He does it again quickly, first one way, then back again, and when he does it a third time without glancing to the water I know something is wrong.

With the camera down I can see the soldiers are now on the bridge running toward Percy. Each group is in a line, two by two, seemingly out for a jog. They're coming from each side, one group from each shore, ten on his right and ten on his left. They're still near the ends of the bridge but getting closer.

This isn't going to be good. Percy probably thinks they're coming for him.

I start running. Any second I expect to hear wailing echoing through the river valley. I'm not only farther away than usual, but with the camera up, I didn't see them move up to the bridge from the shore.

I keep my eyes on Percy the best I can as I go. He's still glancing side to side, frozen except for the motion of his head, standing pressed as flat as possible against the bridge rail.

The soldiers are getting closer to him, moving quickly. They'll reach Percy long before I'm even close. I'm running as fast as I can. I only hope if he starts crying they don't stop and attempt to console him, as that will only make matters worse.

I see Percy glance right, then left, right, then left. I wish a car would come along or a bird would swoop down to distract him. Please. Anything. He turns right, left, right, left, while on each side the soldiers get closer and closer. I wish he would run, but he must be too scared to move.

"Percy!" I yell. "Percy! Percy!"

If he can hear me he isn't acknowledging it.

I keep running. The soldiers are about twenty-five feet away from him on his right and fifteen feet away on his left.

There he is, so small on the big bridge, the shadows of the spans crossing black on his white T-shirt. I'm starting up the hill to the end of the bridge.

The soldiers are close to him now, and I'm sure they have no idea of the anxiety they're causing him. They may say good morning or wave.

He glances right, left. Right. Left. Right. He seems frantic. He turns around for the first time and looks to the water.

"Percy!"

He jumps. With one fluid motion he's over the rail.

I stop running.

Down, down he goes.

There is a long silence as he falls when I can't even think.

He drops like his bottles. Then I wait. I don't even breathe.

He splashes into the water and disappears.

Up on the bridge I hear the soldiers' voices yelling names, a garble of orders. Two men are pulling off their boots and one is already on the bridge rail near where Percy went over, ready to jump. And he does. Several soldiers are running along the bridge back toward me. One has taken his radio out.

"Percy!" I yell.

I race to the shore.

A second soldier jumps in.

My heart is beating so hard it seems it could bruise my chest. It is not supposed to end like this.

Three soldiers run past me to the shore. The two who jumped off the bridge have surfaced and are treading water. They're looking around and waiting for any kind of indication he's there — a sound, air bubbles, a gurgle, a splash.

"Percy!" I yell.

They yell it too.

"Percy!"

Then finally he's there.

Downstream about ten feet from them his head and one arm splash above the water.

"Percy, let them help you!" I scream.

He goes right back under, before I am even finished yelling. The soldiers dive.

I am crying. Sobbing.

One soldier comes to the surface.

Then the other.

The second man has him.

Two of the soldiers run in from the shore and swim out to meet them.

"He's full of water!" one yells.

I have only one thought: the river can't take him.

They reach the shore and Percy is limp.

I rush toward them.

I refuse to think it. I refuse to remember.

They lay Percy on the ground. His white T-shirt is stuck to him. One of the soldiers begins to push on his chest.

I kneel down beside him. His glasses are still tied on and there are water droplets inside the lenses.

"Is this your brother?" one of the soldiers asks. "Percy, you said?"

I nod.

"Come on, Percy," he says.

"Percy," I say.

"Percy," I repeat.

I lean ahead as the soldier gives him air. I stroke Percy's drenched hair.

The soldier is about to press on Percy's chest again when he coughs. He coughs and coughs and looks around.

"Hello Ruby," he says.

"Hello Percy."

Chapter 19

~

When the water finally comes, it flows so slowly that if we hadn't been waiting almost two years for it, anticipating and planning our lives around it, we may not have even noticed it was happening. There is no surge, no urgency, no gush, no rush. It just slowly moves farther and farther inland over days, then weeks. It meanders and takes its time, crawls and creeps. It's deceptive, like a gentle tide you may expect to go back out again. But for every inch the water wets, every blade of grass, every tree stump, driveway, foundation, rock, lawn, garden, it drowns a memory. It creeps over the stump of Mr. Cole's old pine tree, up through Doyle's chopped-down apple orchard, over what was Mrs. Brewer's flower garden, the cemetery, the gas station, the high school, Foster's Store. It covers the foundations of what were Wesley Ball's house, Leonard Black's house, Miss Stairs's house and of course our house. If you waded to your waist you could stand in the space that was our sunroom.

By the end of the first month of school, our river is twice as wide as before. The Pokiok Falls are a quarter their original size and the gorge below is now eighty feet of dark mystery. The new bridge doesn't look so tall anymore. The piers of the old bridge are too deep beneath the water to even bother boats. Except for a few roads that now lead into the water, anyone seeing our river valley for the first time would have no reason to think anything was ever any different.

None of our family saw the old Hawkshaw Bridge blow up, so my image of Percy jumping off it is my final memory. I think of that as the ending anyway. It was as if Percy tried so hard for so long to stay calm and not let the changes get to him, he needed to dive into that water for once and for all to wash his worries away. I also think of it as the end of me wondering about what I saw when I made my own dramatic entrance into the river, well back over two years ago. I'm not psychic any more than I'm weird. Why shouldn't I have seen water when I was in the water? It's really no different than dreaming the phone is ringing, and then waking up to the sound of a ringing phone.

I decided to give the chess set to Percy. After the scene at the bridge, it felt wrong to keep it hidden in a drawer any longer. I didn't hand it over out of the blue though. My mother channelled her extreme emotion over what happened into a big celebration dinner in honour of Percy's final bottle launch. The chess set was his award for five years of dedicated service.

While my mother and I spent the afternoon preparing food, my father sat with Percy in the sunroom and reviewed his whole notebook — something my father had never done before. Percy was able to recall launch after launch with amazing detail thanks to his records. I heard my father ask Percy about the weather on a Saturday morning more than three years ago and Percy talked about it like it was yesterday. Percy showed my father his calculations of possible distances travelled by the bottles, based on their time in the water. My father seemed interested and he even suggested they get out the New Brunswick map, then the globe, to see where they might be now.

For supper we ate turkey and stuffing, potatoes and gravy, peas, yellow beans, and carrots. My mother baked fresh rolls and let Percy take his from the very middle of the pan where they were the softest. I made a chocolate cake with chocolate icing. My mother made divinity fudge and, for good measure, a batch of cookies with dots of her chokecherry jelly.

When our meal was through I went to my room for the chess set. I had carefully stacked all the pieces in a shoe box and wrapped it in paper left over from Percy's birthday. My mother insisted she take a picture of Percy and me before he opened it, but then I took my place at the dining-room table.

"Go ahead, Percy," my mother said. "It's something very special Ruby made for you."

Percy looked up in my direction and something shifted a little in my stomach. I picked up my glass and drank what was left of my water. I knew with Percy there would be no jumping for joy, but I hoped he wasn't disappointed. I watched as he ripped off the paper and lifted the lid. He stared at the box contents.

"Ruby, has something happened to my current chess set?" he asked. "Have the pieces become lost or damaged?"

"No," I said. "I just thought you might like these ones instead."

"Look at them, Percy," my father said. "Ruby carved them. All herself. From driftwood she found in the river."

Percy started taking out the pieces. He lined all the white ones up on his right side and all the black on his left. The expression on his face didn't change and I wondered if he was going to decide he liked his current chess set better, say this one was entirely unnecessary, and give it back.

"You can still use your board," I said, offering it up as a compromise even though I hadn't made another and it was what I figured he'd do anyway.

My mother looked at me and smiled.

"Percy —" she said but stopped when he spoke at the same time.

"Ruby, I am noticing that the queens bear a resemblance to our mother and the kings to our father."

"You're right," I said. "Is that okay?"

He paused before answering.

"Yes," he said. "I believe I will still be able to concentrate on the game without it being a distraction."

"Good," I said. "Good. So you'll use these chess pieces from now on?"

"Yes, I will." He nodded. "Thank you, Ruby, for this gift."

For a split second Percy looked me directly in the eyes.

~

My mother is painting. Even though it's getting late in the year, she's been asked by the provincial centennial committee to paint a series of twelve paintings showing scenes of the changes in our area. She's gone through all her photographs and chosen what to do. She has one painting finished. It's Wesley Ball's house burning. Now she's working on her second. It's Mr. Cole's house sliding down the frozen river, a curious-looking image watching from a cloud in the sky.

Last weekend we went to see Mr. Cole's house at the official opening of the historical village. I thought it would be strange to see it there, and walk through it again in a different place, but it's really no different than ours.

Next weekend is Miss Stairs's wedding, and when my mother isn't painting she and I have been helping Miss Stairs prepare for it.

Mr. Hazen Howard only proposed two weeks ago, but Miss Stairs didn't want to wait. I had wondered what Mr. Howard did with that cottage he bought at the auction, but it turns out it was part of his plan. Miss Stairs insists she never mentioned her wedding fantasy to him, but if not he did some pretty good guessing. He drove into town with the cottage on a trailer behind his truck. No one thought anything of it, because we're all used to travelling architecture. He parked in front of Miss Stairs's house and proposed to her on the miniature porch. He told her that the cottage was a gift — not to be used as a shed as the auctioneer suggested, but a playhouse for their future children.

The wedding will be at our church. Miss Stairs said she felt no need to hold on to the idea of being married near the water since the river already had more than its fair share of attention lately. The "something blue" will instead be the dresses my mother and I wear. She will be the matron of honour and I will be a bridesmaid. Percy is also taking part in the ceremony. He'll be the ring bearer. At eleven he's a bit old, but Miss Stairs asked (carefully explaining the simple task step by step) and he accepted, so that's all that matters. I think it's because Mr. Hazen Howard found Percy's bottle. I bet Percy is doing it as much for him as Miss Stairs. We're all happy about it though, regardless of the reason.

I wrote to Troy to tell him about the upcoming wedding. I mentioned the cabin used in the proposal because it turned out it was the same one he had stayed in those weeks he was here and I thought it was a funny coincidence. In Troy's last letter he said his father did so well selling everything he bought at the auction that he's already talking about making another buying trip down here next spring. I told him about Percy's daredevil manoeuvre on the bridge and the flood that

Acknowledgements

Thank you to my agent, Hilary McMahon.

Thanks so much to my editor, Bethany Gibson, and to everyone at the wonderful Goose Lane Editions.

My sincere appreciation to The New Brunswick Arts Board for awarding me a Creation Grant to complete this novel.

To my parents, Fredrica and David Givan, who raised me in a house on a hill in Hawkshaw, NB, overlooking the St. John River, thank you for explaining to me as a child why there was an old bridge under the water near the Pokiok Falls, and for never letting me forget what had happened to the area before I was born. Thank you both for reading an early version of the manuscript, answering my questions, and giving me your copies of *The Nackawic Bend: 200 Years of History* compiled by Patricia M. Lawson, Gail Farnsworth, and M. Anne Hartley, and *The St. John River and Its Tributaries* by Esther Clark Wright, which were helpful books.

Most of all, thank you and love always to my husband Shane, who read the manuscript almost as many times as I did, and who I know never doubted that this book would come to be.

photo: Shane Nason

Riel Nason writes about antiques and
collectibles for the *Telegraph-Journal*.
Her short stories have appeared in
The Malahat Review, *The Antigonish Review*,
Grain, and *The Dalhousie Review*.
The Town That Drowned is her
sensational debut novel.